The Exile

by Gregory Erich Phillips

ISBN 978-1-63393-765-9

Published by

◣ köehlerbooks™

210 60th Street
Virginia Beach, VA 23451
800-435-4811
www.koehlerbooks.com

THE EXILE

A NOVEL

GREGORY ERICH PHILLIPS

VIRGINIA BEACH
CAPE CHARLES

PART I

EL DESIERTO

1

EVERYTHING WAS DARK.

Though her eyes could see little, her other senses were acute, telling her that she wasn't dreaming. Terror reached down into the pit of her stomach as the sound of whirring jets and the sensation of changing air pressure revealed her worst fear—she was on an airplane.

Hope left her heart as sharply as the air left her stomach as the plane ascended. Was she really being deported? Even after everything that led up to this, it was unbelievable.

She struggled for composure and clarity. Had she been drugged?

Think, Leila. Keep your head.

The shades were down. There was no light besides the tiny dots along the aisles and a bright green "Exit" sign a few rows ahead of her. If only that were a real invitation.

All these years she had worked to pull every detail of her life into her control. That was supposed to protect her, supposed to keep this grim past from reaching back for her. How fast it had all unraveled.

The plane was full but eerily quiet. The air was cool and stale. The hum of the engine reaching cruising altitude overpowered the irregular breaths of her fellow passengers who, like her, must have been too dazed or too afraid to cry. All the crying had been done in the days before.

Leila hurt all over. Her stomach turned with nausea. She was restless from sitting. Her head ached from having her thick hair pulled back for too long. She felt dirty in clothes that had been worn for . . . how many days?

Until now, it had been possible to hope. She'd told herself that she would soon be home, that the mistake would be cleared up in time. She never imagined the despair of a dark airplane, each moment tearing her farther from the people she loved.

Scenes from her life, lovely details which she'd taken for granted, now returned to her as memories: warm nights filled with music, her family's embraces, the sweet smell of azalea and bougainvillea in the spring. She didn't want to believe those times were gone, but her heart knew better and was already cataloging each memory as a treasured marker of a life that was lost.

Her grief was numbing, too heavy and too new to understand.

She blinked away the tears. She would *not* cry. She would *not* give up hope. Somehow, she would get back to the people she loved and be again the person she had worked so hard to become.

This had to be a mistake.

But was it? Perhaps the mistake had been hers all along. After all, what right had she to believe the life she had invented for herself could last? Had she forgotten so quickly who she really was?

As Leila's eyes grew accustomed to the dark, she glanced around. She needed to get her bearings. The men and women who filled the plane seemed resigned. The woman beside her sat with a face like a stone. Why wasn't everyone crying in sorrow or screaming in rage? She could have done either of those things; she wanted to do both at the same time.

Maybe these other people still thought they were dreaming and that they would wake up at home with their loved ones. She envied them, wishing she could believe she'd wake up with her boyfriend's arms around her, with the windows open to the warm morning breeze off the desert. But dreams were over now. This was real.

A sound intruded upon her thoughts—a quiet rattling, almost inaudible. As soon as she recognized it, she realized it had been going on the whole time. Then, quiet as it was, she could no longer ignore it. Naturally, this was the rickety plane. The sound irritated her, then infuriated her, then made her think it would drive her insane.

How did this horror begin? When did her carefully crafted life begin to unravel, leading her to this day? There was the betrayal. There was the accident. But really, it started that night two years ago when she first dared ask herself if life could mean *more*. Hadn't she sensed the danger in that question—that it could lead to this?

Trust. Passion. Love.

She had avoided such things, knowing they could shake up everything she had worked for. But now that she had felt them, how could it be undone?

Surely, she could find a way back. Surely.

Sorrow tore at her heart, but she fought to keep her thoughts clear. Self-pity wouldn't bring her back to the people she loved, and it wouldn't protect her from the dangers that might await her once this plane touched down.

Leila had no sense of how long the flight took. She gasped at the jolt of the landing. It shocked many of the passengers out of their daze. People shifted and stood up. Someone began speaking in Spanish. The woman beside her started to cry.

The rattling noise persisted. She wanted to scream.

The airplane doors opened. Daylight shot in. Leila hurried out into the middle of the crowd, squinting into the sharp sunlight. She was so relieved to be off that horrible, noisy plane. The thick heat was jarring after the air-conditioned flight.

She inhaled deeply—she knew this air. Scenes from her childhood floated toward her, brought by the scents of her never-forgotten past. The familiarity comforted her, in spite of everything it meant.

It had been a long time, but she had not forgotten her childhood home, and it had not forgotten her. If Paulo found out she was back, would he look for her? Despite the heat, a chill danced up her spine. Might he already be *expecting* her?

The tarmac was alive with the sounds of sputtering engines and shouting voices. Across a short fence, two teenage boys with cell phone cameras snapped a picture of each passenger as they passed. Clearly, somebody was interested in knowing who was returning to Colombia today.

They were corralled down a wide hallway into an open room and instructed to sit on the floor. It was stuffy and hot. There were windows on all sides, but from where Leila sat, she could see nothing to help her find her bearings—only blue sky in every direction, broken by a couple of air control towers. The shadows on the towers told her it was midafternoon and gave her a sense of north and south. It wasn't much, but it was a start.

A litany of names was being read, followed by the name of a town and a date of birth. She watched as a face would lift from within the group when their name was heard, but no one was called forward. The men at the computers merely typed some notes before moving on to the next name.

She didn't know whether she wanted them to call her name or not. After all this time, this was the moment of truth. Finally, it came.

"Leila del Sol. Cartagena. November tenth, 1980."

The other man typed something into his computer, then looked up at the man who had read her name.

"Leila del Sol? But that's impossible. Leila del Sol has been dead for years."

2

IT WAS LATE. The moon shone down onto the patio through long palm fronds. A breeze blew in off the desert, cooling the March evening. The sound of two guitars and two voices serenaded the neighborhood to sleep.

Leila smiled at her dad as they finished the song "La Cartera."It was a popular Colombian song about the gifts of love. They set down their guitars in unison. It was a good one to end on; she would let the song ring in her mind for the night."That's still my favorite song. You gave me all those things, *Papá*."

She breathed in the dry Arizona air, scented by spring flowers and mesquite. This was such a nice evening. She had let it go too long since the last time they played together.

Leila looked over at her dad.

"Why did you take the chance on me, after everything you went through? Why take the risk?"

"Love is always worth the risk."

Leila wasn't sure she agreed.

"After my first wife was killed, I didn't expect to love again," Manny said. "I didn't want to. Losing my family hurt too much.

It would have been easy to destroy myself in the revolution. Instead, I set my life on a whole new course, and now here I am. For me, *life* was the risk and death would have been easy. Life has always meant love to me, and so to live, I had to be willing to take a risk on love again."

He made it sound so noble, but she knew it hadn't been any easier for him than it would be for her if she faced the same choices.

"I've made my life be about so many other things," she said. "It's because I don't want to take the risk. I'm afraid of getting hurt the way you did."

They had lowered their voices. The palms brushed rhythmically against the roofs of the single-story houses.

"You have become such an American, my dear," he said. "All work."

The remark took her by surprise.

"I learned the value of work from you."

"Yes, I understand. You had much to work for. So have I. A second chance is strong motivation. But work isn't life. I have worked for you, for Carmen, for a night like this playing music under the stars. But many Americans work for its own sake. Then they try to make themselves happy with a nice car or a big house. They spend money on a lavish vacation or an expensive meal. This weekend, you're going to that fancy place in Sedona to receive an award. It will feel nice, but don't start to think that sort of thing is important. Remember the Latin way, which is better. Work is only so you can enjoy your family and friends with more security and to create the little moments that make life beautiful."

She wanted to believe that.

"Never forget this. Never let your life take you to a place where you're not open to love. Never forget the culture you came from either."

"That all may be true, but don't forget how cruel Colombia was to both of us. Love hardly flourished there."

"But even in the darkest days of the revolution, we were family. We looked out for each other. In your childhood, you children looked after each other as best you could, even with all the cards stacked against you. There was always love. In America, while things are easier, too many people try to go it alone. They close in on themselves. Family is forgotten. Friends are discarded too easily."

Going it alone wasn't always so bad. Leila had everything she needed and nothing she didn't want. Her life was ordered *just so,* and she liked it that way. She didn't want to think that something was missing.

"Life is better here, sure," said Manny. "It's good to have the opportunity to work and build something. I've done it. Now, you're doing it. Just don't forget why."

She looked up through the branches at the stars, abundant above the Valley of the Sun. The moon had passed behind the house but still glowed in the sky.

Leila thought of all the people she worked with, Samantha in particular. Those people were the type of Americans her dad was warning her not to become. She was in danger of embarking on their path—really, she already had—but it wasn't too late to change course. The success was seductive, and once tasted, it swept you along with it.

She turned and looked at her dad in the darkness. "Was love worth the risk for you?"

"Absolutely. My heart still hurts, even after all these years. I won't pretend that you and Carmen have made up for it. I know you understand, but I can't talk to Carmen about it. She's jealous of my old love. But *you* know."

Leila nodded.

"Was Job happy again after God gave him a new family? I doubt it. Who could recover from the loss of a wife and a child? But it's better than not to have loved at all." He paused. "I hope you learn these lessons sooner than I did. Too many years of fighting. Too long running away from myself and arguing with God. Too many years talking about love without living it. My biggest regret was that I didn't change in time to save my wife. My life's main value has been in what I *did* do to save you."

Leila picked her guitar up from where she had set it down against her chair. She hugged it to her chest and closed her eyes. She could still feel the faintest vibration in the wood of the instrument, so recently touched by music. The resonance passed into her. It comforted her but also unsettled her. Music always reminded her that life wasn't as simple as she tried to make it. She was never in control. The lessons of her life should have taught her that by now, even though it seemed like a lesson she had to learn over and over. She was never in control of music either, even if she knew all the words of a song and where to find every note on the strings. Music had a life all its own. It would be frightening to let life itself take on the unpredictable magic of a song.

3

LEILA MADE ONE more pass through her hair, then dropped the brush into the sink, its porcelain spotted with black and tan flecks of makeup. She was satisfied and left her room. Her dad was right—this wasn't what was important, but tonight could be fun. It always felt good to get dressed up and feel beautiful.

It wasn't easy being the curvy girl living in Phoenix, with its workout culture and packed calendar of pool parties. All the girls had perfect abs. Leila tried to embrace her Latina curves, even though she wished she could drop about fifteen pounds. But tonight, in her little black dress, with her dark hair combed back as straight as it would go, she felt confident and proud.

Being here was a big deal. Why downplay it? A girl from the *barrio* was at a Sedona mansion, about to receive an award.

Samantha had rented the entire mansion up in the high desert north of Phoenix for this weekend's event. Leila's room was on the ground floor, in the back. Samantha had absolutely assigned the guest rooms according to status—or maybe based on who she needed to impress. Clearly, that wasn't Leila.

What did she care? It was an honor just to be here. She left her room.

There was Cox in the hallway, also making his way toward the ballroom. Too late to try to avoid him. He stopped and gaped at her.

"Damn, Lei*lalala*. Can I be your date tonight?"

"Do you ever quit?"

"Not if you go looking that hot."

She snapped her fingers. "Up here, Cox."

Leila could not have imagined a more average-looking thirty-year-old man than Cox: thin frame, light-brown hair, pale skin that burned mercilessly in the Arizona sunshine. But his attitude made him anything but average. She grudgingly marveled at the way his boundless ego could command a room. He had no scruples and no shame when it came to making money or getting laid.

Leila walked past him quickly toward the ballroom, aware that if she slowed down a lecherous hand would catch up with the small of her back. The ballroom was decorated with the typical desert décor. The dominant colors were rust and sky blue. On the walls hung paintings of cacti or lonely cowboys. The tables overflowed with a lavish spread of appetizers, dwarfing the little potted cacti. Two full bars served opposite ends of the room. It was noisy. Even up here in Sedona, the room couldn't escape the feel of the corporate event that it was. Leila walked to one of the bars and asked for a Coke. Cox was right behind her and ordered a double Scotch. She turned to face him just in time to avoid his hovering hand.

"It won't hurt you to drink tonight, baby. No one's driving."

"You're not allowed to call me *baby*. How many times do I have to tell you?"

"Why don't you ever drink?"

"None of your business." She smiled at him, then walked toward one of the tables.

"Hi, Paul, so glad you're here."

Paul lifted his expansive frame out of his chair and hugged her.

"Leila, you look amazing."

"Thanks. Did Clary come up too?"

"Yes, he's getting drinks. He'll be back in a moment."

She sat down. Cox had disappeared, just as she'd planned it. Paul and Cox despised each other.

Samantha stepped to the podium and tapped the microphone.

Leila was shocked she hadn't seen Samantha Frye the moment she entered the ballroom. Like Cox, Samantha commanded a room, but no one begrudged Samantha her ego. She had earned it. Standing tall and vibrant in a tight blue dress—cut low enough to display her expensive breasts—Samantha brought all the eyes in the room to her. Her hair may not have been naturally blond, and it was entirely possible that she'd had some face work done to go along with her impressive body work, but there was no denying she looked fantastic for fifty.

"Welcome to the annual awards dinner of Arizona Prime Path Mortgage!" Samantha's voice thundered into the microphone. "Tonight, we celebrate a great year in 2006. Let's make it an even better 2007."

Applause filled the room.

"There are those who say the subprime mortgage industry is unsustainable. Don't listen to them. The companies that failed in this venture simply didn't have the expertise. That's why you work with and work for us. We know this business through and through and will not steer you wrong. Take my word: This business will remain lucrative for *years*."

More applause. Leila smiled and clapped along with the others.

"Later this evening, I will pass out those beautiful awards." Samantha motioned with her toned arm toward the table behind her, lined with glass trophies. "Plus, I have a few special gifts to give."

Murmurs pulsed through the room. Leila hadn't been to one of these events before but had heard from others how generous Samantha's gifts could be.

"I feel like such a proud mother tonight, looking out there at your wonderful faces. We've done a lot together and been through a lot. I love you all, and I'm proud of each one of you."

Leila knew from the glow on her face how genuine Samantha's words were. Her boss was a ruthless businesswoman, but her kindness and generosity for those in her inner circle knew no limits.

"We all work hard at what we do. We work for excellence, for profit, and for the thrill of the business. Everyone wants to be here this weekend. *You* are here because you are the best. I'm looking at Paul Weidman, Jose Martinez, and Julie Jordan, my three top Realtors. I'm looking at my top loan officers, Cox McCann and Leila del Sol. I'm looking at Marshall Berg, our appraiser and best friend whenever we really need a property value. Finally, I'm looking at Christy Strahan of Prestige Title and Escrow, my partner in crime, who makes so many things possible."

Someone started to clap.

"Yes." Samantha began to clap as well. "A round of applause for all my stars."

She waited for the applause to die down.

"We have worked hard all year. Tonight we play hard. Drink up . . . it's all on me. Dinner will be spectacular. Indulge in and enjoy what, I have no doubt, will be a memorable evening."

Samantha stepped down from the podium. The room buzzed from her infusion of energy.

A line of waiters emerged from the kitchen and placed a massive seafood tower on each table. Samantha had not been exaggerating. It was the most exquisite meal Leila had ever experienced. She was full before the main course even came: steak *and* scallops. Now she knew they were going over the top with the food on purpose. The room grew louder as wine was poured liberally at the tables while cocktails still came from the bar.

Let Cox think she was uptight for never drinking; she didn't care. She always wanted to be alert and in control of herself and her situation. She needed to be. Drinking allowed others to relax. For someone like Samantha, who was so high-strung, it helped her unwind. But Leila didn't feel relaxed unless she was sober.

After dinner, Samantha returned to the podium to give out the awards. Leila's heartbeat quickened when she knew her turn was approaching.

"Come up here, Leila." Samantha beamed across the room at her.

Leila stood and walked up to the stage. Samantha hugged her warmly. She always got affectionate when she had been drinking.

"Here she is, my beautiful protégé. Leila is here for the first time, after achieving second place in loan volume during her first full year with the company. You know I only bring two of my loan officers to this retreat each year. So, Leila, this is quite an honor."

She handed a mounted glass plaque to Leila, then turned and smiled at the crowd.

"I have one more gift for you, dear." Samantha returned to the award table with the microphone in one hand. She leaned down to pick up a small box. "A token of my love and gratitude, not only for your sales skills, but for the sweet charm you bring to the office every day."

Leila opened the box and gasped. Inside was an elaborate silver necklace, full of sapphires encircled by tiny diamonds.

"May I?" Without waiting for an answer, Samantha unclasped the simple pendant Leila had worn, lifted her gift from its box, and clasped it behind Leila's neck. "It looks just as spectacular on you as I knew it would. You wore the perfect dress to show it off, too."

Leila was speechless. The necklace must have cost thousands of dollars. She loved it but didn't think she'd feel comfortable wearing it. She wasn't really a sapphires and diamonds kind of girl.

"A girl as beautiful and successful as you needs to show herself off. Never be ashamed of what you've accomplished."

"Thank you."

They hugged again. Leila returned to her seat, carrying her award and the box, with the necklace heavy against her chest. Really, what girl couldn't be talked into being a sapphires and diamonds type?

Paul and Clary leaned in to "ooh" and "aah" at the piece.

Cox had already been called up to the podium.

"Once again, for the third year in a row . . . Cox McCann, the top-producing loan officer of Arizona Prime Path Mortgage."

Leila watched as Cox took his award and new Rolex with all the entitlement she expected.

"Now, for the final acknowledgement of the night . . . come up here, Christy."

Samantha always called Christy Strahan her partner, but Samantha towered over her, both physically and through intimidation. Leila had watched all year as Samantha wrapped Christy ever tighter around her finger. Tonight, Christy got her reward for what she endured.

"I don't have an award for you, Christy. I can't call you our top title rep because you're our only one. But for everything you do, I have a special gift for you." She produced an envelope and handed it to Christy. "Two tenth-row, fifty-yard-line tickets for next year's Arizona State football season."

Christy squealed with delight, slapping her hands against her cheeks.

"And . . ." Samantha shouted, "two tickets for all your Sun Devils' Pac 10 road games!"

Christy almost collapsed from excitement.

Samantha gathered Christy in a hug. "You've earned it, hon."

Leila smiled. In recent months, Christy's patience had been running thin. Samantha had pushed a few loans through escrow on Cox's behalf that never should have been allowed to close. With regulators tightening the screws on the industry, Christy was growing nervous. As big a football fan as she was, though, Samantha had surely just bought herself another year of favors.

That was the way in the mortgage business: high stress, high reward.

Leila listened to the room, loud with clattering forks and boozy laughter. Everything about this weekend was shamelessly superficial. At times, it was all she could do not to despise these people. It reminded her of high school, with all the little alliances and rivalries. Only the stakes were higher now.

What must they all think of *her?* Here by herself, sober and aloof, one of the few without a plus one. She was the outsider, the immigrant in the room at the back of the first floor.

Drinking a little might have helped her look more normal in this American corporate culture. But at what cost? What other social cues would she miss if she wasn't completely in control of herself?

Dessert was served, but no one had room left for it. Leila cringed as the dessert plates were stacked and cleared with the cake smashed uneaten between them. The waste was an accepted side effect of the extravagance in America, but Leila would never get used to it. The memory of hunger never went away.

She resented the wastefulness. She couldn't help it. She had watched children starve on the streets of Cartagena.

The party spilled out onto the veranda as people smoked, drank, and laughed over business stories and gossip. Samantha—

so fierce at the office—was loving and happy, hugging everyone repeatedly.

Leila sat by the fire in the cool evening, savoring the moment. She felt lucky to have won second place this year and doubted she would again. That was okay. She wasn't in this job for the competition. She wasn't in it to care what other people thought of her. It was about the security and confidence it gave her. That meant more to her than anyone at this party would ever understand. She was building toward something. One day, when she started a family, she could give her children a good life. When her father retired, she could take care of him. To think that she had come so far at her age, and to have built so much for her future . . . that was what she took pride in, not how many loans she closed.

Paul came toward her. He usually carried his large frame lightly, but his steps had grown heavier after many cocktails.

"*Dahling*, we are going to make so much money together."

She smiled. "Oh? Do you have something up your sleeve?"

"Perhaps."

"Sit down. Tell me about it."

The Realtor scooted another wicker chair beside her and spilled the still nonpublic details of a major new construction development he would be representing on the outskirts of Phoenix. Leila knew she now had the inside track on making her company the preferred lender for the project.

Clary pulled Paul away, both of them laughing merrily. Leila remained in her seat by the fire. She would follow up with him about the project next week. Sobriety was good for making deals.

Soon, Cox had his arm around Samantha. They were laughing hysterically. Fortunately, Cox seemed to have given up on hitting on Leila, at least for tonight, but it was a little disgusting to see his effort turn toward their boss.

They both eased toward her on drunken legs.

"Oh, Leila, I just can't believe how good that necklace looks on you."

"You picked it out."

"Like I told you earlier, you need to actually wear it." Samantha pointed at her, her finger almost wagging. "I forbid you to sell it and send the money to your family."

"What?"

"Your family back in Mexico. I know you send them a lot of what you make."

Leila's mouth gaped. She was too flabbergasted to say anything. Did Samantha really just go there? She tried to stay calm as her blood boiled. Samantha was just drunk. Cox too, standing there with a stupid grin.

"I'm not from Mexico." It was all Leila could think to say.

"Whatever, whichever one of those countries you're from. I mean, that's why you haven't bought your own house yet, right? I sign your paychecks, so I know you could afford it. But I suppose you have a lot of crop pickers to support."

"My family lives here. My dad works for Intel."

Samantha and Cox had already wobbled off.

Leila lurched up and walked to the edge of the veranda, then back to the same chair. She leaned back and took several deep breaths to steady her nerves.

Unbelievable. Did that really just happen?

These people were a means to an end for her. It didn't matter what they thought of her. But she *did* care what they thought. She couldn't help it. She hated when people—particularly Samantha, who should have known better—assumed things about her just because she was Hispanic.

If only she *did* have someone to share her abundance with. If she did, she would sell this damn necklace too. But the people she would like to help were so far beyond her reach now. They were beyond the arms of the naïve American charities and the corrupt Colombian ones. *Helping* was easier to think than to do in any effective way.

Looking back toward the party, she saw that it had begun to turn.

She had been the only sober one at many parties before, so she always noticed the turn. A critical mass had passed the state of happy drunkenness. From here they would either get sick, begin fighting with each other, or sleep with each other. Not wanting to witness any of those scenarios, she slipped back to her room and went to bed.

4

UP HERE IN the high desert, the morning was colder than Leila was accustomed to. She went back for a baggy sweater before stepping out into the crisp morning. After last night's party, she wasn't surprised that there was no movement in the hall. Everyone else would be asleep for a while. Closing the back door, she walked through the manicured grounds, then out of the property onto the desert path, feeling a few cool grains of sand dance up onto her feet. It felt good. No need to protect her pedicure now that the awards party was over.

She followed the sandy path down toward the valley that the house overlooked. On the rocky hillside, twisted pine trees spaced themselves at a respectful distance. The sand here was brick red. Down lower, it turned yellow, and far to her left it was brown. From behind her, the not-yet-risen sun lit the pink hills in the distance.

Her legs and feet were cold—bare in her shorts and sandals— while her upper body was warm in her favorite sweater. It was strange to feel cold outdoors. She usually only needed the sweater for air-conditioned rooms. She breathed in the crisp, fragrant air. The landscape was so different compared with Phoenix, only a hundred miles away. Here, desert and mountain met. The pines mingled with cacti on the hillsides.

Birds chattered from their perches. These same birds had jarred her out of sleep, but now she enjoyed the raucousness of their springtime passion.

As she neared the base of the valley, she saw a figure stooped toward the ground. Her first thought was to turn in another direction, but a flicker of recognition made her curious. She continued toward him.

Off of the wind-exposed hillside, shorter plants grew around her feet: stubby cacti, catclaw, aloe vera, and broom. The prickly pears had begun to burst with bright yellow flowers. She stepped carefully around the sharp tentacles.

The young man heard her coming and looked up. He had a sturdy bag beside him and held what looked like a paring knife. A larger knife sat on the ground nearby. A small yucca plant had been uprooted.

She remembered now where she had seen him, even though they had never spoken. He was Samantha's son. Leila wished she had walked the other way after all. She would feel angry at Samantha for a while after last night and expected her adult son to have the same prejudices with an extra dose of entitlement. Now, here she was alone on an abandoned hillside and he with a couple of knives.

What was he even doing here, tagging along on his mother's trip?

He looked at her with interest and set down the knife, straightening his tall frame as she approached. He slapped his hands together to shake off the dirt.

She was accustomed to men dropping what they were doing and giving her their full attention. It didn't matter that she was fresh out of bed in a big sweater. Her thick hair must have been a sight.

This morning, when she set out on her walk, she hadn't expected to have to be "on."

"Harvesting some yucca root for breakfast?"

He laughed. The gentle tone of his laughter and the smile that accompanied it surprised her. There was a genuineness about him that she had not expected. She felt more at ease.

"There's a different kind of yucca that grows here in the high desert," he said. "It has many medicinal uses."

"Are you a doctor?"

"Several rungs lower. I'm in nursing school at Arizona State."

"I didn't know they taught that sort of medicine there."

"They don't."

She scoped out a rock and sat down about fifteen feet away from him, folding her arms.

He had neatly cut brownish-blond hair. His face had the glow that came from living in over three hundred days of annual sunshine and spending many of those days outdoors. It was a face that still needed some growing into; he would be more handsome in ten years than he was today.

"I know I've seen you before, but you always avoid everyone when we come to Samantha's house. Why?" Leila asked.

"I'm not interested in her business or that world."

Leila reached into her pocket for a rubber band and tied back her rebellious hair. "Are you staying up there this weekend?"

"Yes."

"Then you're in *that world* whether you like it or not."

He frowned. Not at her, she could tell, but at her words. She laughed, wanting to put a smile back on his face.

"At least a trip to Sedona gives you a chance to collect your specimens." She hoped she hadn't offended him. "I'm hardly one to talk. I'm as wrapped up in that world as anyone."

She thought of all her colleagues and coworkers about to wake up to their hangovers in the house on the hill. Yes, she was part of that world, but she wasn't *of* that world. She never could be. The world she lived in was hers alone. Not even her father was there with her. It was a lonely place, but she was used to it.

"You work for my mom, don't you?"

"That's right."

"What do you think about the mortgage business? Do you feel good about the work you do?"

"Yes, I do. It's all in what you make of it. I love helping people. I always try to do the job with integrity. There are others—"

"Don't worry. I know the way my mom works. You won't offend me."

"I think I already have. But yes, without naming names, there are those who work in a way I wouldn't be comfortable with. The medical profession probably isn't all that different."

He nodded.

"What's your name?" She had never heard Samantha use her son's name in the office.

"Ashford."

"That's a unique name. I'm Leila. I'd shake your hand, but . . ."

He looked down at his hands, caked with sand, clay, and bits of yucca root. They both laughed.

"Rain check on the handshake. It's nice to meet you, Leila. Is this your first time in Sedona?"

"Yes."

"Come with me. I want to show you something." He gathered his tools and folded them into a satchel. He tossed the remains of his yucca plant into the specimen bag.

Leila hesitated, mistrusting. *What is he up to?* After a moment, she stood up. He seemed all right.

Ashford led up the next hill, away from the house. The

trail grew steep. She had wanted a walk this morning, so she didn't mind.

"We'll be just in time," he said.

"In time for what?" She quickened her pace.

"Sunrise on Cathedral Rock."

Just then, the sun cracked over the ridge behind them. Twenty yards farther, they reached the top of their own hill. Leila gasped.

Nearly a mile away across the valley rose Cathedral Rock with its many spires, glowing orange and gold in the morning sun. Each ring of the sandstone formation stood out sharply in varying colors, splashed by the horizontal rays. A forest of deep-green pines, occasionally broken by the orange ground, covered the expanse between them and the monument. The valley was still in shadow. Cathedral Rock shone over everything like a beacon. It looked so strong and ancient, yet also fragile, like it could crumble to dust at any moment.

"Isn't it magnificent?" he asked.

"It is."

She breathed the cool morning scents rising from the forested valley: pine, clay, dewy grass. As if rising with the scents and enveloping the beauty everywhere, a wonderful feeling of peace washed over her. Leila didn't leave much time in her life for peace. She was grateful for the moment.

They stood for a few more minutes in silence as the sunlight spread. It was a strange moment, almost romantic in its way, between two people who had just met—he with dirt all over his hands and she having just rolled out of bed. If it weren't for the dirt, would he have tried to kiss her? That was usually what boys brought girls to places like this to do.

What a scandal *that* would be if Samantha found out.

She turned back to him, smiling broadly. She was glad she had decided to trust him.

"Thank you. I bet this will be the highlight of my trip."

He smiled back at her with a look that she recognized all too well. He was probably calculating the odds of a kiss attempt or at least wondering what it would feel like.

"I'd better get back." She wanted to preserve the lovely moment and carve the peace in her memory before it changed.

She hurried back down the hill and up the other side toward the mansion. Movement had begun on the other side of its many windows. The building with its pristine grounds didn't look so impressive now compared to the glorious monument across the valley.

5

"Oh God, my head hurts."

"Why do you drink so much, Mom? It makes you miserable."

Samantha smirked. "College boy lectures mother about her drinking."

"I'm not lecturing you. Just saying."

The veranda had been cleaned from last night's event, but vibrations from the party lingered in the air. The cold ashes from the dead fire still infused everything with a smoky scent.

Ashford looked across the table at his mother. Despite her hangover, she looked impeccable as always, in a crisp white blouse and designer jeans, with her hair and makeup flawless. At least he had washed his hands after his morning in the desert.

"If you really want to know," she said, "bad as I may feel now, last night was so much fun, it was all worth it. Best night of my year."

"I'm glad you're happy, Mom. I worry about you though."

"I know."

The waiter came back with a sandwich for Ashford and bacon and eggs for Samantha.

"Can you bring me a pamplemosa?"

The waiter looked at her with a blank stare.

"That's champagne and grapefruit juice." She turned back toward Ashford. "I need a little hair of the dog. Can you drive us home, honey?"

"Sure. I like the drive."

"You take good care of me. You always have." She smiled. "I'm not surprised you wanted to study medicine. It suits you."

"You weren't always so encouraging."

"I have high expectations for you. That's why I want you to go to med school. I'd love to see you become a doctor."

"Mom, I've told you a million times—all I want is to be an RN." School for another eight years so he could plant himself on the upper floor of a hospital for the next thirty? No thanks.

"Just give it some thought. I'll pay for everything."

Ashford nodded noncommittally. A high-desert breeze passed their table, refreshing his senses. For a moment, the smells of nature cut through the stale post-party air of the veranda. He looked out past the gate toward the rolling red-sand hills beyond. Birds chirped in the distant trees.

"I've always been reckless with my money," Samantha said. "I'd like to be reckless spending it on your future while I can. I don't know how much longer I'll be driving this gravy train."

"You seem to have it pretty well in hand."

"It can't last forever. My business is diamonds in your pocket one day, debt collectors at your door the next."

They ate for a few minutes in silence.

"I don't know how you got such a steady temperament, coming from me and your father, but I'm glad." She sipped her drink. "You'll make a better career for yourself than either of us did. You might not make as much money as me, but it will be steadier, whether you choose to become a doctor or just an RN." She paused. "I'll be proud of you either way, but I want you to promise you'll think about it."

"I will, Mom." His eyes drifted off again. He didn't blame her for wanting him to be as successful as possible. After she suffered so many disappointments and tragedies because of Stewart, Ashford was supposed to be the son who did everything right.

It was hard to get away from the expectations even when his decision had been made. Now that he was so close, it didn't feel like the time to overthink his career choice. He wanted so badly to get to work and stop relying on his mother's support for everything. She said he had freedom now, but the freedom she thought she gave him was really a handicap. He had allowed that to be the case, though, for her sake as much as his own.

She relied on him too. She had no one else now. The world saw Samantha as the strongest, most independent woman imaginable. Ashford alone had seen the darkest side of her. When he finally moved away, it would be harder for her than for him.

An hour later, he drove his mother's BMW SUV on the winding road down through the Sedona hills. His eyes took in all the landmarks he knew so well. He loved it up here: the beauty, the cool air, the spiritual energy that emanated from the rocks.

He glanced over at his mother in the passenger seat. She would be asleep before they hit Highway 17.

This morning, that girl had told him he was wrapped up in his mother's world whether he wanted to admit it or not. She thought she had offended him, but he appreciated her frankness. If he went to med school, followed by years of a residency, he would remain dependent upon his mother and her world for the rest of his twenties, if not longer. His mother wanted to give him that gift—and he genuinely believed she felt it was the best thing she could do with her success. He yearned to make his own quieter way. Nursing wouldn't make him a lot of money, but he expected that if he could make an impact with his work, he would be happy.

He shouldn't have come with her this weekend. He had been tempted because he loved Sedona, and it was a light weekend for studying, but it was weird to tag along at his age. Deep down, he always worried a little about his mother when he wasn't close by. But he couldn't stay by her side forever.

The road straightened out, and, far ahead, he saw the interstate cutting across his path. Sure enough, his mother was asleep.

It had been seven years since Stewart died. The fact that his older brother had lived that long was remarkable. He'd had a weak heart that should have killed him as an infant. Still, Samantha blamed herself. If she and Stewart had not become estranged, she reasoned, he would have taken more care for his condition. Ashford wasn't so sure. Stewart had been as stubborn as their mother. He had always lived in a way that almost challenged his weak heart to keep up. It was while working on a construction site that his heart finally gave out. If it hadn't been there, it would have been somewhere else.

Samantha had been unprepared for it. The estrangement probably made the news hurt even more. When Ashford got home from school, his mother had been locked in her room with a bottle of vodka. Ashford didn't know what to think, what to do. He hadn't been close with his brother, who was five years older and always treated him roughly. While he tried to grieve that night, he worried more for his mother. He heard fits of crying, followed by angry words. Ashford's father later told him she had called him that night in a drunken rage. It was the first time his mother and father had spoken in years, and they had not spoken again since.

Late that night, Ashford found her bedroom door open. He searched the house for her, finally finding her asleep in her running car as the garage filled with exhaust. He dragged her out to the front lawn and forced her to vomit. She woke up just as the

EMTs arrived, and she refused to go to the hospital. He sat up awake with her the rest of the night. He came that close to losing his brother and his mother on the same day.

The next morning, she was herself again. She claimed not to remember anything that had happened the night before—the phone call to her ex-husband, the smoke-filled garage, the arrival of the ambulance. Considering how much alcohol she'd drunk, Ashford considered it plausible that she had blacked out, but he also wondered if she just wanted to pretend she didn't remember so she could keep her pride. He allowed her her dignity, never telling anyone about what happened, never even bringing it up with her. He never saw her sink to that kind of place again. She seldom mentioned Stewart again either. But Ashford worried about her. He had seen what was possible.

Today, for the first time, the thought crossed his mind that she might be using what happened to keep him close. He wanted to be there for her, just like he always had, but he had his own life to live too. In a few months, he'd be done with nursing school. He would still have a nine-month internship to complete, but he decided to try to find a concurrent part-time job. He'd need to do better than selling dried desert weeds at tea shops and farmers' markets if he wanted a place of his own.

The highway slid through the middle desert with a forked cactus forest on both sides of the road. As he drove down the slope, the color of the sand lightened, the cacti disappeared, and the desert was bare. Even in the air-conditioned car, he could feel that the heat outside had increased significantly. Such sharp changes to the terrain was one of the things he loved about Arizona. Soon, the sprawl of Phoenix would come into view.

6

"HOLA, PAPÁ."

Leila bypassed the front door and walked around to the back of her dad's house.

"Hey, *¿Quibo?*"

Manny set down his tongs and bottle of beer as Leila wrapped him in a hug. A few black specks from his grill transferred from his T-shirt onto her white tank top, but she didn't care.

Glancing up, she saw his wife coming down the back steps.

"Buenas, Carmen." Leila kissed her stepmother on the cheek.

"I just made some iced tea. Would you like some?"

"Sure."

Carmen walked back up the two steps into the adobe house. Leila sat on a padded wire chair and crossed her legs in the sun. The feet of the chair scraped against the small stones of the patio. Two azalea bushes in full bloom climbed up the back fence. In one corner, opposite from the crackling grill, stood a two-foot-tall porcelain statue of the Blessed Virgin Mary. A neighbor's palm tree leaned toward the small yard, but it was too early for it to give any shade.

She watched her father as he turned his meats. Despite his sedentary lifestyle and his age, his frame remained strong. His dark hair only had a few wisps of gray. He always combed it straight back, accentuating his receding hairline, which he embraced without shame. His round belly spoke of his love for good meat and good beer.

"How are your knees?" she asked.

He shook his head. "Never get old, that's what I say."

"I'll make a deal with the devil." They both laughed.

Leila inhaled deeply, welcoming the sun on her face. "March is so perfect."

"Soon, it will be much too hot."

"I don't mind."

Carmen returned and handed her a glass of iced tea.

"When will you convince this man to retire?" Leila asked her.

"Oh, I try to tell him. He won't listen. He loves to work too much."

Leila smiled, remembering her conversation with him only a week ago on this same patio. Maybe he did still love to work, but he kept it in perspective.

"Work keeps me sharp." Manny looked at them as he turned his chorizo and skirt steak. "I was idle as a young man, and it only got me in trouble. If I were idle now that I am old, I would get in trouble again."

Both women laughed.

"I still have a lot to work for. I won't become a burden to you." He looked Leila straight in her eyes. "You kept up your end of the bargain. I have to keep up mine."

Their eyes held for a moment longer. Yes, she knew.

Leila leaned back in her chair and closed her eyes. The air was pungent with the smell of spring flowers and charred meat. She held her cool glass of tea on her leg, where it sweated refreshing droplets onto her skin.

"Is that my Leila I hear?"

Her eyes opened as she looked toward the voice. A dainty head with blond hair and sparkling brown eyes popped up over the wood fence.

"Hey, Jen."

"Hey yourself. What the hell, not calling me?"

"Sorry. Come on over. We're about to have lunch."

"Yes, join us," Manny encouraged.

"You come over here first. I want to talk to you."

Leila took her glass of tea and scampered to the sidewalk and then to the other side of the fence into the neighbor's yard. They should have put in a gate between the two yards years ago. Ever since Jen's family bought this house before her junior year of high school, she and Leila had been friends. They were in the same grade even though Leila was older.

As soon as Leila reached her, Jen ducked back inside and headed to the back of her house. Leila followed.

"I wish you could have come to Lake Pleasant last weekend. We had so much fun."

"It probably would have been more fun than I had in Sedona."

"Oh, come on." Jen shoved her arm. "Big-shot businesswoman. I bet you had more fun than you want to admit."

Leila sat down on Jen's bed while her friend leaned against her desk, scattered with neglected schoolwork. She was a fifth-year senior at Arizona State.

"Did you meet any new boys up there?"

"Is that all you ever want to talk about? I was secluded in a mansion with a bunch of mortgage lenders and real estate agents. Not ideal for meeting boys."

"You can meet boys anywhere."

"Actually, I had kind of forgotten. I did meet a boy there."

"See? Do tell." Jen's eyes danced with intrigue.

"There's really nothing to tell." Privately, she enjoyed

remembering that morning on the hillside. But if she told Jen about it, she'd try to infuse it with meaning.

Jen sighed. "I wish you'd try harder."

"Why do you care so much that I get a boyfriend? You don't have one either."

"Because I want you to be happy, and I think you're letting what happened in high school cloud your judgment."

"I'm just cautious. I don't want my heart to be broken again . . . ever."

"You can't live like that though. Forget about how it was back then. You were in a tough spot from the start. It was a . . . an unusual situation. All those scrawny seventeen-year-olds and then . . . *va-va-voom* . . . here comes twenty-year-old you."

Leila laughed despite the unpleasantness of her memories from those days. Jen was right. The high school boys were all either intimidated by her or wanted to bed her just to brag.

"Not much has changed."

"Have you even given a guy a chance since then?"

"Don't you remember Vince?"

"Oh, I had forgotten about him."

Of course she had. Leila looked at the sharp slant of midday light coming in through her friend's bedroom window. She wished she hadn't brought up the memory, but here it was—how he had made her love him so he could get a few nights of sex. It was a year of her life, being pursued by him, gradually developing feelings for him, and then suffering the heartbreak and shame after it was over.

"Not all boys are like Vince though," Jen said.

"Well, for whatever reason, I always find the boys who want to sleep with me, not the ones who want to love me."

Why did Jen always want to talk about this stuff? Funny, skinny, blond Jen. She had it so easy and didn't even realize it. What made Jen think she needed to be her relationship counselor? Oh, maybe her friend *did* just want her to be happy.

After a minute, Jen stood up and glanced out her bedroom window. "I'll miss Manny and Carmen when I graduate and move out."

"You'll visit your parents a lot, just like I do."

"I know." She turned back toward Leila. "Do you ever regret holding yourself back so far in school?"

"Hmm. Not really. It was tough, and I'm sure if you'd asked me that question at certain points along the way, I would have answered differently. I'm glad now that I took the extra years of school. Remember, when I came here from Colombia at twelve, I didn't speak a word of English and I had barely even gone to school there. I knew nothing."

"Why didn't Manny send you to school in Colombia? I mean, considering Intel sponsored your move, I imagine your dad's well educated."

"Things were different there. There's a reason he worked so hard to get out."

"I guess."

"So, yeah, it was tough to be older than everyone in school, especially because there was no way for me to hide it. I was taller than all the boys in my classes, and these boobs sure didn't help. But I wanted to learn all I could. I wanted to be able to speak English without an accent."

"It's still hard for me to believe you weren't born here. If I didn't know better, I'd think you were one of those rich LA Latinos who don't even speak Spanish."

Leila laughed. "*Eres una tonta. Déjame demostrártelo.*"

"That's right, you have to prove it to me every once in a while."

Leila hopped up from the bed.

"Come on, let's go have lunch with Manny and Carmen."

7

"Let's make some money today, bitches!" shouted Cox as he blew into the open-walled hot box that was Arizona Prime Path Mortgage Company and knotted his tie.

It was 8:35, and the place was buzzing. Leila stood halfway up to look over the partition of her cubicle, across Dennis's desk, just as Cox arrived at his seat on the other side.

"Mornin', baby."

She rolled her eyes. Cox winked at her before throwing his messenger bag off his shoulder and clapping his hands on the back of his cubicle partner. "Dennis, my man. Big five-oh this weekend, huh? I guess I'll share my birthday with your sorry ass."

Dennis winced from Cox's grip on his shoulders. Leila knew Dennis Arkin would prefer to have been born nineteen years to the day before anyone other than Cox.

She sat back down and returned to her day's lead list.

The office was set up with modular desks and only short walls between them. Noise echoed through the airy eighth-story space as the seven loan officers began to make calls. There had been eight loan officers until a sudden and dramatic dismissal in the days before Sedona. Samantha had her own office with a door and a view of downtown Phoenix. Against the far wall sat an empty set of cubicles piled high with junk and half-constructed loan files, neglected in hopes they would never face an audit.

A blank whiteboard hung on the wall with a line of black markers in the lip at its base. Next to it, mounted on a four-foot-tall platform, stood an elaborate red-and-gold Chinese gong.

"Yo, Tommy Wong," Cox called to the next set of cubicles, "how many loans you locking this week?"

After a few minutes, Leila's neighbor on the other side arrived.

"Hey, DeShawn."

The tall man maneuvered into his chair, squeezing his knees under the desk.

"Another day, another dollar." He smiled at her.

Samantha had hired DeShawn off the car-rental lot at Sky Harbor International Airport. His winning smile and witty personality sold Samantha right away, and in the eight months he had been there, he had sold just enough loans to make a good living. He had already passed Dennis in volume, even though Dennis had been in the business twenty-five years.

Dennis knew better than anyone how to structure a tricky mortgage loan. Leila often went to him for ideas, as did the other loan officers, but the way the business worked now, that kind of expertise wasn't valued. Personality was what made the money these days. So, people like Leila and DeShawn were successful, while Dennis struggled to pull in the deals.

Meanwhile, nobody had as big a personality as Cox. "Whoa, there it is! First one of the week." Cox leaped from his seat and ran to the far wall, grabbed the mallet, and whacked the gong with all his might. Next, he took a marker and wrote a name and number on the board: *Mallenson, 103.2.*

Samantha looked out from her office door. "Lock it, Sam!" shouted Cox.

He returned to his seat, gloating. The gong reverberated through the cavernous room.

Although she could not see him from where she sat, Leila sensed Dennis stewing across the thin wall from her. "Was that . . . *John* Mallenson?" he asked Cox.

"Yeah, why?"

"That was my lead. I've been working it for over a week."

"Not hard enough, obviously. It took me one damn phone call."

"Yeah, because I had him half-sold already. How did you get him?"

"Look, buddy, Samantha wants these leads *sold,* not worked. She wants them fucking closed. You had your chance. Better luck next time."

"It's not fair." Dennis's voice rose in pitch. "I wrote notes on my calls."

Everyone was standing up or looking around the cubicle walls.

"Fair?" Cox pointed at the board. "Do you see that? 1-0-3-point-2, fool. You're lucky to get 1-0-1 on your loans. That's why Samantha transfers unsold leads to me. She wants to make money."

"I practically had him sold on Thursday." Dennis's mustache and eyebrows twitched. His plump face had reddened.

"You can't sell shit. You're a walking fucking catastrophe in a shirt and tie."

"You're an asshole. I've been in this business longer than any of you."

"Well, complain to Samantha. I'm sure she'll be sympathetic." Cox snickered.

"I will." Dennis stood up with determination and walked his short frame across the office while everyone watched. The back of his dress shirt was creeping out of his ill-fitting pants.

The loan officers treated Samantha's office like sacred ground. It was with fear that they answered a summons there, and few went in of their own volition. Dennis stood for a moment outside the door, waiting to be invited in. Leila half-expected him to remove his shoes before entering the holy of holies. Soon after he entered, the door slammed shut.

"Ooh," Cox gasped.

There was silence on the phone lines. Everyone was riveted by the closed door. After about three minutes, Dennis came out, deflated. He walked in silence to his desk. Everyone still looked at the office. Samantha emerged—tall, beautiful, and fierce in her doorway.

"Welcome to the mortgage business. Thanks for fucking playing." She wheeled around and slammed the door behind her.

That would be the last time anyone complained about Cox stealing their leads.

Leila dove into her day's work. She spent the majority of each day calling and recalling the leads she was given. It was monotonous. It took a lot of energy to be sharp again and again when only one out of twenty people even gave her the time to talk, but it was how you had to do it. She was making twice as many calls as Dennis or DeShawn on either side of her. Although she could not hear him over the office noise, it looked like Tommy Wong was doubling her own call volume.

Most of the afternoon was taken up by a crisis on one of Rosemary Grant's closings. Samantha had to call in her first post-Sun Devils' tickets favor from Christy at escrow while Rosemary dissolved in tears at her desk. Eventually, Mona Kearse, the processing lead, found a way to save the day.

Leila loved Mona, a stocky black woman in her late forties, wise, confident, and gay. She was the only one in the office who could stand up to Samantha. Samantha may not have liked Mona much, but she absolutely respected her.

The gong rang only once more that day, for Vicky Tran, but by five thirty, there were four loans written on the whiteboard.

Tommy Wong never rang the gong for the two loans he locked. Leila hadn't even seen him leave his seat, but there they were. Tommy was a machine.

"Tough day on the phones." Leila heard DeShawn and looked up as he stood and gathered his things. "How'd you do?"

"I'm going to keep at it a little longer. People are just now starting to get home from work."

"Good luck. See you tomorrow."

A little past six, Leila reached one of the leads she had been working the week before. The office was more than half-empty by then.

"Have you thought about the refinance over the weekend?"

"Your timing is good," said the man on the other end of the line. "I think I need to do this."

Leila reentered her password and opened her mortgage application platform. It was a nice surprise to have interest after a whole day of dead ends.

She listened to the client, then explained the program she could do. He asked her to repeat her company's name.

"Why do you call it that? I mean, you guys are a subprime shop, right?"

"Technically. But we don't like the term *subprime*. The loan I want to put you in will put you on the path to being a prime A-paper borrower in a few years. That's how we got our name— *Prime Path*. Your credit profile isn't very good right now. You're almost two months late on your mortgage, and those credit card payments are killing you."

Cox had popped up on the other side of the cubicle with excitement on his face. Leila muffled the phone with one hand and gestured to him for a rate sheet.

He sprinted to the shared counter and returned, handing the convoluted eight-page stapled document to her.

"The loan I'm going to put you in is a 3/27 ARM. The rate

is only fixed for the first three years. It's the best I can do with your credit profile. This is a cash-out refinance, so we can roll all those credit card balances into the loan and give you a fresh start. Now, you have to promise me that over these next three years you won't miss a payment on this mortgage and you won't run up the balances on those cards again. Then in three years, call me back and I'll refinance you into a thirty-year fixed rate mortgage."

A long pause ensued.

"I'm not locking this rate until you promise."

Cox was giddy, hopping up and down like a child in need of the bathroom. Finally, the man on the line gave his promise.

"Okay, I'll lock it in now, Mr. Collins, and we will definitely get it closed before the end of April."

As soon as Leila hung up the phone, Cox whooped with delight. Leila lifted up her feet and swung around in her office chair with her hand raised to meet his high five.

"That was good. Making him promise. How'd you come up with that shit?"

"I meant it. This loan gives him a fresh start on his finances, or at least it will if he takes it."

"You're such a saint."

"You know I won't do a loan I don't believe in. I couldn't live with myself."

"Get up there to that board, girl."

With a grin, she scampered up to hit the gong, then wrote her loan on the board. Samantha peeked out from her office and smiled. Tommy, the only other loan officer still there, barely glanced up from his desk.

Mona stood beside her desk, ready to leave for the day. Leila walked up to her.

"You'll see that one hit your inbox in the morning," Leila told her. "His current lender is going to start foreclosure proceedings on May first. As bad as his credit is now, if we don't close it by the end of April, it will be shot for years."

"I'll get it done for you, hon." She smiled. "I heard what you told him on the phone. You do this business the right way. I respect that."

"Thanks, Mona."

Leila returned to her desk. She was tired. It was almost seven o'clock. She entered the last of the data for her new loan, then shut down her computer.

Just as she stood up to leave, she heard Samantha's voice.

"Leila, can you come in here for a sec?"

Leila forced herself not to sigh. Why now, just at the end of a long day? But there was no arguing with Samantha. She walked into her boss's office.

"Good job today." Samantha motioned for her to sit down. "I like to see people get rewarded by staying late and getting a loan. You understand how to succeed in this business."

Leila nodded. Samantha leaned against the window frame with the lights in the buildings of downtown coming on behind her.

"Did you enjoy the trip to Sedona?"

"Yes."

"I'm glad. I really liked having you there. You bring a touch of beauty and class, which is often sorely lacking at those events."

"You bring that yourself." Leila jumped on the opportunity to flatter her boss.

Samantha smiled. "I hope you will be there again next year."

Here it comes.

"You know I only bring two loan officers. Cox is always so far ahead, he'll be there every year. But Tommy's already over a million ahead of you this year. If he'd had a full year, he would have caught you last year, even as well as you did."

As long as she still made good money, Leila really didn't care if Tommy Wong beat her for second place—but she couldn't say that to Samantha.

"You're doing some things exactly right. Tonight showed that. But I think you need some fresh competitive motivation. It's been a long time since I've seen you in here making calls on a Saturday. I know that's what Tommy was doing that weekend we were all up in Sedona."

Leila's exhilaration from helping Mr. Collins get out of a bad spot faded. Samantha clearly didn't want her to start feeling too comfortable.

Samantha walked over and took Leila's hand. "You're doing great. That's the only reason I'm talking to you. I want to see you do even better, and I know you have it in you."

The boss's cell phone buzzed on her desk. She glanced over at it. "I've got to go, and I'm sure you're exhausted. My son's waiting for me downstairs."

"Your son's picking you up?" Leila mentally kicked herself for sounding so intrigued.

"Sounds silly, doesn't it?" Samantha laughed. "I loaned him my car for the day while his is being repaired. I don't know why he doesn't let me buy him a new car. He's as stubborn as I am sometimes."

8

LEILA GATHERED HER things and left the office. Everyone but Samantha was already gone.

Wow, leaving later than Cox and Tommy. That's rare.

Wait. Why was she congratulating herself? She never wanted to think that way. That kind of mindset would squeeze all semblance of balance out of her life, making her like Samantha. But the boss was not a model for the kind of woman Leila wanted to be.

As the elevator doors closed in front of her, she saw Samantha's office light go out. She didn't hold the elevator. Samantha always fussed around before leaving, and Leila really wanted to get home.

There was nothing to hurry for. She would heat up the leftovers Carmen sent her home with yesterday, have a cup of tea, and put herself to sleep with a Gabriel García Márquez story. She enjoyed the simple pleasures of her nights after the clamor and chaos of her days.

That was what she had worked for. No use complaining now that she had it.

The elevator clunked to the bottom. Leila stepped out the back door of the building into the parking lot. She stopped. She had spotted Ashford. Their eyes locked. He was parked in an SUV across the lot with the window rolled down.

His face registered recognition, and he straightened in his seat. His crisp blue eyes pierced through the shadows. His expression made it clear that he had thought of her once or twice since their encounter in Sedona.

She stood for a moment beneath the sharp cone of light on the doorstep, holding his eyes. It would be polite to go and say hello. But Samantha might already be in the elevator behind her. She didn't like the idea of her boss coming out of the building right then and learning that they knew each other. That hint of secrecy was strangely stimulating. She smiled at Ashford, then dipped out of the lighted doorway and walked to her car.

It was a small moment. It would be a stretch to call it a flirtation, but it had been a long time since she had given someone *that* kind of smile. She enjoyed it.

The broad streets were quiet, even for a Monday evening. The spring training crowds had dispersed, vanishing as quickly as they had descended upon the Phoenix valley a month before.

As she drove into Scottsdale, she caught herself still smiling. She laughed.

Her life must be *really* boring if such a little thing could excite her. But a boring life was what she wanted. She was better off without excitement, which had proven to be a double-edged sword. The last thing she needed was any excitement involving her boss's son. Her life was too steadily speeding down the right track. Things were just where she wanted them.

Her friends called it a lonely life, but she didn't like that. *Loneliness* was a form of self-pity in which she chose not to indulge. She had other priorities.

Yet she couldn't help being drawn by the image of those blue eyes shining out of the shadows and the face of a young man she barely knew.

She pulled her Toyota into the desert-tan apartment complex, parked, quickly glanced around the empty lot from her car, then got out of it and hurried up the outer staircase to her second-floor unit. An indignant meow greeted her as soon as she opened the door, and a black shadow darted away toward the bedroom.

"Romeo, come say hello."

When she had put down her things and taken off her shoes, the cat came back and rubbed against her legs, crying for his dinner. Her tardiness would be forgiven after a can of tuna.

She had lived in this same little apartment since saving up enough money waiting tables after high school to move out. It was an easy drive to work and to her father's house. Now that she was doing so well, everyone told her she should buy her own house—mortgages were her business, and she could afford it. But home prices had increased so much in Phoenix this last year that she was hesitant. So, she saved as much money as she could, content with her little rental.

After eating her leftovers, she opened her coat closet and took out the guitar case that leaned upright inside. She took the instrument out and checked the tuning. Close enough. She sat back down and plucked out one of the Colombian folk songs she remembered from her childhood. The beauty of her homeland tugged at her heart through the song.

It was a children's song, a lullaby. She wondered how she heard it the first time and who might have sung it to her. She had barely known her mother, who died when she was so young. Leila remembered her through feelings more than images. She liked to think her mother had sung this song to her as an infant.

She imagined that she was singing it to her own child. Deep in her heart, the destiny of motherhood tugged at her. She sometimes dreamed of her child—a daughter, usually—with such vividness that she felt it was reality. Her love for this imagined child was so strong that it made her afraid. Pain could cut deepest across the strongest love.

Most of the time, this future seemed distant, but music brought it closer. Making the dream a reality would require risks. Would she ever be brave enough?

She put the guitar back in its case and prepared for bed. She opened her bedroom window—the night breeze in springtime was so nice. This evening, it felt warm enough to leave the window open for the night. She took her earplugs out of the bathroom drawer so the city noises wouldn't keep her awake.

Leila had chosen this simple life. She worked her tail off to earn it. It gave her what she needed and kept her from getting hurt.

But what about now? She had done the work. She had "made it." Was it time to believe life could mean more?

9

"I'M SO GLAD you're coming with me to this."

"Me too," Jen said. "It'll be fun. I get to meet these characters you keep talking about."

"Watch out for Cox."

"I know. You've told me."

Leila brought her friend into her small kitchen. "I'm almost ready."

Jen hopped up onto the countertop, dangling her legs as one of her sandals fell off her foot onto the floor. She looked at the sundress Leila wore.

"You better have a bikini on under that." The bright-blue halter strap of Jen's own suit showed under her tank top.

"I'm more comfortable in this. It's a pool party, but I doubt I'll want to swim."

Jen scowled at her. "It's not about swimming. I know you have a bikini. I was with you when you bought it, remember?"

"I need to work out some before wearing it. My stomach isn't fit for public exposure right now. Maybe by summer."

"Come on. You look fantastic. Rock your curves, girl!"

"Fine, I'll bring it." She only agreed to shut the skinny bitch up. "Not promising I'll put it on."

They drove in Leila's car to North Scottsdale. Here she went—to a work party on a Saturday. Samantha told her she should work more Saturdays. What else was this? At least she had a friend with her this time.

"So, it's two people's birthday party?"

"Yeah. Cox and Dennis share a cubicle and a birthday, so every April there's a big party. This year, it's Dennis's fiftieth. The two of them couldn't be more different, so it will inevitably be weird."

"Can't wait."

"Don't get your hopes up. Promise me you'll come salsa dancing with me tonight. I'm going to need to blow off some steam after this party."

"Deal."

Leila glanced over as she ascended the hill. Jen's eyes grew large at the million-dollar homes lining the road.

"Your boss lives up here? Wow."

"I told you." She turned up the driveway.

Samantha's house was of the vaguely Spanish design so common in Phoenix, with light stucco and orange-tiled roof, but it stood taller and grander than most. Leila thought it reflected Samantha's personality to perfection. The sturdy pines that lined the driveway were too tall to have grown up with the house. They must have been brought in and planted as mature trees. All this greenery must have demanded an astronomical irrigation budget.

Leila parked and walked with Jen around to the back. The large pool was surrounded by a spacious gray-stone patio, perched above the Phoenix valley. Potted bougainvillea and geraniums splashed the deck with spring color, while azalea vines climbed the fence, bursting with lush purple flowers. There was a bar to one side with a hired bartender. Music blared.

Jen gaped at it all. Leila grabbed her hand.

"Come on. I'll introduce you to all these characters."

Cox bounded up to them. His skinny, hairless torso was heavily doused in sunscreen. "Is this my birthday present? You shouldn't have."

"This is *my* friend, Jen."

"Really? What *kind* of friend?"

"Huh?"

"You hold hands. What else do you do?"

Leila sighed, dropping Jen's hand, which she had inadvertently hung on to.

Cox slapped his forehead. "Now I get it. You're into girls."

"That's the only way you can reconcile that I won't sleep with you?"

"It all makes sense now that I know you're a lesbo."

Jen snickered.

"Please don't embarrass yourself. I told you, Jen and I are just friends."

Jen's snicker had turned into full-on laughing.

"I bet you at least, you know . . ." Cox began making lewd hand gestures.

"Oh God," Leila muttered. She marched away from Jen and Cox, angry at them both. She was upset with Jen for encouraging him with her laughter. But Jen followed her.

Dennis greeted them next, already reveling in his birthday party while his wife followed him disinterestedly. DeShawn sat by the pool. Rosemary was splashing around in it. Tommy Wong lounged in the shade in dark sunglasses, jeans, and a designer shirt, looking completely out of place and clearly not caring a bit.

Samantha walked out of the house in a white bikini and gold sarong. To Leila's surprise, Ashford walked next to her. They each placed a tray of food on the long table. Leila left Jen and walked over to them. She intended to greet Ashford by name to make it clear they had met before. She didn't want to hide anything from Samantha.

"Hi, dear." Samantha beamed and hugged Leila. "Meet my son. Ashford, this is Leila."

Leila and Ashford looked into each other's eyes.

They each said hi and shook each other's hand. Leila remembered that he had asked for a rain check on the handshake in Sedona. There was still a moment to make it clear they had met before.

"Come," Samantha cut back in. "I want to meet the friend you brought."

The moment passed, and an inadvertent secret was born.

Before they got back to Jen, who had started up a conversation with DeShawn, Vicky Tran arrived, followed shortly by Mona and her partner. Samantha walked over to greet them. Leila stepped back toward Ashford. A line of tall mesquite trees rose from the slope below the patio and cast their broken shade over the area where they stood.

"Look at you, coming to a mortgage party in broad daylight," said Leila.

"Maybe I hoped to see you again."

"Bold of you to admit that."

"It's true."

She hadn't needed to hear him say it. She saw it in his eyes the moment he came out of the house. She was curious about him, but cautious.

"So, Ashford Frye, did you manage to get all your specimens home from Sedona?"

"Well, first off, my name's Ashford Cohen."

"That makes sense. Samantha and your father have been divorced for quite a few years, haven't they?"

"Yes. And all I'll say about the specimens is that you should have seen my mom's face when I opened the trunk at home."

Leila laughed. "I can only imagine. But what do you do with them all?"

"Sometimes, I sell teas to a local shop or at the farmers' market."

A loud splash erupted as Cox cannonballed into the pool. After a quick glance that way, she looked back at Ashford.

"I'm imagining some kind of mad scientist laboratory set up in your bedroom."

"You're not far off."

"Yet you're studying nursing, not medicine. Why?"

"They go hand in hand . . . with a little imagination."

"I'm not sure the hospitals will like you brewing exotic teas at your patients' bedsides."

"I'll wait awhile before I bust out the teas. I'm trying to follow the rules while I take my grad-school lumps." He adjusted the folded-up sleeve of his striped dress shirt, untucked above blue shorts.

"So, is the nursing itself more of a means to an end for you?"

"I want my work to mean something. Nursing will allow me to have an impact."

"Interesting. Most people go into nursing for the human element—to help people."

"It's the same thing."

"Not exactly. Being impactful is about you, not them."

Ashford's forehead crinkled. Leila couldn't tell if he was upset or simply wrapping his head around what she had said. Probably some of both. She wished she had held her tongue.

"There, I've offended you again. Twice now in the two times we've talked. I'm sorry."

"It's nothing."

She turned away and looked out toward the sun-drenched valley.

Sometimes, Leila thought she subconsciously sabotaged her conversations with boys because she didn't want to risk her emotions. Here was a handsome and compelling young man who was clearly attracted to her, and she had called him out for having selfish career motivations, as if she would have any idea—or any room to talk. She would not have blamed him if he just walked away.

Instead, they stood side by side in silence. She wasn't going to walk away first, and he was probably just as stubborn. Ashford grabbed several corn chips off the table behind him. The crunch of his bites sounded artificially loud against their silence. He brushed his hands together to get rid of the salt.

"How did you end up with all these people?" he finally asked. "It doesn't seem like you fit in any better than I do."

"They must have thought I would." She looked back toward him, glad for the invitation to talk again. "I fell in with them a lot like everyone your mom recruits. I was waiting tables at an upscale steakhouse not too far from here. One night your mother, Cox, and a few others came in. They spent over a thousand dollars that night. It was astonishing. Cox, naturally, was hitting on me mercilessly, and by the end of the night, he offered me a job. Samantha laughed and said, 'Why not?' The next morning, I showed up. And after I sold a couple of loans, I quit my waitressing job."

Ashford laughed. "A stroke of good luck."

"Maybe."

But luck had nothing to do with it. She had strategically climbed to better restaurants and better shifts so she could meet successful people. Even when she was hired, nothing was guaranteed. Over these two-plus years, she could no longer count the number of people to whom Samantha had given a phone and a lead list who flamed out after a few weeks. She didn't pay anyone a base salary except for the processors.

"Obviously you've done well with it."

How could she respond to that? Guys often made that kind of comment to her. Yeah, she had done well, but what did that really mean? Doing well at her job didn't define who she was.

Or did it? What else could define her right now?

She looked at the people clustered around the pool. Dennis was still attempting fake joviality. Fifty was, after all, a depressing age for a man to turn when his career and marriage were stagnant.

Rosemary was talking to Cox, who was disinterested. She craved attention from the playboy, but she was past the age and physique where she could interest him. It was sad to watch. Jen was down to her blue bikini, sitting on the edge of the pool with her feet dangling in, flirting with DeShawn as he floated nearby.

As Leila looked across the scene, her eyes met Samantha's. Although she was all the way across the patio and they both wore sunglasses, Leila could tell that Samantha's eyes were on her, and there could be no doubting that their eyes had met. A tingle of apprehension danced up her spine.

Leila couldn't put her finger on exactly why, but from the start she had sensed Samantha wouldn't like seeing her getting to know Ashford. It wasn't her place. This look from across the patio confirmed it.

"I'll talk to you later." She left Ashford, walked to the bar for a Coke, then went to sit in a pool chair next to Mona.

She chided herself. Surely, Samantha noticed her son's rare appearance at one of her parties as well as his and Leila's awkward greeting. She didn't miss much. Now, she would be suspicious of Leila. Leila wished she had been quicker to reveal their acquaintance when she had the chance twenty minutes ago.

Why even bother talking to the guy? If her ego needed stroking by a man's interest, she could get that from any sleaze like Cox. Ashford's interest in her was probably no better. He just had more class. No sense risking her job for a man who would surely let her down.

10

LOOKING BACK, IT was clear how it had all started. Good intentions had led many into the same trap. Leila always made her business be about the people, not the money, thinking that would keep her from wrong. But in the final reckoning, how could she honestly claim she had been different?

The office was abuzz from early on that day. Interest rates had taken a dip, and the loan officers were calling on every old lead they could find. Dennis was the first one to lock a loan. He made sure everyone saw when he went up to ring the gong and write his loan on the board. But the lower rates meant previously locked loans were at risk of being poached by other lenders.

It was Monday, April thirtieth.

"Your Collins loan is funding today, right?" DeShawn asked Leila. "What does that make for you this month, six? Gonna be a nice check in a couple of weeks."

"Yes. I'm so relieved. I had to babysit that one all the way through. But we got it done. How many for you?"

"Only two."

"Two is better than none."

"Keeps me in the business another month."

He laughed wryly, and she understood. Such were the fine lines of the mortgage business. One or two closings, and you could keep your head above water. Three or four, and you were making a decent living. Five or six, and you were earning six figures.

The phone rang. She answered. It was Christy from escrow.

"Leila, I have some bad news. Collins can't close today."

"What do you mean it *can't close*? It has to." Her blood started heating up. "If his old loan doesn't pay off today, the bank will start foreclosure proceedings tomorrow."

"I'm sorry." Christy's voice shook. "There's nothing I can do. The right of rescission wasn't signed till Thursday."

"No. He signed Wednesday."

"But his wife didn't sign her papers till the next morning. The notary saw that the rate lock wasn't expiring for another week and thought it would be fine. Now, it has to roll to tomorrow, the first."

"That's unacceptable! I trusted you to get this right. Of all the files, this is the one you couldn't screw up."

"I'm . . . I'm sorry."

"There's got to be some way."

"Please, Leila, you know the rules. Three full days. You can't cheat your three days like Jesus did."

"Dammit, Christy. This is no time for jokes."

Hanging up, Leila's whole body shook. She was furious. It was all she could do not to pick something up off her desk and throw it.

She hated how after she did the hard work of a sale, a loan file passed totally out of her control. She had to rely on underwriters, the appraiser, and processors. At the end, she had to rely on escrow. They all made mistakes, and sometimes, there was nothing she could do about it. Yet she was always the one who had to break bad news to the clients, even when it wasn't her fault. That was how it worked. That was why she made the big bucks.

Leila knew the regulation. A cash-out refinance couldn't close until three days after the right of rescission notice was signed— no exceptions.

Christy said they'd close it tomorrow, but she wasn't looking at the whole picture. Leila wasn't so sure the loan *could* close tomorrow. This family was in trouble, and it was about to get far worse than they realized. Once foreclosure had started, the end investor wouldn't buy the loan from them. Samantha wouldn't agree to fund a loan without an investor lined up to buy it immediately afterward. Otherwise, their firm would be stuck with over $200,000 on their warehouse line of credit with no way to move it off.

She tried to concentrate, to focus. The other loan officers' voices pounded against her ears. Usually, she could make them all fade into a background buzz, but today she heard every word. The voices were grating, infuriating. She leaped out of her seat and walked into Samantha's office. Her boss listened, patient and unmoved, while Leila told her the whole story.

"Calm yourself, hon. Stop panicking."

"I don't know what to do."

"Yes, you do. Don't pretend you don't know how these things get handled. Do you have the co-borrower's signature?"

"Well, yes. She signed the opening paperwork."

"Then what's the problem?"

"But—"

"Solve it!" Samantha glared at her. "I'm tired of you acting like you're too good to do what needs to be done. You like to say you're in this business for the people, as if you're different. Well, prove it. These people need your help right now. Get it done!"

Samantha turned back to her computer screen, signaling to Leila that they were finished.

She walked back to her desk. Yes, she did know how to solve it. Did the fact that she had looked the other way so often when Cox and others fudged customer documents make her any less guilty just because she had not done it herself? Cox would blatantly revise income figures on loan applications to make it appear people qualified for higher mortgages than they really did. Then he would brag about it. Leila would never do something like that. But this was totally different. She was trying to get her clients out of a bad situation, not put them into one.

She already knew what she was going to do, but she still needed a few minutes to come to terms with it. It was for their own good—to save their home. Isn't that what Mr. and Mrs. Collins were trusting her to do for them? She wasn't going to commit fraud—lying about a borrower's income or assets or fudging an appraised value. Other loan officers did those things regularly. Yes, it would technically be forgery, but it would reflect the customers' true intentions. If she did nothing, they might lose their home. In this one case, surely the ends justified the means.

Leila found one of the original disclosures that had a clean signature, then printed up the original right of rescission page from the final doc package. Taking both into the copy room, she cut out Mrs. Collins's signature with steadier hands than she expected. She taped it onto the new document and dated the document for Wednesday instead of Thursday. She made a photocopy. It looked good. She took the page with the taped-on signature and slipped it into the shred bin. She scanned the new page to Christy at escrow before she would have time to rethink her action.

Christy closed the loan without asking any questions. Later, Mr. Collins called Leila, profuse with gratitude for the fresh start she had given his family.

Leila was exhausted. Despite the opportunity of the low rates, she couldn't muster the energy to make any calls that afternoon. She left early and drove to her dad's house.

After eating dinner together, they sat outside in the warm evening. Carmen had stayed inside. The air was pleasant now that the whole yard was in shade. Leila put on her light leather jacket. Birds chirped in the palm trees.

"I don't know how much longer I can do this business," she said. "It takes a lot out of me."

"You're a tough girl, though."

"I worry what I'll become."

"Always keep your integrity. I learned that the hard way."

She might have to learn it the hard way too. How much of her integrity had she already sacrificed? It was difficult to know what to think about what she did today. She had a hard time even thinking it was *wrong*. The three-day rescission rule was silly. But people had lost their careers over less than she'd done.

In her position, she had risked more than her career. Her dad always warned her that as non-US citizens, it was imperative that they live by the letter of the law. Any slip could be the end of this life they'd built on so much sweat and tears.

Leila breathed deeply of the hot night air. The dry desert heat was so different than the humidity of Cartagena, perched between the jungle and the sea.

"A few months ago, I had a dream," she said. "My face was on one of those pictures I told you about seeing in Paulo's house in Cartagena. All the women looked dead in the pictures—I've never forgotten that part. In my dream, my face looked dead too. Thinking about it makes me wonder what I'm doing with my life."

Manny snorted. "The portraits looked dead because Paulo was never any good as an artist. That's all."

"That's not the point. I'm afraid I'm not really living. Maybe the mortgage business isn't for me."

She wished she could work in a lower-pressure career, one that wouldn't suck the life out of her. This morning, DeShawn had reminded her how nice her paycheck would be in a couple of weeks. It was hard to think about quitting when the money kept flowing. How much would be enough? How much of herself would it cost?

Samantha turned off her light and looked out across the empty office. It had been a good day—four closings and eight new names on the board. She began to shut off lights. In the copy room, she took a key out of her purse and opened the shred bin. She didn't look in it every night, but on a wild day at the office like this, one never knew what goodies might be found in there.

It didn't take her long to come across the rescission document with Mrs. Collins's taped-on signature. Her eyes were well trained.

Samantha smiled. "Good girl, Leila."

She folded up the page and put it in her purse, just in case it might be useful to her one day. She locked the shred bin and turned off the rest of the lights.

11

"ASHFORD."

He knew her voice immediately. His eyes searched the crowded square on this hot June night in Old Town. The place had a festive atmosphere, befitting his mood as he celebrated with his classmates. A Latin band played under a large awning, and several couples danced on the pavement.

He found her. She was sitting on a bench in a black dress with two other girls. Her legs were folded at an angle down to her strappy sandals. Her curly hair flowed over and behind her head. She was stunning. She smiled as he walked over.

"It's good to see you again, Leila. I hoped I would."

"Did you?"

"May I buy you a drink?"

"No, thank you."

Her two friends watched with interest. He remembered the blonde from the pool party at his house.

"Sit down for a minute," Leila said. "I'll try not to say anything rude this time."

He sat on an adjacent bench. Strings of lights reached from the lampposts toward the buildings behind, creating a starlike pattern above them. The lights shimmered off the windows of the restaurants and clubs.

"I graduated today," he said.

"That's wonderful. Congratulations. So did Jen."

The blonde smiled. They congratulated each other.

A small breeze rose off the canal, softening the heat of the night. Out of the corner of his eye, Ashford saw his classmates walk into a crowded bar across the square. He was in no hurry to catch up with them.

"I owe you some thanks." He looked back at Leila. "You gave me a good challenge the last time we talked. It made me think."

She looked skeptical.

"The week after the pool party, I had an encounter at the hospital with a patient who really shook me up. It forced me to think of my role as a nurse differently, in a good way."

"I'm glad to hear that. I think you'll be a good nurse. Just go easy on your magic brews."

He laughed.

"So, what happened at the hospital?"

"I don't want to go into it now."

"But I'm curious now, and I don't know when I'll see you again."

"I hope we'll see each other again soon. Really, I would like to ask you out."

"So ask."

"I'm afraid to."

"It would be bold of you, all things considered."

"How would you answer?"

"I don't know. Going out with you would be pretty risky for me. I suppose it depends on how you ask."

Ashford's heart thumped. Now was the time. Her two friends bored holes in him with their eyes. "Will you go out with me?"

"No. That wasn't good enough."

He laughed even though it felt like he had been led into a trap. He fidgeted and glanced toward the bar his friends had entered.

She placed her hand on top of his, where it rested on his knee. "You have to give a girl a reason to say yes. An enticement . . . something to look forward to. I'd need more incentive before taking such a risk."

"I'll try again."

"Too late, you missed your chance. But I'll dance with you."

"I don't know how to dance salsa."

"This isn't salsa music. It's bachata. Come, I'll show you how." She hopped to her feet and reached her hand toward him. He couldn't resist taking it. He followed her down in front of the band where the other couples danced. The music was inviting: beautiful with its melody while pulsing with its rhythm. Leila's shoulders had already started moving to the beat.

"See how they're moving?" She nodded toward the other couples, still holding his hand. "Try it—side to side, one two three lift, one two three lift."

He tried as she watched him.

"Bend your knees. Get low. That's it." She turned in front of him. Her face was inches away. "Now, hold me behind my shoulder blades."

He put his hands behind her. Their eyes were locked. She began to sway. He supported her back as she leaned into his hands.

"Feel the way I move. Now, move with me. Remember the steps: one two three lift."

He followed her, feeling the rhythm through her back against his hands. Their eyes remained locked. She had dark, wise eyes.

"Now closer. Let our knees move in between each other's."

Without waiting for his lead, she moved in close to him. He could feel her hair against his cheek and smell her fragrant skin. Her cool, bare legs were against his. Her chest brushed against him as they moved from side to side. Her back muscles pulsed against his hands. The dance was sensual, visceral—her body and the music inviting him into the movement.

She was singing softly in Spanish. Her voice moved him with its beauty and drew him closer to her in the intimacy of the moment. He understood the rhythm now, moving naturally with her. Their legs were entwined. Their chests moved in unison without being pressed together.

By the time the song ended, Ashford had fallen in love.

She looked back up into his eyes. Surely, she had felt the same thing he did. For the briefest moment, he saw it in her eyes before she looked away.

"That was nice. You're a natural." She began to walk back toward her friends. He reached for her hand.

"Leila, I have to see you again."

She turned her head and smiled at him. There was a distance in her eyes now, a lonely melancholy. The connection from a moment before was gone. "It's only a dance, darling."

She slipped her hand out of his grasp and walked back across the square.

It was late, but the girls weren't tired. Leila scampered ahead of Jen and Brandy and pirouetted on the canal path. The warm night air felt good against her skin. She waited for her friends to catch up.

"Nobody would believe you're the sober one." Brandy laughed.

"She's drunk on love," said Jen.

"No, I'm not."

"Lie all you want. We saw how you looked at that boy and how you danced with him. It was hot."

Leila walked on. She felt happy and alive. She wanted to enjoy the moment without thinking about it too much.

"Please give that boy a chance."

"I can't. He's my boss's son."

"Then why did you dance with him like that?"

"A dance isn't a promise."

"You're leading him on."

As Leila walked, she moved to the bachata rhythm in her head, remembering the feeling of Ashford's strong hands on her shoulder blades and the scent of his neck. She *did* like him. That was why she had to be so careful.

The warm breeze rustled through the close palms beside the path. The canal shimmered in the light of the few stars bright enough to break through the glow of the city.

"How bad could it be if you went out with him?"

My goodness, Jen, just let it go!

"Maybe his mom wouldn't even mind."

"Oh, she would."

"So? Get a new job. Mortgage brokers are a dime a dozen around here. Wouldn't it be worth it?"

"No." She turned and looked at Jen, finally starting to feel annoyed. Surely, Jen remembered. It wasn't only the issue of Ashford being Samantha's son. Leila wasn't ready to open her heart to anyone. The risk to her heart scared her more than the risk to her livelihood.

Even if she was ready to love, surely she could do better than *him*.

Jen looked sad for her. Leila couldn't help feeling a little melancholy too.

"Let's get out of here," Brandy said. "My feet hurt."

Leila took Brandy's arm, and they walked back up the path the way they had come under the tall palms. Jen followed a step behind.

Soon, Leila was driving her friends home. With the windows rolled down and the radio cranked up, they sang at the top of their lungs, pleading along with Justin Timberlake that *this just can't be summer love.*

Later that night, Leila kicked off her shoes as soon as she walked back into her apartment.

It had been a fun evening—the kind she should make the time for more often. It wasn't time she lacked, but energy. Her job sucked so much out of her that planning and preparing for a night out had become a daunting task. She couldn't even imagine dating.

Jen was right. There were more important things than work. Love was certainly one of them. But why take a chance for something she couldn't trust?

Lying awake in bed as Romeo settled himself heavily on her legs, the melody of the song she and Ashford had danced to came back to her mind.

She *was* lonely. She could admit it to herself, if not to anyone else. But somehow, even loneliness had become comfortable. Her childhood trained her in loneliness as a means for survival. Those lessons had served her well. But her heart wanted to trust people, to believe in them. She wanted to feel free to take a risk. She longed for companionship—to let someone hold her heart and trust it wouldn't be broken.

For a moment tonight, when she leaned into Ashford's hands and felt herself held securely, she trusted him. How wonderful it would feel to be held now as she drifted off to sleep.

If only it were that simple.

12

"ARIZONA PRIME PATH Mortgage, this is Leila."

"Leila, it's me. Ashford."

"What? You can't call me here." She looked around, hoping nobody had heard her.

"I have to see you again. Can you come downstairs?"

"You're here? At the office?"

"I'm at the Starbucks across the street."

She was angry. She didn't want to meet him, but she couldn't talk on the phone. DeShawn had already glanced over. She was clearly not on a sales call.

Minutes later, she took the elevator down and crossed the busy street at the stoplight, glancing up even though she knew none of the loan officers had desks at the windows.

Ashford stood up from his table when she walked in. Her eyes shot daggers at him. He tried to smile, but her look wiped it off his face.

"Don't be angry."

"I am angry. You can't put me in this position."

"My mom isn't even there today."

"But it's not just her. What if someone else sees us here?"

She sat down but refused his invitation for coffee. Just as in the office a few minutes before, the room buzzed with many voices, but she could have heard a pin drop, afraid her every word would be overheard.

"I'm sorry, Leila. I had to find a way to see you again. I've been dying since that night we danced in Old Town. You're unlike anyone I've ever met. I can't think of anything but you." His words came quick, with agitation.

"Have you thought this through? Think of the position it would put me in."

"Maybe my mom wouldn't mind as much as you think."

Leila was glad he didn't say, "She wouldn't have to know."

"Don't you know your own mother? I'm an immigrant with no college education. She has high hopes for her son, and one of them is for him to marry well. She's picturing a nice white girl from a good family for you. Now, maybe that sounds too heavy for you. Maybe you're only looking for a girl to have a good time with, and here I am talking about who you'll marry. But for me, it *is* heavy."

It wasn't something she could explain to him if he didn't already know. After two years working for her, Leila thought she knew Samantha pretty well. Samantha cared about her, genuinely, but Samantha also categorized people.

Samantha expected people to remain in their roles. She saw no disconnect in hiring an immigrant while at the same time railing on the politicians for failing to secure the state's southern border. Leila had a legal visa, but she had no doubt that Samantha would employ a nondocumented immigrant if they were good on a phone. The same deeply held categorizations allowed her to be good friends with Paul Weidman and hold genuine professional respect for Mona Shaw, yet at the same time laugh when Cox made hurtful, homophobic jokes behind their backs.

Leila had been in the country long enough to see these assumptions in people's eyes. It was the kind of racism you couldn't even call out. She wouldn't have been able to explain it to Ashford. "There are things about me you don't know," she said instead.

"I want to know everything about you."

"I know. I can tell. I even wish . . ." She let the thought trail off. "If I agree to date you and it doesn't work out, I'm risking both my career and my heart."

"I won't break your heart, Leila. I promise."

His words rushed in and grabbed at something inside her. She looked into his eyes. They were serious and true. She believed him. But his confidence was unwarranted. He had no livelihood of his own. Even if they truly loved each other, if Samantha fired her and kicked him out of her house, they would have nothing. She didn't like him *that* much.

She placed her hand on his across the table. "I believe you won't try to. But it might be out of your hands."

They sat in silence for a few minutes longer. There was nothing else to be said.

Leila stood up and walked to his side of the table. He stood up too. They hugged. She closed her eyes, realizing that they were moist as she savored his embrace. She could almost believe she was safe in those arms. She stepped back and squeezed his hand between both of hers.

"Goodbye, Ashford."

Through the summer, Leila buckled down and worked. It was her only focus. She spent long days at the office and even started coming in on Saturdays. Nobody wanted to be outdoors in the summer in Phoenix anyway when the heat hit you in the face like a wall and took your breath away. Opening the front door felt like opening the oven. July had been her biggest closing month ever, and August was shaping up the same way. She was gaining on Tommy Wong for second place.

Paul was acting as the listing agent for a huge new subdivision on the edge of the city being built right out into the desert. Thanks to Leila's efforts, which had started that night in Sedona, Arizona Prime Path Mortgage was named the preferred lender. Plats had begun to sell above asking price before ground had even been broken.

The political mood in the country was turning against the subprime mortgage market, but business boomed on. Rates were low, and the housing market was hot. Regulators had eliminated a few loan programs but not enough to seriously impact business. A handful of the most risk-inclined lenders went bankrupt that summer. Rather than worry, Samantha reveled in the reduction in competition.

A slight dip in house prices threw people into a brief panic. Articles in *The New York Times* and *The Wall Street Journal* started referring to the housing market as a "bubble." But Arizona Prime Path had an ally in their trusted appraiser, Marshall Berg. Samantha's loan officers always got the property values they needed. There were strict regulations meant to prevent collusion between lenders and appraisers, but Leila had little doubt those had all been thrown out the window. She didn't even want to think about the implications if the rumors were true—that Samantha had started sleeping with the appraiser.

Toward the end of the summer, closed mortgage loans became more difficult to place with investors. While Leila, Cox, and Tommy kept selling loans to new borrowers, Samantha would spend most of her days on the phone with investors who had become reticent to buy subprime mortgage paper. Leila marveled how she always managed to find someone. There was still plenty of willing investment money, even if it came from odd places and the securitization of the mortgage debt grew more creative by the month.

"It's a temporary blip," Samantha told Leila when she dared ask what she *really* thought. "The economy is as strong as ever, and the stock market is at all-time highs. The mortgage market needed this. It helps clear out the people who just got in the business for easy money."

Leila couldn't help but be a little concerned, despite her stunning monthly commission checks. The easiest thing was to work and not think too much.

Early in September, Samantha stopped at Leila's desk at the end of the day. "Do you have plans tonight, honey?"

Plans? Since when did she have plans on a Wednesday night?

"Come to dinner with me. My treat."

Leila wrapped up her work and accompanied her boss down the elevator. They took Samantha's SUV to downtown Scottsdale.

"Do you remember this place?" Samantha asked as they walked in.

"Of course."

The room was dark, with high ceilings and modern chandeliers slung low over the tables. The pervasive smell of the grill filled the artificially cool air. Leila wished she had brought her sweater from the office. It was the restaurant where her waitressing career had ended. All the little sounds of the place—the clatter of dishes, the sizzle of the grill, the whir of the air conditioner—registered themselves with her memories.

"I wanted to bring you back here to show you how far you've come. I'm incredibly proud of you."

Leila smiled. An extravagant gesture like an expensive dinner was typical of Samantha.

As the hostess led them to a booth, the men at the bar all looked up from their drinks. Leila knew they both looked good that night—herself in black pants and a flattering black blouse, Samantha in a fitted button-down white shirt tucked into a pinstriped pencil skirt.

They started with oysters and an enormous martini for Samantha. Leila ordered the sea bass, the most expensive fish on the menu. She knew Samantha's generosity would be offended if she didn't splurge.

"I see a lot of myself in you," Samantha said after the oyster shells were carried away. "Neither of us grew up rich. Neither of us went to college. We made our own breaks. Now look at us, queens of this city."

Leila smiled again.

"Most Mexicans never get out of the kitchen of a place like this."

"Samantha!"

"I'm sorry. You're right. That wasn't very PC."

Leila shook her head, appalled, though she didn't know why it even surprised her anymore. She focused on her fish, which was delicious, although it took her a few minutes to regain her appetite. The cover band in the corner started a new song.

"I've so enjoyed the renewed focus I'm seeing in you this summer," Samantha said. "You're really coming into your own and turning this job into your business. Successful loan officers do that—they make it into their own small business. Things are getting tougher, but you'll survive it."

"What do you think will happen, really?"

Samantha took a long sip of her cocktail. "It all depends on the politics. I'll be the first to admit that the housing market looks like it could be in a bubble. If so, we'll have a little downturn and then get back to business. But the politics scare me. Last night on Fox News, they were talking about a bill in Congress banning subprime mortgages. That would be a disaster. Think of all the people we gave those low adjustable rate mortgages to with the promise that they could refinance in a couple of years. What will happen if they can't? Mass foreclosures."

Leila thought of Mr. and Mrs. Collins and so many others. She had never thought about this possibility before, but Samantha was right, not that politicians wouldn't look at it that way.

As the martini began to hit Samantha, her eyes moved downward the way a man's would. It wasn't the first time, and Leila had to admit to having been guilty herself a time or two. It was about power, the way they noticed each other, not sex. Samantha would have given anything for hers to be natural, while Leila marveled at Samantha's lift, even when she didn't wear a bra. They were each envious of the other . . . but only a little.

"Paul's Desert Villas complex is having their first occupancies later this month." Samantha's gaze returned to Leila's eyes. "How many are you closing in the first batch?"

"Three. And I have four more in contract for later in the year."

"That's fantastic. Which reminds me, Paul's hosting a gala Saturday after next to serve as an unofficial launch. It will be a beautiful event at the Wrigley Mansion. I'd love it if you could go. Paul adores you."

"I wouldn't be intruding?"

"Not at all. Think of all the Realtors who will be there. A huge opportunity. I can't take Cox after what he said to Paul last year."

Leila laughed. "Is Cox truly oblivious, or does he just not care?"

"Some of both, I'm sure. Afterward, he claimed he didn't realize Paul was gay when he said it. If that's true, then he really is oblivious."

"His loss, my gain."

"So, will you come?"

"Sure. It sounds like fun. I've never been to the Wrigley Mansion."

"One condition: You *have* to wear that sapphire necklace I gave you. I want you to sparkle and glow."

"Okay." Fine, she would be Samantha's exotic dress-up doll for one night. That was still the roll Samantha had assigned her to, no matter how many loans she closed. She was the immigrant success story who got out of the kitchen, damn her.

Everyone always spoke highly of Samantha—an example of a powerful woman succeeding in a man's world. It would be harsh to say that Samantha did it for the wrong reasons. Perhaps the power and the admiration of the community were what made Samantha happy, and if so, who was Leila to judge? But Samantha was no role model. She had succeeded by using all the same dirty tricks that men had been using for years—along with a few added tricks that only women knew. She subtly encouraged the misogyny that pervaded their business, because she knew how to use it to her advantage. Samantha had no interest in empowering Leila or other young women. If Leila's success or aspirations ever threatened Samantha's, she would quickly be made an adversary.

They finished their meal.

"For the gala, will I be your plus one?" Leila asked as they walked back toward Samantha's car.

"No. Bring your own date if you like. I'm bringing my son as my date. He looks so handsome in a tuxedo."

Leila stopped for a moment before falling back into stride beside her boss. She was glad Samantha wasn't looking at her face. It wasn't the right reaction, but she found herself looking forward to the event even more.

What would she wear? What would she say to him when she saw him again, with Samantha inevitably standing right there beside them? It would be a dangerous moment.

"Here." Samantha handed her keys to Leila. "You drive us back to the office. I'll go up and work some more to sober up."

13

LEILA TRADED PLACES with the valet outside her car door. She had been looking forward to this night, albeit with some trepidation.

The two-story white stucco mansion with dark wood trim and Spanish tiling glowed in the sunset. It sat at the hilltop, up a long, twisting drive from the base of the valley. From here, she could see the entire Valley of the Sun, spread out in all directions, to the distant mountains that surrounded it on all sides. She looked back toward the mansion, feeling several sets of eyes look toward her from the entryway.

The party was in full swing. She was late, but it was worth it. It took time to look this good.

It had been hard to decide what to wear. Since Samantha had insisted on her wearing the sapphire necklace, she needed to wear something it would complement. Nothing in her closet would do, so she and Jen had gone shopping. She'd found a gorgeous, cream-colored dress with stitched detailing. It fell just below her knees, with half-inch straps and a sweetheart neckline. It was the most money she had ever paid for a dress; she knew she wasn't supposed to care. A pair of blue heels tied in with the necklace perfectly.

The valet drove off. In her sunglasses, with a small clutch in her hand, she looked up to the second-floor balcony. There he was.

He *did* look good in a tuxedo. She smiled upward, feeling a little flutter inside and then she hurried in.

She entered the grand lobby beneath a high rounded ceiling of ornately painted wood. It felt regal walking in there, like stepping back into the 1930s.

"Leila, darling!" Paul Weidman hurried toward her from the parlor.

She regrouped. Her thoughts had drifted away. She forced herself back into business mode and kissed Paul on the cheek. He held a glass of champagne, which was clearly not his first.

"You look absolutely ravishing. I was beginning to think you weren't coming."

"I wouldn't miss it."

"Have you been to the Wrigley Mansion before?"

"No. It's beautiful."

He offered her his arm and led her back through the hall, past the library, into the parlor, which served as the main gathering for the gala. Two young real estate agents milled eagerly with sales packets while Paul worked the room. It was easy to spot the investors and business partners, who looked at ease in the setting and had dressed appropriately. By contrast, those two junior agents—in dresses better suited for the nightclub, with new money they hadn't learned how to spend and new breasts they hadn't learned how to carry—looked as out of place as the bright real estate posters on the walls beside the stately paintings by Dutch masters.

Paul excused himself, leaving her with Clary and going to talk with one of the investors. Clary looked a little too tan in his white dinner jacket.

"By dinner, he'll have the development a hundred percent sold," said Clary, watching his partner with pride. "You may need to take some loan applications on napkins."

Leila laughed. "It wouldn't be the first time."

Samantha and Ashford entered the room from the bar, each holding a glass of champagne. Samantha glowed in a floor-length yellow gown with a plunging neckline. Ashford, in his classic, fitted tuxedo, was easily the most handsome man in the room.

"You wore it." Samantha rushed toward her. "How gorgeous you look. That dress is perfect for your figure."

They embraced. Leila's eyes were on Ashford.

"Naturally, you two need no introduction," said Samantha.

Leila leaned in toward Ashford. Considering the setting, it felt appropriate to greet him with a touch of their cheeks. Maybe she just wanted to. "Hello, Ashford." She lingered close to his face, breathing in his scent. "It's good to see you again."

"You too, Leila."

Samantha took her son's arm, unwilling to relinquish her escort. Leila walked beside them. She glimpsed Ashford stealing glances toward her, but she forced herself not to look at him. She felt drawn to him as if by a magnetic force. Her whole body tingled.

Why him? He was only a boy: raw, naïve, untested by the toughness of life.

Soon, dinner was served. The dining room, directly off from the lounge, glowed with soft light. In contrast to the lounge, the inner walls of the dining room were white, with bronze curtains framing the two long walls of windows. The sun had gone down, and the city shimmered in lights. Far in the distance, the mountains formed a glowing pink silhouette against the dark sky.

Leila was seated with Paul and Clary, along with several investors and the lead contractor. Dinner conversation buzzed with business talk. If they could sell Desert Villas so easily, why not build farther out into the desert? No one mentioned the dip in home prices or the tightening regulations on mortgage lending.

Though Leila took part in the conversation, she couldn't concentrate. Against her will, her eyes kept being drawn toward Ashford's. He was all the way across the room, but their eyes met several times throughout the meal. He was clearly looking at her as much as he thought he could get away with. The first few times she caught him looking, he shifted his eyes away. After the main course had been carried away and dessert was being served, he dared to hold her gaze. They looked at each other for several long seconds, just like they had as she arrived, but this time neither smiled. She saw the longing in his eyes and wondered if her eyes gave her away too. Finally, it was Leila who looked away.

He had never been able to hide his attraction for her. But the way he looked at her was different than other men. His eyes were filled with kindness instead of lust. He looked inside her, inviting her to reveal what was there.

She yearned to give love a chance. She was tired of this life and its false validations. With the right man, perhaps she would be ready to try again. But why did she have to be drawn toward *this* man?

After dinner, the party spilled back into the lounge and through the dining room to the bar on the other side. It grew noisy. Wine and champagne had flowed freely, and now more cocktails were being poured. This was the time for the deals to get made. Leila, normally so good at using her sobriety as an advantage, struggled to keep her focus. Her mind was on anything *but* business. She needed a moment to herself.

She passed through the lounge, back toward the lobby entrance. It was a beautiful building with things to see on every wall and in every corner. From the lobby, a staircase spiraled up toward the ornate ceiling. She walked up, curious about what treasures were to be found on the second floor.

Soft lights from the city below and the stars above shone through the windows of the dimly lit bedrooms. Oddly shaped passageways led from one room to another. The whole building creaked and sang. The old pipes echoed in the walls. Soon, she came around to a landing above the noisy bar. The commotion drowned out the songs in the old building's walls.

Leila glanced over the dark wood banister. Samantha held court below, with contractors and real estate agents wrapped around her finger. Leila stepped back and sat on a dark-velvet couch, looking out the windows through the palm and mesquite trees toward the glowing night.

Samantha sold with such ease. Leila could hear her, pretending to flirt with the men who had gathered around her, who had no idea the sale was well underway. It was almost too easy. Leila could do it too, if she wanted to, but she didn't like doing business that way. It grew harder and harder to keep doing it the right way.

Her father was right—everything else was worthless unless there was space for love in her life. What else had she been working for all these years?

A footfall sounded on the stairs, coming up from the bar. It was him. She knew it even before she saw him.

"I wondered where you were," he said.

"I'm tired of it all."

"I know."

He sat down on the couch beside her. After a few moments, he placed his hand on top of hers. She reflexively squeezed down around his fingers, surprising herself. She had craved his touch more than she realized.

"I think about you every day." A whisper was all he dared. "You told me it could never work between us. Maybe you're right, but I can't help it."

He paused, seeming to gather his courage. She tried to steady her racing heart.

"Leila . . ." Her name hovered on his lips.

She turned toward him, her breaths coming quick. Her decision had already been made.

Samantha emitted a sharp laugh close below, as if to warn them of their folly.

In a moment, the care with which she had ordered every detail of her life would be shattered. She wasn't worried anymore.

The space between them broke. Their lips met. Her arms were around his neck, her chest crushed against him. Her tongue darted and found his between their parted lips. She closed her eyes and relaxed into his arms. He kissed her with passion. It felt so good, she could have cried.

She pulled back for a moment and looked at him, beaming as she studied his face.

"I love you," he said.

"Kiss me again." She grabbed the back of his head and made him.

Another footfall sounded on the stairs, coming up.

Leila leaped off the couch, taking Ashford's hand and snatching up her clutch. They ran noiselessly into the nearest passage out of the landing. As soon as they were away, they began laughing. She kissed him quickly, kicking her leg back behind her. Still clutching his hand, she led farther through the strange passageway as it twisted first right, then left. They found themselves in a lavish old powder room, ornately tiled in green. To one side was a long, inset seat, covered in antique, brocade cushions. The green tiles darkened the whole room.

Leila reclined onto the cushions. Ashford leaned over her. His kiss was soft and tender now. She wrapped her arms around his back, pulling him into her, kissing him harder. She couldn't get enough of him.

His hand touched her cheek then her neck beneath the fancy jewelry. His fingers moved lower, tracing the neckline of her dress.

That was when she realized the right straps of her dress and bra had slipped off her shoulder. She didn't try to pull them back up, but her heartbeat quickened. Ashford helped it farther down her arm, folding her dress and bra down and taking her breast in his hand. It was shocking to feel his warmth against her there. She relished his courage. It made her tingle everywhere. She wanted more.

He had removed his jacket. She tugged at his bow tie and undid it, then undid the top few buttons of his shirt. She kissed his neck, lingering by his collarbone as she took in the delicious scent of him, which she had first noticed the night they danced together and again when she greeted him earlier that evening. She could feel him hard against her. She fought against the abandonment of desire.

She stopped herself from unbuttoning his shirt any further and hugged him tightly against herself. "Hold me like this for a moment." Her heart was binding itself to him. She could feel his love. It was beckoning her to plunge in with him. She had to be careful, or her heart would be lost. She pushed him up so she could look into his eyes.

"I want you so bad, but not here. Not like this. You said you love me. I need you to prove it."

The wrong kind of man would have taken it as a rejection, but Ashford grabbed her cheeks and kissed her. "That's all I want."

She was aware of his eyes on her as she pulled the side of her dress back up. His gaze made her feel shy but also beautiful. Also aroused.

"We'd better get back before we're missed," she said.

He picked his bow tie up from where it had fallen on the green tiles. "Do you know how to tie one of these?"

"No. Did Samantha tie it for you?"

He nodded.

"I'd better learn how." She stood up and draped it, untied, around his neck. "You'll look good wearing it like this at this stage of the evening. It's sexy."

She took a business card and pen out of her clutch. She circled her cell number and drew a heart next to it. "I'll go down first and head toward the parlor. You go back the other way, to the bar." She pressed the card into his hand. "Call me tomorrow, okay?"

She kissed him one more time, then placed her finger against his lips, smiling broadly. She dashed out of the room.

14

ASHFORD DID CALL Leila the next day, and every day from then on.

He took her out, first to coffee, then to dinner, then out to the night clubs on Saddlebag Trail. She invited him to a bachata and cumbia lesson, and they danced at a Latin club. She made sure they went to a club Jen and the other girls didn't frequent. They made sure that their dates stayed secret. The only way they could ensure that Samantha didn't find out was not to tell anyone.

Leila loved the feeling of being courted, but she was still hedging her bets with Ashford. As she got to know him better, she learned that his kindness was real. Maybe he was naïve, but at least he wasn't jaded by love. He was eager to give, eager to serve. He would be a good nurse, she knew now. She had judged him harshly at first. He would be a good boyfriend too—if she let it come to that.

Business slowed sharply for Leila and for the whole office. She didn't mind at all, even though several others grew nervous, particularly Dennis and DeShawn. Leila still had a few loans closing each month, which was plenty. It was nice to be able to leave a little early and not feel pressured to come in on the weekends. It gave her more time to spend with Ashford.

He also had plenty of time on his hands. He was working as an intern at the university hospital while looking for a permanent nursing job. Until he got one, he wouldn't be able to afford a place of his own, which he assured Leila was an urgent priority.

Leila savored those weeks, feeling warm in her heart and content. Ashford was so much fun to be with. He made her feel beautiful and cherished. She wanted to take things slow and enjoy this time when dating felt so easy and fun. She knew the easiness couldn't last. She wouldn't have wanted it to. If Ashford was right for her, then it would have to grow more serious and then they would have to face the consequences of their romance.

He was head over heels for her. She had been worried about her own heart being broken. If she ended things now, it would be *his* heart that would break. She didn't want to do that to him. But neither did she owe him anything. She still had to take care of herself first.

In October, Samantha was asked to speak at a west regional convention of subprime mortgage lenders in Los Angeles. As the leader of a still-thriving independent mortgage brokerage, it would be her job to dispel the larger investment banks' fear that the subprime mortgage business had begun to implode. She would be gone three days.

Ashford asked Leila to come over on Friday evening when Samantha was out of town. He would cook her dinner. They could swim.

It felt wrong somehow, but the idea of the secrecy tempted her. And why shouldn't she go? It was his home too. He had the right to invite over the girl he was seeing. She accepted.

What should she wear? What should she bring? She couldn't be so presumptuous as to pack an overnight bag, but she wanted to have all her necessities available if she *did* end up spending the night. She never liked being caught in a situation unprepared. She tried to get ready before leaving for work that morning, but she couldn't decide what to wear. Instead, she left the office early to change and freshen up. She wore shorts and a pretty yellow top that she would feel okay about wearing home the next day if she had to, and stuffed her largest purse with her swimsuit, a change of underwear, and all the toiletries she might need.

She drove up to his house—her boss's house—later than he was expecting her. He greeted her at the door with a happy kiss, not seeming to mind her tardiness. His face was smooth and soft, clean-shaven for the evening.

"How about a swim before dinner? It's beautiful to swim here while the sun is setting."

"Is that what you do with all the girls?" She smiled to let him know she was joking, even if she *was* curious.

"You're the first girl I've ever brought here. My mother is a difficult person to bring a girl home to."

"I can imagine." She believed him, and that felt nice.

Leila looked out toward the low sun against the mountains. She was savoring each moment. "We met over a sunrise. Now a sunset. I like it. I'll go change."

This was the kind of night she had been waiting for. She may have been at his home, but she felt comfortable and safe—as in control as would ever be possible at this early time with him. Unlike those rushed, reckless moments at the gala, tonight she thought she knew what she could expect. She needed that to feel relaxed.

In the bathroom, she put on her black bikini. She had been in this bathroom before, at Samantha's parties. She took an extra moment to get her bearings and assess where everything was. She pulled her hair up high on top of her head. Hopefully, she could keep it dry during their swim. Otherwise, it would go *everywhere*.

She rehearsed her smile once in the mirror and looked at herself. Jen was right—she should wear this suit more often. It did favors for her that bikinis didn't usually do. As long as she breathed from her chest instead of her stomach, she looked *amazing*. She walked out and met Ashford by the pool.

She smiled at him, then walked down into the cool water and swam forward with her head above, in the warm air. He unbuttoned his shirt, kicked off his sandals, and did a full dive in toward her. She bobbed in place until he came close, then reached out her hands to him. He held them and pushed away from her, pulling her after him in the water. They came to the far edge of the pool, looking west over the valley. The sun had just started to dip behind the mountains. They leaned over the rim and watched until it disappeared, turning everything in its vicinity golden. In the foreground, the palm trees looked black, each trunk and frond creating crisp lines as if drawn in pencil against the clear sky. The mountains on the horizon made a dark rim of the western sky, which went from bright yellow, rising to pale blue, and, higher still, darkening and filling with more stars until directly above and behind them the color went deep navy.

Leila pushed back from the edge. Ashford swam beside her. She fell toward his body, inviting him to wrap his arm under her lower back beneath the water as she put her arm around his shoulders. He carried her that way, slowly, in wide circles around the pool. She placed her head on his shoulder, feeling safe and content.

"Ashford, I want you to make love to me tonight."

He smiled at her with his gentle eyes. She lifted her head from his shoulder and kissed him. As she reclined against him in the water, she felt him getting excited. Now that she had said it, she didn't want to wait any more than he did.

She swam away from him toward the steps and got out of the water. She dried herself off with the towel he'd brought for her, then untied her hair and shook it out. She started toward the house, smiling back over her shoulder.

Was it so bad to want to be touched, to want to be loved? He had told her he loved her. Was it so wrong to want to find out if he had it in him?

The doors from the pool were flung wide open, bringing the dry night air into the house. The tile of the patio continued past the glass doors, into the spacious, open kitchen and dining rooms to the right. To the left, the sitting room looked out over the valley.

Ashford dried himself off and followed her in. When he reached her, she threw her arms around his neck and kissed him. He pulled her upward and toward him, caressing her mouth with his own.

She took half a step back, reached behind and untied her top, letting it fall to the floor, then pressed herself into him again. His body had warmed faster than hers after the swim. She savored his warm skin against her cool, damp breasts. She closed her eyes as his tongue responded to her kiss. His mouth was sweet, inviting.

Leila stepped back again, then untied his wet shorts and pulled them down. With her hands on his sides, she guided him toward the nearest couch and pushed him down, sitting on top of him and pressing herself against him as his hands and lips explored her body. Grabbing her hips, he flipped her over on the couch and pulled off her suit bottom. The plush couch was cool against her back.

She put her hand on his chest. "Darling, do you have a condom?" She had brought some in her big purse but didn't want to admit it to him unless she had to.

"Yes."

He got up and walked away from the couch. She watched his firm behind and the arch of his lower back. *What a gorgeous man.* He only disappeared for a few moments, returning with four Trojans connected on a line.

"You have high hopes for tonight."

He laughed, nervously perhaps, but he still carried himself with confidence. She felt so sexy lying there naked with him looking at her, desiring her.

She had half-expected him to be a hesitant lover—a boy lacking experience. But so far, he seemed like a man who might be able to handle her. She was about to find out and could hardly wait to know.

He tore a condom off but didn't unwrap it. He kissed her again, then let his hand run across her neck and slowly over her breast and stomach until it rested against the wetness between her legs. Her insides roiled with every touch of his body against her skin, his lips against her neck, his hand between her legs. She was aching for him.

Leila's entire heart and body went out to Ashford as they made love. She was no longer afraid, despite all the obstacles in their way. She wanted to trust him. She wanted to stand on the precipice and then dive into this love, without hesitation or regret. She was offering her heart as a gift to him; it was his to do with what he would.

When it was over, Ashford smiled down at her, his body slick with sweat. She bit her lip with pleasure.

"Stay inside me for a moment longer."

He *did* make love with confidence. She already wanted more, but considering how long she'd made him wait, she wasn't surprised it had been short. She would get hers soon enough.

They had plenty of time, all the time in the world, even *forever*, she hoped. But she wouldn't say that to him yet.

They lay together on the couch in an intimate embrace. Leila had never felt so happy. They might never have moved if both of their stomachs hadn't started to grumble. Leila laughed. "You invited me for dinner. I suppose I should let you make it for me."

She put back on the clothes she'd arrived in and sat at the

kitchen bar top watching as he boiled pasta and made an olive oil sauce. He served it with sliced chicken he had grilled that afternoon over a bed of arugula. It wasn't a complicated meal, but Leila was impressed. She didn't recognize a few flavors in the sauce; it tasted fresh and new. She wondered if his knowledge of local plants and their uses extended to his cooking. Hopefully, he would cook for her often.

They talked and laughed late into the night. She helped him wash the dishes, and then they sat back down on the couch where they had made love. Leila felt their bond growing stronger with every hour. She chose not to be afraid.

At midnight, they made love again. Then she pulled the blanket off the top of the couch and slept there naked, with her back to him and his arms wrapped tightly around her. The doors were still open to the warm night. Even when the cool night breeze came in, she felt warm with his hot body behind her, touching every inch of her backside. She fell asleep in the comfort of his embrace.

Leila awoke with the sun on her eyes. How good it felt to wake up in someone's arms. It amazed her how well she had slept. No unfamiliar noises woke her during the night. Ashford was apparently not a snorer, thank God.

It was starting to get hot. She rose from the couch and walked to the double glass doors, pausing for a moment with the sun warm against her bare skin, then pulled the doors shut. The air-conditioning came on automatically, triggered by the closing doors. She picked up Ashford's shirt and buttoned it up halfway, glancing down at him, still asleep but beginning to stir.

She opened several cabinets until she found the coffee. She started a pot. Before the smell of the coffee flooded the room, she could smell his scent still on his shirt. The front flaps brushed against the bare skin between her thighs, where every nerve had been awakened.

As she walked back to the couch, Ashford opened his eyes. She sat down and smiled at him. He reached up and touched her neck, then caressed her breast through the thin shirt. She was tingling and had to have him again. She pulled his shirt up over her head. She pulled the blanket off of him and straddled him. Reaching back to the side table, she unwrapped a condom and put it on him. It fit tightly.

She guided him inside her, closing her eyes and breathing in deeply. She grabbed his hands and put them on her ass, showing him how she wanted to be loved. "No, there, let me lead. Yeah, that's it. Right there."

She moved herself on top of him, making him find all her spots. Her body welcomed him into her, joining his flesh to hers. This time, it was she who didn't take long. She screamed with delight. Her own pleasure brought him there with her until he joined her in climax. She fell onto his chest. He grasped her, still pulsing.

Something had happened inside her. It felt like the whole world shifted at that moment.

She sat back up, slid herself off of him and reached to remove the condom. She gasped again, this time with dread. A chill ran through her as she clapped her hand to her mouth.

"What is it?"

"Shit."

He looked down and saw the broken condom.

Leila hurried to her feet. "This is bad, Ashford."

She gathered up her clothes and rushed to the bathroom. She leaned forward on the sink counter for a minute. She knew where she was in her cycle. Maybe that explained why she had wanted him so badly, but it was stupid, *stupid* not to think of that. When she came back, Ashford was standing by the couch in his shorts looking bewildered. She didn't want to tell him about the strange feeling inside of her. It wasn't something she could explain. But she thought she knew what it meant.

"I'm not angry at you. It's not your fault. This has been wonderful. But I need to go home. I need to be alone right now."

He reached for her hand. For a brief moment, she resisted, but he grasped first one hand, then the other with such strength that she relaxed. His touch assured her. He lifted her chin to make her look in his eyes.

"Leila, whatever happens, I'm here for you now. I'll protect you and take care of you. Don't worry about my mother or anything."

She forced her breath to steady. "Months ago, you promised me you wouldn't break my heart. I need to hear it again. I need you to really mean it."

"I promise. I love you. I will never hurt you. I will never break your heart."

Leila believed him. As she looked at his face, the tears that had been on the verge of falling dissolved in her eyes.

She fell against him, and he wrapped his arms around her. There was safety in his embrace. Suddenly, it was the only safety she had, and she needed to trust it. All the security she had built around her life had been lost. Such was the price of choosing love.

PART II

LA JUNGLA

COLOMBIA, 1985

15

"TELL ME THE story, Manny. How did you pull it off?"

"It was a great day for the people, young *revolucionario*. Tomorrow will be another, and you will see the power of justice with your own eyes."

Daylight had been slow to reach through the moist foliage to light the rebel camp. Only thirty miles outside of Bogotá, the jungle was thick. They had been here for almost a week. Word was this would be their last day waiting amongst the mosquitos and beetles in sweat-soaked green fatigues. The time for action was coming.

Manny poured himself another cup of coffee from the battered tin pot, then tipped it across to his companion's cup. "Have you ever shot that gun of yours, San Juan el Bautista Velasquez?"

"Only in practice. But I'm ready."

"You'd better be." Manny looked at the boy with his thin frame, skinny arms, and hairless face. How old could he be—seventeen? He wondered if he could even *lift* his gun. Manny decided to treat the child like the man he would need to be.

"Be ready not to think, only to act. It's a shock to fight for the first time, but if you stop to think, you'll be the first one killed."

Manny looked up as a tall, thin woman stepped out of his tent, dressed in the same green fatigues as he wore, with her black hair pulled tight into a bun. He smiled at his wife. Even dressed as a soldier, her face etched with sadness, he thought Marissa was the most beautiful woman in the world.

"What are you men up so early talking about?"

"Manny is going to tell me the story of when we took the Dominican Embassy. Were you there too?"

"No. But my father was, along with Manuel. I was pregnant at the time."

"If I had known, I would have stayed home."

"*¡No te comas sus cuentos!* Nothing could have kept him away."

Manny laughed. "*Quizás. Bueno,* do you think the boy with the cumbersome saint's name deserves his story?"

"Oh, leave him alone about his name." She turned back into her tent.

San Juan el Bautista Velasquez fidgeted. Manny knew he was embarrassed by his parents' strange choice of a name.

"Picture it." Manny stretched out his hand. "Ambassadors from around the world gathered at the embassy for a celebration. They were dressed in their finest regalia, all their pins and medals, eating and drinking. We surprised them in tracksuits." He laughed. Two other men, stationed to watch the road, took a few steps closer to listen. Manny nodded at Carlos and Pasqual before continuing.

"That was the day the Colombian government finally took us seriously and saw us as the voice of the people that we were. M-19 had waited ten years for a day like that. Even the United States' ambassador was there, so you can be sure the world took notice.

"We released all the women the next day to show we are a movement of the people and only held the diplomats. We are a political movement after all, not animals. I'm proud that not a single hostage was killed. The president tried to make us out as terrorists, but the people were behind us the whole time. When it ended, the crowds cheered us as heroes."

"Was the mission a success?"

"I suppose it depends on your point of view. Not all our demands were met, but we showed the government that the people will stand up, that we are willing to fight and die for justice. We made the name of M-19 famous in Colombia and around the world."

Manny paused, then looked from Juan to the other two men. "I believe this new mission will be an even prouder moment for us, our *proudest* moment. Even if we die, it will be for the honor of the people of Colombia, and others will follow in our footsteps."

Someone grunted. Manny thought it was Pasqual but couldn't be sure. He had spoken the heroic words they all wanted to believe, but none of them felt eager to die, himself included.

"Did you go to Cuba with the others?" asked Juan.

"Yes. Most of the group is still there, including Marissa's father. Since I wasn't one of the leaders, I was allowed to return to Colombia in less than a year."

"In time for the birth of your child?"

The question brought a pall over Manny's good memories. His face darkened. "Yes, in time for the birth of my child."

San Juan el Bautista stopped asking questions. But after a moment, Manny continued talking anyway. He wanted to share his story, even the painful parts.

"I had many dreams in those days of what Colombia could become once its people were free and also of the family I could have. I wanted to start a better life for myself—that was what we were fighting for, after all. I used my share of the ransom money to start a course at *Universidad de Cartagena*."

"What did you study?"

"Computer programming."

Juan started to laugh. "Computers?"

"Don't mock the future. Unfortunately, God had other plans for me. I quit the program, and now here I am."

The day was growing hotter. Humidity hung thick in the air. Droplets gathered on the wide green leaves of the foliage that encircled the camp.

"Okay, enough of your stories," said Pasqual. "My feet ache. Time for you two to take a watch."

"Fair enough." Manny leaped to his feet. "Grab your rifle, Juan. Don't let it weigh you down."

The relieved watchmen sat down. Pasqual shook the empty coffee pot in disappointment as Manny and Juan walked toward the edge of camp.

Early that afternoon, after his watch had ended, Manny retired to his tent, hoping there would be time for a *siesta* before the others arrived.

Marissa handed him a mug of water. He took it and held her hands around it. She looked into his eyes for a moment before slipping her hand out and walking back across the tent. He would not get the kiss he had hoped for. Manny knew he was sticky and unshaven, with his mustache overgrown—hardly the handsome husband she had married long ago. But he also knew that wasn't why she had walked away. He could not be blamed for his appearance after a week in a jungle camp.

It wasn't he who had changed. Their pain affected him, but he was still the same man, full of hopes and dreams. His heart ached for their lost child. But it also still ached with love for his wife, even though the spark was gone from her eyes. He wouldn't push for her love. He believed it was still there, deep in her broken heart, and would return to him in time. He missed her, even now when they stood beside each other. He missed her most at night when they lay together, when sometimes she even allowed him to make love to her, but he could tell her heart wasn't in it.

"Do you really believe everything you told that boy earlier?" she asked.

"What do you mean?"

"Nothing changed after your *success* at the embassy in 1980. Nothing will change if we are successful in the days ahead."

"We must believe it can. If people like us don't work for a better future, Colombia will be lost."

"A better future—I used to believe in that."

Manny came up behind her and took her bony shoulders in his hands. She flinched at his touch, but he held firm. He would never stop trying to restore the connection that had once been so intense between them. "Have hope, Marissa, both for our country and for ourselves. We can have another child."

She twisted out of his grasp. "Do you think another child can make up for the daughter we lost? This hole in my heart is not something that can be plugged with a new thing to love."

"I'm sorry. I didn't mean it like that. I'll never forget that loss either. But it doesn't mean you can't love again."

"Look at us. Look at our lives. This is no place to raise a child."

"We can walk away from it, like we did before. I'll go back to the university and finish the course."

"This thing we're doing will always follow us. It would have poisoned our daughter's life if she had lived, and it will poison another child's life if we have one."

"It doesn't have to." Manny sighed, desperate to make her understand. "Don't you want the chance to love again? It wouldn't be to undo the pain. A heart is big enough to carry love and pain together. Pain alone will kill you."

"Maybe it already has."

Manny sat down on his cot. There was nothing more he could say. It had been three years since their baby died. Marissa had to find the will to heal in her own heart before his love would have a chance to reach her again.

How he wished she would try, even if only for him. He had loved their baby too—so much. He would never forget. But he wanted another chance at fatherhood. His heart burst with love that had nowhere to go. Without a child, and with a wall of pain between him and his wife, there was nothing left but to channel his energy toward the cause of his people.

He believed Marissa's heart could still love too. He remembered her before, in the intimate early days of their marriage and during the happy months with their daughter. He believed motherhood could bring back the woman he loved. If only she would give it a chance.

The rumble of trucks sounded sharply from the distant road. Manny jumped up from the cot, instinctively reaching for his rifle. Marissa remained calm.

"They're here," she said. "The time has come at last."

16

MARISSA LIFTED THE flap of the tent and looked out.

"*¡Dios mio!* Look at all those guns and explosives."

"Who is it?"

"The *comandante* and his whole gang." She paused. "It looks like Paulo came with them."

Manny stiffened. "What business does that *traqueto* have with this?" He walked up beside his wife, watching as three crowded trucks rumbled into the center of camp. The men leaped out, stretching their legs after the long, cramped drive into the jungle. Yes, there was Paulo Varga, looking full of energy for a fight. The men began to unpack their arsenal.

Marissa turned back inside. "Don't let your imagination turn that man into a rival, Manuel."

"It's his own doing."

"Let it go. I told you, nothing happened when you were away in Cuba."

"I saw the picture he painted of you."

She rolled her eyes. "I was all alone and pregnant. You were off trying to save the world. Paulo was kind to me, so I was kind to him too. He asked if he could paint me, but it wasn't romantic. You saw the picture. He made me look like a frumpy old woman in that stupid folkloric dress. He's not a good artist." She lifted the tent flap again. "Jealousy's not attractive on you, Manuel. Come on. There's work to do today."

Manny followed her out as the entire assembly instinctively gathered for orders from their commander.

The comandante was last out of the truck. Everyone's eyes fell on him. He was built like a stone, not the largest man, but the one who would surely be the most difficult to move off his spot. His own eyes, quick and clever, surveyed those who waited on his words. He had a mustache almost as broad as his shoulders, and bushy hair squashed down from his green cap.

"It is time, my friends," he said. "Tomorrow, we fight for justice, for Colombia!"

A cheer went up, which the comandante quieted with his arms. "There is still much planning to be done. There will be time for celebration later. An hour first to rest, then let us gather to plan our attack."

The group dispersed reluctantly. Everyone who had been waiting in the jungle was anxious to begin.

Manny and Marissa walked up to examine the new supplies. M-19 had never been short on weapons, but this new arsenal was still impressive.

"Well, there's my favorite man and wife," Paulo said, appearing from behind the truck.

Manny took Marissa's arm. As one of only a handful of women in their militia, and the most beautiful, Marissa always remained under Manny's watchful eye. Most of the men respected him and admired his wife honorably. But Paulo didn't respect him, and Manny doubted he had any honor.

"Welcome, Paulo." He tried to muster a warm tone. The last thing he wanted was to appear intimidated.

"I can't wait for a good fight tomorrow." Paulo punched his palm and licked his lips.

"Hopefully, it can remain peaceful, just like in '80."

"Your past exploits do you credit, Manny, but this time will be different. I hope you have the stomach for a fight. Go through and pick some weapons."

"I already have a gun I trust."

Paulo whisked a strand of oily black hair off his forehead, then looked at Marissa. *"Linda Marissita,* I have missed your pretty face. It's so much better alive than in the picture I have of you in my apartment." Manny saw Paulo's eyes rest on his wife for an extra second before he reached into the closest truck and pulled out a box marked with a red medical cross. "This is for you. Don't let your husband fool you. Your job as a nurse will be busy. Men *will* be wounded."

He took a medic's armband out of the box and reached to put it on Marissa's arm. Manny snatched it out of his hand and affixed it himself. Paulo laughed.

"Don't think that will protect you though," Paulo said.

"I have a gun I trust too." Marissa turned and walked back to the tent.

Manny couldn't help asking the thought that had been on his mind since the trucks drove up. "Who financed all of this?" He swept his arm across all the weapons and crates of ammunition.

"We have always had powerful friends."

Manny looked Paulo straight in his dark eyes. "Are they *our* friends or *your* friends?"

"I've told you before, I never worked with Pablo Escobar."

"But you know him."

"Many people know him. His cartel reaches far and wide."

"The mission of M-19 is justice and freedom. I won't have drug lords polluting our cause."

"You're a soldier, Manny. A good one. Let others worry about politics and finances. Do your job, and maybe tomorrow night you will still be alive to lay with your wife."

Manny scowled up at the taller man.

Paulo cackled, patted Manny on the chest, and sauntered away. "Either way, she won't be lonely."

Manny forced himself to stay calm. This was no time to fight with a comrade. He may have been respected within M-19, but Paulo had many more powerful friends.

Whispers circulated in the camp as the afternoon progressed. The target was the Colombian Palace of Justice in Bogotá. Beyond that, nobody yet knew the scope of the plan. When the sun was almost down, the comandante gathered them all together. The men sat on benches while their leader sat on the bumper of one of the trucks.

"My friends, my brothers, tomorrow we will take the Palace of Justice by force. The Supreme Court is in session, and all twenty-five judges will be present. If any of you have been there, you know it is built like a fortress. Once we have secured the building, it will be nearly impossible for the army to retake, should they attempt it. Regardless, we do not expect them to retaliate given the prominence of the hostages we'll hold. After the initial standoff cools down, we'll force a trial of President Betancur for his crimes against the people of Colombia. Presided over by the Supreme Court, this trial will stand in the official records."

"Isn't that merely symbolic?" someone asked.

"Yes!" The comandante was emphatic. "Much of what we do is necessarily symbolic. We have thirty-five men and a few women here. The military has hundreds of thousands. We can't beat them in battle. What we do is meant to inspire the people to rise up with us, showing that brave men and women will not take injustice lying down."

He paused to let his words sink in. Manny had to admit, he was an inspirational leader. It sometimes took such a man to remind them of why they had given their lives to this cause. The comandante continued.

"I will lead the main assault through the basement. We should be able to get the trucks in with little resistance and overwhelm the guards down there. Avoid bloodshed, if possible. A smaller group will be on the first floor, having entered in civilian clothes. Our goal will be to secure the entire building, but the fourth floor is where the justices meet and all legal records are held. So, that is our primary objective."

A flurry of questions followed, and the lieutenants began to assign tasks. Manny felt a rush of excitement. This sounded much like the successful embassy siege five years ago.

The comandante's voice boomed again over the chatter. "Enough with the questions. You all know exactly what you need to know and not more. Now, let us eat and enjoy a peaceful evening. This may be our last one for a long time."

The group began to disperse, returning to their tents to make ready for the morning's departure. Manny started back toward his own tent but stopped when he felt a hand on his shoulder. He turned. It was the comandante.

"Manny, I want you to lead the group in civilian clothes through the main entrance tomorrow."

Manny nodded.

"Your valor in '80 has not been forgotten. Neither has your skill. You are the only one here today who was on that mission. I think that experience will serve you well in gaining access undetected."

"Thank you for your confidence in me, Comandante."

"Which men do you want to take with you?"

"I'll take Pasqual, Carlos, and San Juan el Bautista." He didn't like the idea of being separated from Marissa, but as the nurse, her place would be with the main group.

"How about bringing Paulo with you too? He's a strong fighter, if it becomes necessary."

"No. I don't trust him. He's a loose cannon. I don't know what he might do."

The comandante nodded.

"Also, forgive me, but I wonder if Paulo may be more interested in his own ends than those of the revolution."

"You may be right, Manny, but it's unwise to question your comrades. We may die tomorrow. It would be better to die as brothers."

Manny clasped his leader's hand and nodded. They embraced.

"Get a good shave tonight," said the comandante as he walked off. "Your disguise won't work if you look like such a dirty guerrilla."

Manny stood alone in the clearing. The benches were empty. The trucks waited heavily on the matted earth. The comandante was right. He might die tomorrow. In 1980, he had been too young and foolish to realize how lucky he'd been. Until today, he felt sure that the next venture could be equally successful and bloodless. Unlikely. Would the government allow them the same success twice? He had studied enough of his country's history to know that these adventures seldom ended well.

The smell of fresh stew filled the air. Soon, it brought the men out of their tents. They gathered again on the benches to eat their dinner. Manny wondered if it would be his last dinner. His anxiety had sapped his appetite, but he took his bowl and ate it anyway. He needed his strength. As night fell, a jug of wine was passed around along with tales of past glories and future dreams.

"Manny, where's your guitar?"

He went into his tent and brought it out, feeling better as soon as he strummed the old strings. San Juan el Bautista sat beside him and began to sing. Manny smiled. The boy was untested as a fighter, but he sure could sing. Others soon joined in, singing the songs of the revolution they all knew so well. One by one, they went off to bed, comforted by food, wine, and song, trying not to think about the dangers of the next day.

Marissa was already on her cot when Manny entered their tent. *"Mañana,"* she said. "Are you ready?"

"I suppose. I wish we didn't have to be apart for the attack."

"I can take care of myself. So can you. We both have a job to do, and we will do them well."

Manny knelt down beside her cot and took her hand. "For some reason, I have a bad feeling about this mission."

"There's always danger. That is the cause we've chosen."

"You're not afraid?"

"If we die, we die. All my fears have already come to pass. Why should I be afraid of escaping this life of sorrow?"

Manny kissed her cheek and walked across the tent to his own cot. He had lost just as much as Marissa. But he didn't feel ready to die. He still believed his life could be worth so much more.

"Are you afraid, Manuel?"

"Yes." He sighed. "Yes, *mi amor,* I am afraid."

17

"Well, don't you look the part, San Juan el Bautista. No one would believe you are a violent revolutionary."

The boy scowled and pulled his shirt up to show the pistol in his belt. Manny laughed.

"After today, I promise I'll never make fun of you again. This is the day that will make you a man."

Manny led his group across the square and up to the main entrance of the Colombian judicial headquarters. The comandante was right . . . it did look like a fortress. The building was long and square with heavy walls and few windows, an ideal spot for their mission.

The main entry was unguarded. Though the men had prepared background stories for why they were there, they were not asked. The place bustled with morning business. They waited in the cafeteria, avoiding any parts of the building that would require them to pass through metal detectors. It surprised Manny how many people were there. The crowd made their entry easier, but it would also make the building tougher to secure.

For a moment, the previous night's uncertainty crept back.

He pushed it out of his mind. There was no place for fear on a day made for action. The others looked excited. He was glad not to see fear in their eyes. He tried to make their excitement his own, but the knot of fear remained in his stomach.

He looked at his watch. "It's just about time. Listen carefully."

Almost as soon as he spoke the words, Manny heard a rumble beneath him—the trucks entering the basement. He glanced at Carlos and nodded. Carlos walked toward the entryway. Suddenly, rapid machine-gun fire sounded below. Someone in the cafeteria screamed.

"*¡Mierda!* Something's gone wrong." Manny knew that shots fired this early couldn't be good news.

Pasqual had his gun out.

"Everyone on the floor!" he shouted. "Stay calm, and no one will get hurt. This is not the time for heroes."

Pasqual and Carlos secured the cafeteria. They had to stick to their plan, even though the group in the basement had already strayed from theirs.

"Come on," said Manny. With guns drawn, Manny and Juan ran to the security desk, which blocked the path to the judicial chambers. They leaped over the turnstiles as the bewildered guards weighed whether it would be worth it to reach for their guns. Another *rat-a-tat* from a machine gun sounded below.

The staircase door burst open, and their comrades rushed into the room from the basement. At least one of the guards had started shooting at the intruders. A man fell in the entryway. Others rushed through. Manny's head swiveled, desperately looking for the guard who was fighting back. His gun was in his hand, but people flew around him everywhere—rebels entering the room, overmatched guards, frightened civilians running for cover or falling to the floor in the confusion, and somewhere in the chaos, a guard with a gun.

Manny looked back at the doorway just as Marissa came

through. She reeled from a bullet.

"Marissa, no!" Manny tried to step toward her, but the crush of bodies pushed him back. "Oh God, no, no, no."

San Juan el Bautista had found the guard who tried to be a hero. Manny saw him run up and shoot the guard at point-blank range, then follow the men as they rushed upstairs.

Manny grew dizzy. It was all a blur. He tried to stay calm as men pressed past him. Someone on the floor grabbed at his feet. He forced his way through toward the doorway. He couldn't get to his wife, prostrate in the open doorway, until all the rebels had made it up the stairs.

By then, she was dead.

Manny took her head in his arms, letting his head fall onto her lifeless shoulder. He couldn't breathe. He couldn't even cry. How could he lose her this fast, without even a final moment to say goodbye?

When his breath returned, his tears also broke free. A voice within him whispered that he had to hurry upstairs. There was no time to grieve. It was dangerous to stay here. The military would arrive soon.

Marissa's face was at peace. In a way, this was what she had wanted. There had been no fight in her today, no resistance in her body to the bullet. It killed her without a struggle.

It angered him. His anger was not at her but at the God who let her lose hope while forcing him to carry it still.

He was also angry at the comandante for devising such a reckless plan and at whoever it was that had started the shooting. This was not supposed to be a violent takeover. There were dead civilians too. Each minute now, it grew more likely that they would all die in here.

Manny eased Marissa's head back to the floor, unwilling to leave her, even though her heart had long since flown away from him.

He stood up but couldn't bring himself to go upstairs. The mission felt odious. It went awry as soon as the first shots were fired. How could it succeed now?

"This way, *hermano*. Hurry." A woman's voice came from a nearby hallway.

Manny turned his head. He felt disoriented, his vision still clouded by tears. He managed to focus on the voice, expecting one of his comrades. But he didn't recognize the woman who had spoken. She looked about fifty, a worker in the justice offices.

"There's a room this way where we can hide. You must hurry."

Confused, Manny glanced down at his own clothes: civvies— his disguise. In the confusion, he had dropped his gun. Nobody knew who he was. This woman never guessed that he had helped start this tragedy.

He looked at the stairway where his comrades had gone, then back at the woman in the hall. He was being offered a way out. Perhaps he would die either way. If Pasqual and Carlos found him hiding down here, they would surely kill him. But he now felt certain that death awaited those who had gone upstairs. Things had started too badly to end well. He looked at his dead wife one last time.

No, he would not embrace death as she had. He had so much life he still intended to live. He ran after the woman into the hallway.

Hiding for hours in a dark, windowless office, Manny tried to numb his emotions. Fear, shame, and sorrow swirled in his heart. Other people huddled close by him, but he was utterly alone. His wife was dead, and he had abandoned his comrades. If these people he hid with knew who he was, they would be outraged, even kill him if they could. If he survived this day, he would have no one in the world. He tried to pray, but even God seemed distant. What use had God for the prayers of a man like him, who in the same hour had brought death upon innocent people and deserted his brothers?

The people shifted restlessly, not daring even to whisper. Discomfort increased. How long could they hide before thirst and bodily needs became unbearable? If they knew it would only be hours, they could endure it. But what if they had to hide all night, or even for days? Manny listened to the subtle sounds of distress, watching in the faint light.

Meanwhile, there were other sounds: shouting upstairs, a helicopter above, then the rumble of gathering tanks and troops in the square. Twice, he heard Pasqual shouting at the hostages in the nearby cafeteria. From what he could tell, the militants had secured the upper floors, presumably capturing the entire Supreme Court, while outside the army laid siege to the building.

The silence in the room was broken. *"Líbranos del mal,"* chanted a man as he rocked back and forth, sitting on the floor against the wall. Someone tried to hush him, but the man was delirious. *"Líbranos del mal. Oh, señor, líbranos del mal,"* he chanted quietly, over and over until Manny felt the rhythm of the prayer in his body.

He was this evil the people prayed against. He had joined the revolution to help the Colombian people, yet instead had inflicted death and despair. The fight wasn't against these people here in this room—workers whose only fault was taking a government job, and who could blame them? Millions of the poor in this country would have given anything for a job like this, for the education that spawned the opportunity. He possessed such an education but had chosen violence instead. How wrong he had been.

He wanted to pray too, to connect to God. But he could not. He had never felt more distant from God than in that moment as he waited with the countrymen and women he had wronged. He was angry at God, fresh off the death of his beloved, whose body might even still lay in the hallway close by. He was still angry at God for taking his daughter three years ago and for never giving Marissa the peace to move past it. But God was angry at him too, surely, for this horror he had wrought. Who was he to expect fairness from a peaceful God?

He couldn't talk to God, but he could make a promise to himself. He determined that if he escaped this day alive and free, he would finish his education and use any opportunity that came to him to fight for his people with love, not blood. This was the best he could do. The promise allowed him to hope for escape without being leveled by his guilt.

Manny had no sense of how many hours passed in that room. What noises could be heard above sounded unnatural and severe. He closed his eyes, wanting to bring Marissa's image back. He tried to remember her as she had been when he first met her—as a feisty daughter of the revolution or smiling with love on their wedding day. But the only image his mind brought back was of her sad face in the years since they lost their child. He cried against the wall, glad that no one would notice his tears against their own emotions and the continued, solitary chant, *"Líbranos del mal."*

A hideous crash sounded close by, followed immediately by gunfire. People gasped and huddled closer in the office.

The door burst open. Manny struggled to see through the blinding hallway lights. A soldier stood there in his rounded helmet and fatigues.

"¡Vengan, gente!" whispered the guard. "Hurry."

The people rushed out. Others came from the office rooms down the hall. Manny rushed through the cafeteria with the crowd, looking for Pasqual and Carlos, who must have fled upstairs or been shot.

Out in the square stood about two hundred people rescued from the ground floor of the building. It was never their intention to take civilians as hostages. The comandante was always willing to let the ground floor go. Manny still couldn't help rooting for their success, even though he had now staked his own survival against them.

Manny slipped out of the crowd and kept walking. His emotions were too raw to rest. He had lost more than his wife today. He had lost his own identity. Who was he without M-19? What would he do now that he had left them? Would he even be allowed to leave?

All day, he wandered the streets of Bogotá. When weariness overcame his emotions, he fell asleep under a bridge.

The next day, his curiosity brought him back to the Palace of Justice. He stood far off and watched as the army rolled a tank up the front steps and through the palace entrance. Soldiers followed it while militants shot down at them from the roof. This was no peaceful negotiation.

Shortly afterward, soldiers stormed the front entrance while tanks fired directly at the building, bombarding the upper area. Heavy gunfire rained down from above. Soldiers lay dead in the square.

Manny wanted to turn away but couldn't. It was going to be a massacre. Did the lives of the hostages mean nothing? Suddenly, tall flames burst from the top of the building. Gunfire and screams could be heard from within.

Was this what he had been fighting for all these years: death and destruction? He was a fool to have believed peace could be won through violence. No wonder it came to an end like this.

Manny's heart ached for his wife and for his friends whom he had abandoned and would likely soon be dead. Most of all, his heart ached for Colombia. It was out of love for his homeland that he had joined M-19, yet he had done his people more harm than good.

Finally, Manny was able to pray. He begged God for the chance at redemption—to fulfill the promise he had made to himself—even though it was not a chance he deserved.

18

"WAIT FOR ME," shouted a young girl as she ran after three boys. At first they tried to shake her, but at twelve she was in the middle of the growth spurt that the boys hadn't had yet. She caught up with them at the next corner.

"Why did you try to go without me?"

"It might be too hard for a girl."

"¡Qué *ridículo!* I'm faster and stronger than any of you."

"Fine, *Alta.* You can come."

"No, *chicos.* You come with *me.*" She set off on the dirty street between low homes built of plywood and aluminum as the boys followed. She knew they were getting tired of being led by a girl. But they would be glad to have her. They always had more fun when she was there. She came up with ideas they wouldn't dare without her.

She had grown up with these boys—orphans just like her. It had been a rough childhood in the barrio. She never knew where her next meal was coming from. But people here looked out for each other. Even the prostitutes and pimps treated the orphans like their own.

Sometimes, she would venture toward the harbor and gaze up at the old colonial walls, or she would go to the beach and look across the bay at the row of hotels that lined the Bocagrande peninsula. One day, she would feel welcome in such places—this was something she had determined since she was old enough to understand it. But for now, she and her friends had to survive however they could. They were not above stealing food or working small jobs for the thugs who ran their barrio.

Something would have to change soon. She felt it in her body as acutely as in her heart.

La Alta—the tall girl. That was what her friends called her. It was a fitting nickname, because she had shot up faster than the other children. But she was starting to look different. She wanted to welcome the changes, but she feared them too. There was a place for a child in the streets. People gave her odd jobs in exchange for a room to sleep in for a week or two at a time. But once she was a woman—and she was beginning to look like one—everything would change. Men would begin to lust after her, and women would distrust her. Those neighborhood bosses who looked out for her as a child would soon try to groom her for a new career. Her mother had been a prostitute, but the girl believed there was a better life for her. If only she could get a chance to work for it.

She led the way toward the center of the city. Cartagena bustled on this hot Saturday afternoon. If the boys had gone without her, they would have limited their adventures to their own streets. She smiled to herself. She always had more ambitious adventures in mind.

"Look." She pointed at a gathering crowd. "There's a *fútbol* match today. Let's sneak in."

After several attempts, stadium security proved equal to the children's resourcefulness. When a security guard threatened to arrest them, they gave up. But they found an abandoned ball in the parking lot and played their own game between the cars, listening with delight to the roar of the crowd when Real Cartagena scored the only goal of the game.

They took the ball and started back toward home. It was a treasure to have a ball in such good condition. She knew they would play with it every day until it got run over by a truck or stolen by other children.

"Let's see if Manny's home."

Manny's house was on a nicer block in their neighborhood, right on the main bus line into downtown. It was part of a row of concrete houses with a market and bar at the end of the block. The children of the barrio were always welcomed at Manny's house. His refrigerator—a luxury in itself—was always full of lemonade or Coca-Cola.

"Hey, *muchachos,*" called Manny from his doorway as the children approached. "You found a *fútbol!*"

The girl smiled. Manny was the only adult who was consistently kind to her without an ulterior motive. He was the only person in the world she trusted. Even these boys—her best friends—would betray her for a slice of beef if they were hungry enough. They usually were.

Manny met them on the street, below the web of electrical and phone wires that passed overhead. He intercepted the ball with skill that surprised the young boys. He passed it to the girl, and without words, teams were established—the three boys versus the man and the girl. Despite the odds against them, the girl was delighted that she and Manny could successfully keep the ball away from the boys. They played until the traffic in the street grew too heavy and the honks became indignant, then ran sweating into Manny's house for cold drinks by the fan.

Manny laughed. "How will you become the next El Pibe if you can't dribble past an old man, eh?"

After greedily swallowing from bottles of Coke, the boys were back out in the street with their ball, mastering their skills while annoying a new set of motorists. The girl stayed inside, savoring her beverage.

"How are you, *niña*? Have you been able to go to school?"

"I go one or two days a week."

"I know it can be tough, but keep with it as much as you can. If you get an education, you might get a job when you're a little older. I'll help you if I can, but I can only get you so far."

"I want to work in one of the hotels."

"I know. But you have to speak like *de clase alta* for that. You need to know English too—for the tourists."

She frowned. "Do you speak English?"

"Yes."

"How did you learn so much?"

"I only learned English these last few years, after I returned to school."

"I don't have that much time, though."

"No, you don't." He paused and looked her in the eyes. "Get the knowledge that's available to you now. First speak Spanish as well as you can so you can get work in the city—perhaps in a shop or a café. Colombians are very proud of their Spanish. If you can speak it well, you can get a good job. A job means money. Money means an apartment. An apartment means a new life."

She liked that he was honest with her. He knew what would become of her if she didn't find a way off the streets—soon. She hated to think about it; she wanted to stay a child.

It had been a few months since she had bled for the first time. The women of the barrio had prepared her for what to expect. But it was traumatic in what it meant. Childhood was ending fast. She could not naïvely hope these changes would never come; they were already happening to her. She had witnessed the fate of girls not much older than herself, making her wiser than she wanted to be. She envied the privileged children who she imagined could remain blind to the darkness in the world.

"*¡Vamos, Alta!*" shouted the boys from outside. "Let's go home."

She hopped up from her seat.

"*Chao, Manny. Gracias por la Coke.*"

Manny watched the children as they disappeared down the block, the ball bouncing between their feet. He enjoyed their visits so much.

His life had become steady and predictable in the eight years since he had walked away from the revolution, leaving it in a fiery explosion in Bogotá. He had poured all his energy into building his new life—first finishing his degree, then working at the jobs it helped him to get. After he managed to save a little money, he went back to school at night to get a graduate degree, which had recently led to a better job.

Now, he was one of the most skilled computer engineers in the city, maybe the country. Already, he was receiving more job offers, some as far away as Mexico and the United States. Going abroad was intriguing, but Colombia had always been home. These were his people. He had sacrificed so much for his country. It would be difficult to leave.

It had not been all study and work. There had been friends with whom he would share some fun or a few beers. There had been women, too—who shared his bed but to whom he wouldn't reveal the secrets of his heart. But what others might have called *living,* Manny knew as *distraction.* He had known life in a way that these friends and lovers could never understand. He had once fought for something and lost everything.

Recently, the distraction of friends and even sex had ceased to entice him. His only real friends now were the children. He focused on his work, wondering what it would lead to, but he never questioned his path. That was for God to decide, not for him to ask. The work allowed him to keep the ghosts of the past at bay—the ghosts and the guilt.

Manny was back on speaking terms with God, despite the old resentments between them. He wasn't ready to ask for forgiveness, since he still didn't feel like forgiving God. But he had decided to let their past be water under the bridge. He felt deep inside himself that God wasn't finished with him yet, so he must have still been listening. Despite everything, he still believed in a God of love and that love would give him another chance if he remained open to it. Some days, he felt as if his life was over—on others, like it was only now about to begin.

He left the window and walked into his hot kitchen, barely cooled by the open windows and whirling fan. He had been in this small house for three years. It worked fine for him. Not everyone would have considered it comfortable, but he had known worse. It was cheap enough, safe enough, and right on the bus line to his work. He had no desire for anything more elaborate without someone to share it with. He poured himself a glass of cold water from the pitcher he kept in the refrigerator and sat down at the table. He smiled at the four empty Coke bottles on the counter.

It had been love that drove him into the revolution long ago— love for the people left on the margins of a country controlled by the rich and the strong. That same love had stirred again as he watched the children walk away today, especially the girl, *La Alta*. It was destinies like hers that he had tried but been woefully unable to change. He already knew the tragic story of her life. Worse, he could tell she knew it too.

When he saw her, he wondered what his daughter would have looked like. She would have been about the same age now.

His anger over such injustice could have led him straight back to the fight; but he no longer believed fighting would do any good. He had learned that huddled in the dark room at the Palace of Justice with those frightened people he had endangered.

If justice could not be won through blood, what other way was there? He didn't want to watch while those innocent children were pulled into the underworld as their only means to survive.

If he could use what he had worked for to change one life such as that girl's, all his sins would surely be forgiven.

A heavy knock on his front door startled him. His first thought: Perhaps the children had returned. But that was not a child's knock.

19

MANNY OPENED THE door, then jumped back with surprise.

"Well, well, Manny del Sol. *¿Qué cuentas?*"

Paulo Varga pushed past him into the house.

Manny wanted to feel happy to see a familiar face after all this time, especially of someone he had presumed dead. But Paulo's malevolent grin as he sat on the couch and regarded his surroundings reminded Manny that Paulo had never meant well. What malice had brought him here after all these years?

"Paulo, what a joy to see you alive. I never found out how many survived."

"Only a few of us. It was a bad day." Paulo stretched his arms across the couch. "You're a hard man to find, Manny."

"I haven't been hiding."

"Hiding in plain sight. Like that day in Bogotá . . . in your civilian clothes."

Manny said nothing. He closed his front door but stayed near it.

"You seem to have done well for yourself. No worse for wear. A nice little house, a good job, as if the past never happened."

"What about you? Do you live in Cartagena now? You're not from here."

"I do live here. The beauty of the Caribbean Coast inspires me. I started painting again while I was in prison. It amazed me that they allowed me the canvases and the paints. A more malicious man could have mixed a poison from the oils. But they were generous, and it gave me a way to pass the time. I kept painting after I got out. I've become a much better artist."

Manny said nothing. He always thought Paulo's paintings were terrible and expected that they still were. His portraits never had any life in them. Even that one of Marissa, who at that time had been so full of life . . . but he didn't want to think about it.

"I started a business after prison too," Paulo continued. "There's money to be made in a city like this."

"*Your* kinds of business will land you right back in prison."

Paulo laughed. "I've gotten smarter. Look." He took a card out of his pocket and reached his long arm toward Manny from the couch.

Manny took it and read: *Estrella de Indias: Ascenso de Talento.* "Talent acquisition? Is that what they call it now?"

"In Cartagena, the opportunity is endless. There are so many young people who need work and so much money coming through every day on the cruise ships. I first hire the girls as models, and they love having their portraits painted. Once they trust me, they are receptive to doing more. The money becomes very attractive to them. I'm starting small, but I have big plans."

Manny handed the card back. He was disgusted. "Are you still with M-19?"

"Loosely. But everything's changed. It's a political party now more than a revolutionary movement. I keep involved as far as it might help me get a civil position one day. But surely you know that. You read the news."

"Not really. Reading the news depresses me."

"Why don't you do something about it? That's what you would have done before."

"I stopped believing anything I did would make a difference."

"And when did you stop believing?" Paulo leaned forward where he sat. His grin had turned into a scowl. "Was it before or after you walked away as your comrades died in a burning building?"

"That's not what happened that day. My presence couldn't have changed the outcome."

"Oh no? Was it that easy for you? Haven't you wondered what happened after you 'disappeared'? Do you have any idea what it was like up on the fourth floor once the soldiers started firing on us? It was a massacre."

"Who started the massacre?" Manny walked across the small room, then back again. He was on edge. "I heard the shots from the basement as you came in. It damn well sounded like your gun. That wasn't the plan. I've heard stories about what happened on the top floor too."

"Have you? Did you listen to the stories the president spread about the judges we burned in hot oil or the trial records we burned? A fine time for a man like you to start believing government propaganda. What about us, helpless up there as they fired missiles at their own palace? They burned us together with their own Supreme Court to make an example."

Manny stood still for a moment and looked at Paulo. He was a harder man now. He looked ruthless. At once, Manny believed all the stories he'd heard.

"Well? Did you torture the judges?"

"It was war up there, Manny. There are no more rules once it's war. You do what you must to win and survive."

"That was never the way I saw it. We used to stand for something. Everything changed that day."

"Always such an idealist."

"Revolution is about ideals."

"No, it's about power. Ideals are for the weak."

"You were never there for the same reasons as the rest of us."

"You were always the pawns. I'm one of the players."

"I know that now, so I've left it behind." Manny felt a wave of sadness, remembering everything he'd once believed in and how useless it was to fight for those things.

"You abandoned your precious ideals at the first sign of trouble. You think you know revolution, but you were never in a real battle. It's easy to speak of ideals when there are no bullets humming by your ears. All those thoughts go away when weighed against survival. What did we care for the hostages when a fireball crashed through the wall and enveloped the room? By then, we were only fighting for our lives. So yes, I killed those judges and I didn't care. Cruelty became a way to cope with the fear. I suppose hiding is another way to cope. You chose your way. I chose mine."

"How did you get out?"

"San Juan el Bautista and I shot our way out together. But Juan was slower than me and was blamed for the dead policemen in the path we'd run. He got the harsher sentence when we appeared in court. He's still in prison."

Manny imagined that Paulo had somehow tricked Juan to take the fall for him. Poor young Juan had been pretty naïve. Still, it pleased Manny to know the boy had survived.

"I bet it helps to have friends like yours in prison. Especially if it's true what I heard, that all the Escobar files were burned in the fire that day."

"As I said, in war you do what you must to survive."

"Well, I did what I could."

"Yes, you did." Paulo stood up and surveyed the room. His eyes rested on the empty Coke bottles. He tapped four fingers in a row on the countertop, counting them. "Not a bad little life.

You even have friends."

Manny stiffened.

"So, this is what it's like to live in shame."

"I'm not ashamed."

"Oh no?" Paulo turned toward him. "You walked away from your brothers. You hid while we fought to the death. You have been free, living well, it appears, while I spent five years in prison. If you had stood your ground and done your time, you could live proud now, but you took the easy way."

"I watched my wife die. Don't talk to me about sacrifice."

"That's your hardship? Do you know what prison's like, Manny? Can you even imagine what your young friend San Juan el Bautista has endured there?"

Manny turned toward the window. The late afternoon traffic grew heavy. He didn't want to be reminded of those times. He had worked so hard to move on, but somehow he always knew that life would reach back at him.

"This is an evil land we live in," Paulo said.

"It's made evil by men like you."

"And *you*!"

"Perhaps." Manny sat down at his kitchen table. He was shaken, afraid. Paulo leaned back in his seat and glared at him.

"You have a debt to pay, Manny. Surely, you know that."

"How can you say that after all I gave to the revolution? After 1980?"

Paulo spat. It landed with a thud on the tile floor. "You've hung your pride on 1980 for too long. That can't excuse you from your cowardice. What you heard about the judge who burned in hot oil was true. I poured it on him myself. In prison, I dreamed of doing that to you. Believe me, I thought of you every day in prison. The others—and there weren't many who lived—assumed you were dead, but I knew you were out there somewhere living as a free man."

Manny stood up sharply from his chair. Paulo laughed.

"Doing what we can to survive. That's what I did in prison too. So, yes, Escobar helped me get out early, and your young friend, San Juan el Bautista, helped me pass the lonely nights."

"You sick bastard!"

Manny grabbed a kitchen knife and took a step forward. Paulo braced his sturdy frame with amusement in his eyes. Manny knew he would be no match for Paulo, not after these sedentary years.

"I know you want to kill me," Paulo said, "but think before you do something stupid."

"What do I care? Everyone I love is dead."

"Are they?" Paulo took a long look at the four empty Coke bottles.

Manny felt sick to his stomach. Paulo had watched the children come to his house, perhaps more than once. He now remembered what people had said about Paulo in the early days—his work for the drug lords and prostitution rings had solidified his influence on the streets. *Talent acquisition*—a fancy phrase for pulling young kids into prostitution and drugs. Now, Manny had unwittingly put those children in danger of Paulo's recruitment. He would surely have noticed the girl. It was clear she would be beautiful. He put the knife down.

"Get out of my house. I don't want to hear any more from you."

"But you will. Next time you see me, I will not come alone. And I will have a proposition for you. Think hard about how you can afford to answer."

After Paulo left, Manny sat back down at the kitchen table. He sat there for a long time, as the traffic died down, the sky darkened, and sounds of night filled the city. He didn't bother to turn on a lamp.

Images flooded back into his mind: Marissa, so beautiful on the day they wed, so sad on the day she died; his infant daughter, whose very face had grown hard for him to remember; the faces of his comrades who died; poor Juan, who perhaps wished he had; the exploding building in Bogotá as he watched with the crowd. The last image that came into his mind was from that afternoon, of the young girl they called *La Alta,* with her innocent smile that was slowly hardening with the wisdom of fear. She was the daughter he had not been allowed to love and who he would be unable to protect from the evil of the world.

Finally, he stood up and walked to the bar at the corner of his block. He drank a beer and ate a *choripan,* which made him feel better.

Returning to his house, he turned on a lamp and opened the drawer of the small wooden desk next to his bed. He pulled out the letter and read it again. It was an employment offer from Intel, in the United States. The salary offered was an unfathomable amount compared to what he had earned in the jobs he had worked. When he received this letter a week ago, he had been afraid. It was the kind of opportunity he had been working for. But could he leave his homeland? Could he be happy in a new place? He loved Colombia.

But Colombia did not love him. It never had.

Now that Paulo had found him and set his mind on revenge, there would be no peace for him here. He had no choice but to accept this offer.

And the children? Perhaps leaving would be the best he could do for them too. His love had only put them in danger. What could he really do for them if he stayed? They would have to learn to survive on their own with or without him.

20

"HEY, *CHICA,* COME here a minute."

The girl turned and looked toward the voice. Night had just fallen. The man who had spoken stood in a lighted doorway—an unusual sight on this block. She had seen him around the neighborhood recently. He was always nice, but not *kind* like Manny, who she knew was looking out for her. He watched her with a different kind of interest. She didn't like the look in his eyes now. She felt wary but didn't want to offend or anger him. She stepped toward him but stayed in the street while he stood in the doorway.

"What's your name?"

"They call me *La Alta.*"

He laughed. "You are becoming too much of a woman for that name. What's your real name?"

"Cristina."

"I'm Paulo. Won't you come in? I won't hurt you."

"No, gracias."

His look turned mean. "I asked you to come in. It's rude to refuse an invitation."

She was afraid. If she tried to walk away now, he might force her to come in. She was quick, but she doubted she could outrun him. She stepped toward the door.

"Don't be afraid. I'd like to show you my pictures." He was acting friendly again. His cruel tone had only lasted a moment, but it didn't fade in her ears. What would be worse—to go into his house or make him angry?

As soon as she stepped through the door, it closed behind her. She clenched her fists. It was a strange house for a man like him. Was it even his house? It didn't look lived in. There was no furniture, but brightly colored paintings hung on all four walls of the front room. An entryway to what looked like a kitchen opened from the wall ahead of her, and another hallway opened to her left.

She didn't know much about art, but it was easy to see that the paintings were all done by the same hand.

"Do you like the pictures? I painted them myself."

There were six of them in that empty room. Each was a portrait of a woman. They wore brightly colored clothing against weirdly colorful backdrops. The clothing went up all the way to the women's necks, and no lines made them look sensual or even really all that feminine. Though they were all clearly different women with different features, each of them looked strangely similar.

Her eyes were drawn away from the pictures on the walls as she realized that the man was looking at her, examining her.

"I would like to paint a picture of you. Would you like that?"

She would *not* like it but didn't want to tell him so. She didn't want to look like those women on the walls. They weren't ugly; some of them even looked pretty. But something disturbed her about them. She tried not to look at the pictures, but neither could she look away.

"Look at yourself. A beautiful *muñeca*. You shouldn't have to rot in these slums."

She realized what it was. The girls in the pictures had no life.

They looked dead. She almost thought he had dressed up and painted corpses. A chill ran up her spine.

"I want to offer you the chance at a better life."

"I need to go."

"Listen to me first. It's not what you think. I'm offering you a new start, a chance to see the world, a glamorous career. Don't you have dreams? A girl like you could choose where she wants to go. Just imagine it: New York, Los Angeles, Buenos Aires, Paris, Tokyo. I know you'd like to see those places."

She did, but how did he know?

"Imagine yourself wearing lovely dresses every night, eating in nice restaurants . . . the feel of silk against your skin. You can have a beautiful life. Why would you refuse that?"

She felt his finger touching her hair without having seen his hand rise. Another chill passed through her. She reached for the door, but he was quicker. He wrapped an arm around her stomach, pulling her toward him as his other hand suddenly covered her mouth. She hadn't planned to cry out, but now she wanted to.

"You're a young and foolish girl. But you're not naïve. You know what your mother was and that you have no choice but to follow in her profession. Do you know it was AIDS that killed her? Did the other women tell you that?"

Her eyes unwillingly returned to the portraits of the women with the dead faces.

"Do you want to die young in these slums like your mother, or will you embrace your beauty and live a glamorous life? I'm the man who can make that a reality for you."

She writhed and struggled against his arms, but it was no use. He was too strong.

"It's time for you to begin your training. The best start young."

He moved his hand down between her legs and pressed it against her jeans so hard that it hurt. She forced herself to steady her breath. He seemed to believe that she was relaxing. His hand moved off of her mouth.

"Okay, *patrón*. Tell me what you like."

His arms relaxed and she turned toward him, just in time to see his eager grin before her hand slashed it away, her nails scraping against his face so sharply that she drew blood.

He cried out in pain. She reached for the door and was through it in a flash. She ran to the street without looking back.

She made it to the street corner and turned. She was still running when a hand grabbed her wrist, whipping her out of her run. She gasped, as if the wind had been knocked out of her. He pushed her against the nearest wall, now with her arms crushed behind her and his knee in her crotch.

He smiled maliciously, then licked the blood she had drawn off of his lips.

He didn't have to speak; his look said everything. She could run, but she couldn't hide—not from him, not from her destiny. Her breath came in startled spurts. If he wanted to rape her or kill her, there was nothing she could do about it.

Instead, he let her go.

She ran again, desperately through the tight street, too stunned even to cry.

Why run when there was nowhere to go? She could never get far enough away. For her, there was no escape, no way out.

She wanted to get as far away from this place as she could, but already she knew she would have to go back. How could she stay alive somewhere else? Where would she sleep? How would she eat? More importantly, how would she avoid her awful fate? At least here she knew how to survive.

That was why Paulo had let her go. In a way, it was the most terrifying thing he could have done to her. He knew she had no choice but to come back.

All the dreams of her childhood, both the fanciful—seeing the world, wearing pretty clothes—and the practical—working in one of the big hotels—had been twisted and corrupted by this man. She wondered whether she would ever be able to indulge herself in dreams again.

She had known this day would come but thought she had a couple more years of childhood. There had not been time to come up with a plan, even to learn to speak better like Manny said. Her time was up.

Finally, she stopped running. She looked across the street at Manny's house. There was a light on inside.

Trust felt lost, but she *had* to trust someone. It was too exhausting to be alone. Surely, if anyone could help her, it was Manny.

She knocked, and he opened the door. His expression told her that she had made the right choice. He seemed to understand what had happened.

"Was it Paulo?"

She nodded.

His face reddened with rage. "I won't let him hurt you. If it costs me my life, I won't let him do this."

She almost asked how he knew, but it didn't matter. Not right now.

Manny paced the room while she sat at his table. His expression was serious, thoughtful. She felt good being there, safe. He would think of something. But his first words were not at all what she'd expected.

"Listen, my friend." He stopped his pacing and looked at her. "I'm going to be leaving soon."

"Leaving this house?"

"Leaving Cartagena. Leaving Colombia."

Her mouth fell open. Manny couldn't leave! Then she truly would have no one. She felt like she would cry.

"That man Paulo has evil plans for me too. Just now, I was writing my acceptance letter for a job in the United States."

"No! What am I supposed to do?"

"Well, I just thought of something. It's a crazy idea, but it might work. I would give anything to protect you from Paulo, to give you a good life, with real opportunities. You deserve it." Manny paused. "Maybe I could take you with me."

She hopped up in her seat. "Could you? Really?"

"Maybe. Did I ever tell you about my daughter, who died as a baby?"

She nodded. Manny had told her about his own daughter several times.

"Her name was Leila. She would have been about your age now. I still have her birth certificate."

Her heart beat faster, anticipating what he was going to suggest.

"Nobody in the United States knows that she died. You could take her place. I will tell the company that I can only accept the job on the condition that they also give a visa to my daughter. You and I will both start a new life in the United States."

She could hardly believe what she was hearing. Was this a dream? Yet her instincts told her to be cautious. Manny looked at her seriously.

"If you come with me, I need you to know that you can trust me completely. I will adopt you. You will truly become Leila del Sol, my daughter. I will protect you and care for you. I will never lay my hands on you or be anything other than a father to you. Tonight, you have seen how evil men can be. I hope you can also believe how good and honorable a man can be."

She did believe it. Of all her dreams, having a father was one she had never dared.

She spent the night on his couch. It took her a long time to fall asleep as she dreamed about the future in the United States. What would it be like there? She had heard so many stories. What would *she* be like as this new person named Leila?

A loud knocking on the door woke her with a start. Disoriented for a moment, she remembered where she was and everything that had happened. She bolted off the couch and hid in Manny's bedroom closet before he even rose from his bed. She caught his eye as she passed and saw that he was afraid too. She didn't like seeing him afraid.

"Is she here?"

She recognized that voice all too well. Her heart was in her throat.

"What are you talking about?" Manny asked.

"The girl. I know she's here." Paulo's voice was calm, steady, terrifying. "She's hiding from me."

"I'm here alone."

"Let me look around."

"No! Who do you think you are, the police? You're a damn bully, and I won't have you snooping around my home."

"You better not be hiding the girl from me."

She heard shoving in the next room followed by a string of curses. She shook as she cowered against the closet wall.

"Get the hell out of here."

"This isn't over, Manny. I'll be back."

The door closed. She dared to crack the closet door open. Manny sighed when he walked into the room.

"We need to leave. Today."

Her fear turned into excitement. Her new father had already proved himself to her. The adventure was about to begin.

Manny wouldn't let her go home to pick up her few possessions. It was too dangerous. Those were things of her old life anyway.

Leila. That is my name now, she told herself over and over as the bus took her through Cartagena toward the sparkling old city, with its fine hotels and fancy restaurants. She said the name again and again under her breath as she waited on a plush yellow couch in the lobby of the small inn Manny had chosen. *Casa Azul*, it was called. Everything looked so luxurious, even though Manny had said this was one of the simplest inns of the neighborhood.

Leila. She liked her new name. It sounded pretty, and she liked what it meant. It meant a history, a father—family. She would do the name proud.

Manny walked back to her from the hotel desk.

"I mailed my acceptance."

She smiled brightly.

"I sent them Leila's birth certificate too. Now, we have to wait, hopefully for two visas and two plane tickets."

"How long does it take?"

"I don't know. This is a new experience for both of us."

He sat down on the chair across from her. "I rented two rooms here. It's expensive in this part of town, but Paulo won't think to look for us here. We have to stay as long as it takes because this is the address I gave." He looked at her earnestly. "From now on, to everyone we meet, you are Leila, my daughter. The past is our secret. Nobody else can know."

She nodded. "I want to be Leila. I *am* Leila."

"Pray this works. There's no going back now. I called my job and quit. I couldn't risk going back. If Paulo came to find me there, after abandoning my house, he would know. I just hope my savings holds us out as long as this takes."

"It will." She had no idea what a place like this would cost, but she also couldn't imagine someone like Manny not having enough money.

"Come. We need to buy you some things to make you comfortable here."

Her eyes were wide with wonder as they walked through

the colorful streets of Old Cartagena. She had only ventured past the colonial walls a couple of times before. The old stone buildings were painted in vibrant oranges, reds, and blues, with hanging baskets of flowers dotting the balconies. The hot air felt fresh here, closer to the sea, perfumed with the scents of wealth instead of the squalor of poverty. They had only gone a few miles, but she had stepped a world away from her old life. She wasn't worried about the visa application, or whether Manny's savings would run out, or even if Paulo was still looking for her. The old life was gone, and now she had a father to protect her. She could not be happier.

They stayed at the inn a month. Leila enjoyed her private little room, with a window looking out toward the pretty buildings of the old neighborhood. During those days, Manny began teaching her English and how to play the guitar. She learned the latter much quicker.

For the first time, she had everything she needed: enough food, clean water, clothes, shampoo, soap. Everything about this felt like a dream.

Finally, the response came from the United States: two plane tickets and two approved visa applications.

She kept waiting to wake up from this incredible dream. She didn't deserve any of this. She felt lucky rather than blessed. She vowed to become worthy of this chance. She would work so hard to earn it, for Manny's sake, who gave it to her, and for all the poor girls who would never get the chance at a new life.

PART III

EL PARAÍSO

21

FOR THE FIRST weeks, Leila tried to talk her mind out of what her heart already knew. She had felt life take hold inside her even before she saw that the condom was broken. It was impossible to know that fast. Anyone would have told her that. She couldn't explain the sensation she felt. It was something she would cherish alone.

The unborn child she had dreamed of for so long was suddenly close, alive not only in her heart but in her body. A deeply spiritual shift had taken place within her, faster than the physical conception. The feeling was wonderful, even though it shocked and terrified her.

Soon, her missed period and the appearance of two horizontal lines on a paper strip confirmed it. Motherhood was her dream, but this wasn't the right time. She wasn't ready. What had become of all her carefully crafted plans? She couldn't even begin to fathom the consequences.

She could tell that Ashford was worried, even though he was polite enough not to ask her about it. He called her almost every day after their night together, and while she took his calls, she wasn't ready to see him again. It was too complicated. If they were together, they would be drawn to each other, but she couldn't be intimate with him again yet. She couldn't tell him what she felt. She doubted he would understand. She still didn't know much of anything about him. How would he take the news? He had said all of the right things to her, but men had said the right things before. Words alone couldn't be trusted. Would Ashford want to be a father at this age, before he had launched his career? Would he disappear like so many men did, committing to send a check each month in lieu of love?

Worse, he might pressure her to get an abortion. That would surely be Samantha's advice if—*when*—she knew. But it was never an option for Leila. Ready or not, how could she destroy the child who had long been alive in her dreams, who she had already sung to on her quiet evenings at home?

She had to prepare to face motherhood alone. Maybe Ashford would prove himself, but she couldn't be sure. She wasn't even sure how much she liked him. She feared he would turn out to be the untested, self-centered boy she first expected. She wanted a *man* who could hold her in his strong arms and make all her fears go away.

This all happened too fast. She didn't have time to find out if Ashford could be that kind of man.

She asked Samantha for a week off from work. Things were slow, and Samantha allowed it, even though vacations were always frowned upon. She asked Ashford not to call while she was gone, telling him they would meet when she returned, and by then she would *know*. She disliked being dishonest with him, but she needed time to know how to tell him and be prepared for any response.

She packed warm clothes, a few books, and her guitar. She drove west, to the California coast, then north, beyond the vast tentacles of Los Angeles. She stopped in a quaint village along

Highway 1 and rented a room in a beachside inn. The autumn air was cold and salty. She wore her sweater every day as she walked on the sand. Seagulls called out continuously as they flew low over the frigid surf.

Every night, she sang to the child who would soon begin to grow, cradling the guitar against her womb. Her life was on the verge of changing forever. There were so many practical considerations and not a lot of time to put things in order. She recalled the last time her life was turned upside down in a single moment—when she left her childhood in Colombia to become this new person. That day, she'd had no time for practicalities, but her past life had been simple, making it easy to walk away. This time, it was different. She had built a life through sweat and tears that she wasn't willing to walk away from.

She didn't want to worry about practicalities and plans yet. There wasn't a lot of time for those things, but she hoped there was at least *enough* time. Instead, during those days by the ocean, she gave license to her dreams, imagining a happy life with Ashford and a child. Was it such a stretch to think this could turn out wonderfully?

When she returned home, she would take a hard look at her savings and find out where she stood. She needed to write up her resume and start looking at options. Ashford talked about wanting to become financially independent from Samantha. It was even more urgent for Leila to do so.

But losing her job was the least of her worries at Samantha's hands. Worse was the fear that Samantha would turn Ashford against her, leaving her to raise the child on her own. When the moment came, how could Leila, who had spent a single night with Ashford, be sure he would choose her over his mother?

How much deeper might Samantha's anger run? Samantha was cunning. What if she started digging and found out about Leila's past—that she wasn't really who she said she was?

Her concern was for the future, but the past also reached back toward her on those cool, solitary days. Her mind kept wandering back to her childhood. Vague memories of her mother stirred in her heart. She remembered the children she grew up with. Those had been hard, frightening years, but there were good times too: playing football in the streets, dancing in the plaza at night, spontaneous swims in the ocean before they had any idea how dirty the Cartagena Bay was. There was a freedom to being a child of the streets, but there was no future except for the dark underworld offered by Paulo and similar men. She knew that at a young age and never regretted giving up the freedom for the opportunity Manny had offered her.

Leila wanted to give her child both—opportunity and freedom. She wanted to give the security of not wondering where their next meal would come from or fearing that any day they would be dragged away by cruel arms. She wanted to give her child *everything*.

She placed her hands on her stomach, realizing that she was eager for the day when she would feel it beginning to expand. Yes, she wanted this child, *needed* this child. She was scared, but it was a fear she had longed for.

On Friday morning, she left the seashore inn. It had been a good respite, but she could only run away for so long. She called Ashford before leaving and asked if they could meet for coffee the next morning. It felt like too casual of a suggestion, but she didn't know what else to do.

While driving east across California and into Arizona, she realized that, while Ashford had been there abstractly in her vision of a future family, she hadn't really thought about *him* much at all this week. Circumstances had so quickly taken her thoughts beyond the joy of what they had shared, all too briefly, with each other. It wasn't supposed to be like that. That warmth of first attraction should have lasted longer. It was gone for her already.

Before eleven a.m. on Saturday, she sat at an outside table at a small café beside an outdoor Scottsdale shopping center, uncharacteristically early as she watched for him. She had suggested this place because it was near his house but wished she had picked somewhere less crowded. At least she had found a table around a corner so they would be able to talk with some privacy.

It was early November; the daytime weather had cooled from sweltering to pleasantly warm. Snowbirds had begun their flight south for the winter. She saw them mobbing the nearby mall in their shorts and sandals. In other places, the leaves changed color in the fall; in Arizona, the license plates changed color. She watched them driving in and out of the parking lot: Minnesota, Michigan, Illinois, the various provinces of Canada.

Ashford appeared across the parking lot. She saw him coming toward her before he saw her. He wore jeans and his characteristic untucked, button-down shirt with the sleeves rolled up. It was the first time she had seen him since that night at his house. Her heart went out to him. Yes, the attraction was still there, even if it wasn't new and carefree anymore. She remembered the feel of his hands on her, his kisses, the passion with which they made love, all his tender words. Something of him had remained inside her. Their relationship was still brand new, but it was inseverable now.

His eyes found her, and he smiled. She felt less afraid.

She stood up and hugged him—their bodies together again, the scent of his neck, their intimacy remembered. She held him for several long seconds, then reached up to kiss him.

"Go ahead, get yourself a coffee." She already had hers.

She waited until he came back with his cup and settled into the wire chair across from her.

"So, Ashford Cohen, how do you feel about being a dad?"

Perhaps it wasn't the most elegant way for her to tell him, but there it was.

He took some time to process the news. She waited, forgetting for a moment that this had been her reality for several weeks while he had only been able to wonder. From his look, she surmised that parenthood had not been a dream of his the way it had been for her. She tried her hardest not to judge him for that.

"I'm scared."

She appreciated his honesty. "Me too. But I also feel joy. We've never talked about it. We barely know each other. But I've always seen myself as a mother, so I'm not sad, even if I don't feel ready."

He nodded. She wasn't sure if he understood, but she had needed to say it.

"I don't suppose I can ask much from you at this point. I don't even know what we are to each other. We haven't talked about it."

"You're my girlfriend. I insist now." He reached across the table and grabbed her hand.

"I like that."

"This will be my baby too. I'm freaked out about it. Wow, I'm only twenty-five! I don't even have a job. But it happened. I love you. When I told you I would be here for you, I meant it. We'll make this work."

Leila yanked her wire chair noisily across the concrete until it was beside him, then tucked her head under his arm and placed it on his shoulder. It felt so right to be back in his arms. The weeks since they had seen each other melted away. The future looked less frightening.

"We have to keep it a secret for a while. Not just the pregnancy but that we're together at all. I need to start looking for another job. It would be good to get one before I'm showing. It's supposedly illegal to make a hiring decision based on that, but you know it happens. The mortgage business can be pretty screwed up."

"My mom will be upset, but are you so sure she'd actually fire you?"

"We'll see." *Does he not know his mother at all? He'll be no match for her.*

"I have some good news too," he said.

She turned to look at him.

"While you were gone, I interviewed for a nursing job at the hospital in Glendale, and I think it went well. It would be a part-time assignment for now, which is perfect because I need to finish my internship at the university hospital. They said it could transition to full time once my internship is complete."

"That's wonderful! When does your internship end?"

"March."

The two wire chairs pushed together were not the most comfortable, even though Leila liked to be next to him.

"Let's walk."

They took their coffee cups and walked toward the nearby shops holding hands. His hands were larger than hers, and as they strolled, she rested her head on his shoulder, a little higher than her own. It was comforting. It made her feel feminine and secure.

"It's funny," he said, "all my life I've had whatever I needed, but I've never had any money to my own name. My mom just bought me anything I wanted. She still pays for everything. If I want something—even if I just need cash—she gives it to me. But I always have to ask, which never feels good."

"Makes it hard to date."

"Having a job will make a huge difference, but I'm pretty far from being financially independent."

He started laughing. It surprised Leila, but she enjoyed hearing it, particularly at a time like this. He had such a kind, musical laugh.

"What is it?" she asked.

"Earlier this morning, I stopped at this naturalist's shop nearby—a great hippie named Minerva. I often sell her my herbs for teas. This morning, I brought her a couple of pounds of stuff, mostly dried yucca and dandelion root, the result of two months of collecting. She paid me sixty bucks. Right now, those sixty bucks, minus the price of this cup of coffee, is basically all the money I have to my name. It was so funny to think about that I had to laugh. Yet there's something about it that's decidedly *not* funny."

Leila almost told him how much she had saved over these last few years, to assure him that he could lean on her if his mother kicked him out. But this wasn't the right time. Telling him he could rely on her wasn't what he needed to hear. He needed to know he could make his own way. She needed that too. The security of his large hand and strong shoulder were false comforts. She liked that he was going through these sorts of thought processes. Despite the shock of the pregnancy, he was starting to plan, which was important for the man who would be her child's father. That was *real* comfort, *real* security.

"Has Samantha ever mentioned Stewart to you?"

"No. Who's Stewart?"

"He was my brother."

Leila stopped and looked at him. "Was?"

"He died almost eight years ago."

Leila was amazed. Samantha had never mentioned having a child other than Ashford.

"Mom didn't handle it well. I mean what mother would? But it *really* messed her up. It happened during my senior year of high school and while I had been considering going away to college, after that I decided to stay and go to Arizona State. She needed me close. Now, though, it makes it even harder to break away and become independent."

So much more made sense now. Leila didn't want to ask him any more about it—he would offer if he wanted to tell her. She felt closer to Ashford, knowing the loss he had suffered. She'd thought he hadn't had much to test him in life. She had been wrong.

"Do you miss him, your brother?"

"I do. We weren't close. He was a lot older than me. He had a physical problem—an irregular heart—and he overcompensated by feigning strength. I was an easy target for him to pick on. I was glad when he moved away, but after he died, I only remembered all the things I loved about him."

Leila squeezed his hand. She couldn't really imagine having a sibling, much less losing one.

"I never grew up as an only child," he continued, "then suddenly I was one. I felt a lot of responsibility for my mom after that. Maybe too much, when I think about it. I'm seeing now how she's used that to keep me close. Dad told me she'd make it hard when the time came that I'd want to leave. I never really listened to him. I didn't need to until now."

A sudden breeze kicked through the palms that lined the sidewalk.

"You've never told me about your dad. Where has he been through all these years?"

"He lives in LA. He's a wonderful person, but not really a model for who I want to be. He can't hold a job for long and never can save any money."

"How odd to think of someone like that with Samantha."

"Not really. He's a charmer and an artist. Mom was young when they married. I think it took a few years until she realized that she didn't want the life he offered. After Stewart, and when I started school, she went into sales. She was great at it, and after a few years, she was making far more money than Dad ever had. He spent all of her money he could get his hands on and seldom contributed much in return. So, she divorced him."

"Interesting."

"She was always fair to him—I'll give her credit for that. She never asked him for child support, which wouldn't have made any sense. She knew that Stewart and I would be better people for having a relationship with our dad, so she let him see us whenever he wanted."

He looked over at her with a smile. "It was my dad who got me started on the plant-based medicines."

"Really? I can't picture Samantha with anyone who liked to grind up yucca root."

"He's an incredibly creative person—full of ideas and full of love, but always with his head in the clouds. Stewart was that way too."

"I want to meet him."

"You will. Hopefully soon. I think you'll really like him."

"I want to know everything there is to know about you." She squeezed his hand again, pressing her body toward him. "I like having a boyfriend."

They spent the rest of the morning talking and walking through the shops. They ate lunch, then drove back to Leila's apartment. Her complex was growing fuller with Phoenix's expanding winter population. Soon, she would have to start leaving notes on the cars that took her assigned parking spot. She showed Ashford the correct guest parking area. Romeo ran and hid when they entered the apartment, unsure of the stranger.

They made love all afternoon.

The crisis had happened. There was no undoing it. They were united now for better and worse. Leila wanted to let herself fall all the way in love with him.

Ashford left as the sun was setting. Leila wished he could spend the night, but it was too soon for that. She stood in her doorway at the top of the stairs, covered only by her bathrobe, watching him drive away.

Samantha could fire her. She could kick Ashford out and cut him off. But if she tried to turn him against her, Leila would fight her tooth and nail. Maybe Ashford was no match for his mother, but Leila sure as hell was.

22

LEILA HAD TRIED not to think about the work that would await her when she got back to the office on Monday. Hopefully, she wouldn't have to go much longer. She had updated her resume the night before.

She arrived just after nine, hoping to slip in quietly. To her surprise, everyone was there already, but nobody was working. Not a single phone receiver was off its hook. Samantha's office door was shut. Leila looked around.

"What's going on?"

"You picked a bad time to go on vacation," said Cox.

"Things were so quiet when I left."

"Well, they're not quiet anymore."

She sat down at her desk and opened her email, but didn't start sifting through any yet, scared of what she might find.

Samantha's office door opened and two men in suits walked toward the elevators, not making eye contact with anyone.

"Do you think they're the feds?" Dennis asked.

"No way," said Cox. "The feds always come on Fridays, and they wear black suits. That guy's suit was gray."

"What the hell are you talking about?" Dennis was clearly on edge.

Samantha appeared in her doorway. "Leila!"

She obeyed the summons, terrified. The door shut behind her.

"You sure left me in a hell of a mess."

"I'm sorry." Leila sat down, not able to imagine what was going on. Samantha leaned back against the front of her desk. She looked exhausted for a Monday morning.

"The least you could have done was answer your cell phone."

"I was out of coverage range. What happened?"

"Desert Villas is in crisis. The new houses aren't appraising for half what the first batch closed at. Buyers are walking away from their earnest money deposits. Better than taking a bath by closing, I suppose."

"Isn't Marshall Berg still doing the appraisals?"

"Fuck Marshall! That ass has betrayed me for the last time. I'll have his license before this is through. Leila, I need you to call Paul. He'll listen to you. He panicked when you were gone last week. He needs to hear your voice. Tell him everything will be fine with the two Kumar loans and we'll find a way with the others."

"Kumar? But the Kumar loans funded over a week ago, before I left."

"We've still got them on our warehouse line of credit. The investor pulled out. I've tried everywhere. Sun Trust won't touch them. Neither will Countrywide."

"Shit. Who was that Kumar guy anyway?"

"Amit Raj Kumar. He's a British investor. He bought two of the biggest houses with five percent down payment on interest-only loans."

"Well, if the new appraisals are right, he already owes more than they're worth. How long can we afford to keep them on our warehouse line?"

"Not this long. It's bad. When you left a week ago, we were a healthy company. Now, we're a whisper away from insolvency."

"What are you going to do?"

"Well, I have a potential investor in Sweden."

"Sweden?"

"And if that doesn't work out, there are those guys you just saw walking out of here. I can't talk about it yet, but they're my last resort."

"How are you funding the other loans?"

"The smaller ones we still have room for on the line."

"Three big ones are supposed to fund on Wednesday."

"I'll have to cover some of that out of my pocket."

"Can you do that?"

"I have to. If the feds find out, they'll be here on Friday to put handcuffs on the doors and we're done."

Leila stood up and walked toward the door.

"What should I tell Paul?"

"I don't know. Use your charm. Whatever the hell you do, don't tell him the truth."

Leila put her hand on the doorknob but turned around one more time. She couldn't help it. "What *is* the truth?"

Samantha exhaled audibly. "Nobody wants to live in those houses they built in the desert. They sold to investors and speculators, but who are *they* going to sell or rent them to, coyotes and rattlesnakes?"

Leila walked back to her desk. Not two months ago, they celebrated Desert Villas as the new frontier of Phoenix real estate. How quickly it all came crashing down.

It was a strange week in the office. Samantha hardly spoke to anyone. There wasn't much action on the phone lines. Cox and Tommy each managed to lock a loan, but those were the only two names on the board. The three loans funded on Wednesday. Leila wondered if anybody else knew the strings Samantha had pulled to get it done. Fortunately, the investors came through the next day. Meanwhile, the Kumar loans remained on the books. Time was running short.

Leila began sending out her resume.

On Friday morning, the two mysterious men were back. They were in Samantha's office for over an hour. At the end of the meeting, they shook hands in her doorway, all smiles as everyone watched nervously.

"May I have everyone's attention, please?" Samantha said after the men left. She wore a big smile that would have looked fake if not for the relief it showed. "I am thrilled to announce that our company is merging with Alamo Trust Bank, a super-regional that has a big presence in Texas and New Mexico. They already have a small mortgage office in Phoenix and are excited for the opportunity to grow in Arizona. Next year, they plan to open a couple of deposit branches here."

Did Samantha really think she could fool any of them into thinking this was good news? Across the short cubicle wall, Leila heard Dennis snort, "What a shit show." Samantha was undeterred.

"The advantage is that as a bank, they fund all their loans in-house. We have access to all the capital we could ever need. The flip side of that is our product offerings will be smaller. This merger is effective as of today, but we will retain our name through the end of the year. Our lease in this space runs through another two years, and there are no plans at this time to break it."

She paused, and her smile disappeared.

"Now, for me to get this deal through, I had to agree to become leaner. Our loan volume over the last two months doesn't justify this fat of a staff. A few of you have not been carrying your weight." She looked down at the floor, then back up and exhaled sharply. "Dennis, DeShawn, Rosemary . . . thank you for your contributions. You are hereby terminated. You may take a moment to pack up your things."

Nobody moved for a second. The shock was still sinking in.

"I mean now. Don't bother to try to save any of your files. Your log-ins have already been canceled. I'd like this to be as painless as possible, so please just go."

Rosemary burst into tears. Dennis began putting things in his briefcase. DeShawn stood up.

"It's been fun," he said quietly to Leila.

She offered her hand. "Good luck."

He walked out without taking a thing. Dennis and Rosemary remained at their desks.

"Kristen," Samantha called toward the junior processor, "this is your two-week termination notice. Mona can handle all of our processing from here on, but I'd like you to stay and finish up the files you're working on."

Finally, Rosemary and Dennis made their painful exits. Samantha addressed those who remained.

"The rest of you are officially on notice. No crap, no games, no more vacations. This is do-or-die time. Now, get on those phones and sell some goddamn loans or you can pack your things too."

They obeyed. Sales were hard. Voices on the other end of the line were indignant, sometimes even threatening, but the four surviving loan officers kept at it. They had to.

For a few hours, Leila's mind was back on the pressure of this job, even while she plotted her escape. She felt bad for those who had been fired when she planned to quit as soon as she had a good offer, but she couldn't offer her place to another even if she wanted to. It didn't work like that. Every loan officer was judged on his or her merit alone. That was something she loved about it.

It was past one o'clock, and she hadn't eaten all day. She hadn't brought any food either. She stepped out to get some lunch. Crossing the street and heading for a reliable deli, she passed the Starbucks where she had met Ashford a few months back. Dennis sat at an outdoor table. There was no coffee cup in front of him. He must have considered it a suddenly expendable expense. He stared with glazed eyes across the street at the office building. Leila guessed he had been sitting there all morning.

"Hi, Dennis."

"Oh, hi." He was jolted out of his daze.

Leila didn't really want to, but she sat down beside him, thinking it was the polite thing to do.

"What am I going to do?" The pitch of his voice rose the way she remembered it always did when he became agitated.

"You'll get another job soon. You have great experience."

"It's not like it used to be. What happened here is happening everywhere. There's no place for a guy like me anymore. Maybe for you or Cox. Maybe even DeShawn. He's young. He's got a big personality. That's the only thing that's valued anymore. An over-the-hill guy like me, though? I'm screwed!"

She didn't know what to say. Sadly, he was probably right. She couldn't imagine where he would find a new job with his skill set in *this* economy.

"It's too late for me to start a new career. All I know is the mortgage business, and this business is going to shit. I bet my wife will leave me too."

"Don't say that."

"It's true. She's wanted to for years. If I'm unemployed, what does she have to stay for? Our kids are grown. None of them need me anymore."

It wasn't only the business that had moved past Dennis. The *world* had moved past him. But he had let it happen. She did feel for him, even as his self-pity reeked of a lifetime of entitlement and privilege. Maybe he was right, that the days of an older white man being handed another soft landing were over. His real problem was that as a privileged white man, he had never learned to scratch and claw for his chances.

She stood up. "I can't be away for too long. Samantha's cracking the whip up there today. Dennis, I'm really sorry. You have my number. Let me know if there's anything I can do to help."

She started to offer her hand, but Dennis had returned to his daze. She hurried to the deli for her salad, then brought it back to eat at her desk.

A day at a time, she told herself. A day at a time before she could find a new job . . . *if* she could. A day at a time before she and Ashford could live their love openly. A day at a time until her child came into the world. Until then, she would pick up the phone and fight to survive, even if the housing market crumbled around her.

23

LEILA WALKED UP to Samantha's house knowing it might be the last time. Only two and a half years had passed since the first time she walked up this stone drive, wide-eyed and wondering if she was in over her head. Perhaps she had been all this time.

The evening was cool. She had left her scarf in her car and hurried up the steps toward the house, expecting it to be warm inside. The city sounds echoed upward against the hills. Christmas lights sparkled around the windows and on the large tree inside the house. Samantha's Christmas party had always been a big event. This year would be different, as their office staff had been sliced in half and the entire subprime mortgage industry circled the drain. But Samantha would find a way to make everyone feel happy, or at least pretend to. She always did.

Was it December already? Time was flying by, and Leila still didn't have an exit plan. She would probably be showing in a matter of weeks now.

Ashford didn't have an exit plan either. She knew he didn't like talking about it with her, but he had been turned down for the first job in Glendale, and no other hospitals had offered him a position. Leila wasn't surprised. After all, he still had his internship to negotiate. She knew he was embarrassed, still being dependent on his mother. She had to admit she wanted to see how he managed once he was out in the real world. She was still a little unsure what kind of a man she had gotten herself tangled up with.

She hoped he had made plans elsewhere tonight. She knew he would stay away from the party, but if he was here, alone in his room, she would sense it. It would be better for him to be away. Yet part of her heart couldn't help wishing that he *was* here. She hadn't been with him in several days. She missed him. She wanted to be near him, even if she didn't see him.

The house was full of new faces. Leila only recognized about half of the guests. Warm light from the tree gave the party a festive, happy feel. The house even smelled like fresh-baked Christmas cookies. Samantha must have asked the caterers to do their baking here. She thought of everything.

Samantha herself was affectionate as ever when she greeted Leila and introduced her to the new people. But something was different. Something had been lost. Even if Leila had never gotten involved with Ashford, this life was ending anyway, not just for herself but for all of them. Samantha was hanging on to it by a thread, gathering new people to replace those who fell away. There were always willing moons to orbit her. Once Leila left, she would be replaced too. But how long could Samantha hold on to her place in the sky?

Leila made an effort to engage with the guests. She smiled, said the right things, and laughed at people's jokes. But she was detached from it all. It made it harder that her whole body felt uncomfortable. She had never fit in here, and now she didn't care enough to try.

As she tried to be friendly with the guests, a wave of nausea rolled over her. The place smelled awful. Alcohol on people's breath, combined with the sweet baking smell from the kitchen, was too much for her to take. The clatter of plates, rising voices, and loud music beat against the inside of her head.

"Leila, are you okay?"

Startled, she glanced up at Samantha, who stood next to her with a cocktail in hand. Her voice sounded distant amongst all the other noises.

"Yeah, why?"

"You don't seem yourself."

Leila got nervous. She couldn't hide anything from Samantha. "A lot on my mind, I suppose."

"I understand. Things are changing fast, but it will be okay. Please do try to mingle. Use your charm. There are executives from Alamo Trust Bank here, as well as some new real estate agents. It's important for us to widen our sphere of influence."

"I'll try."

Samantha smiled, but Leila saw something wrong in her smile.

Leila did try, but only while Samantha was watching. She had to keep up appearances for Samantha if for no one else. She needed an exit strategy fast, but until then it was crucial to retain her boss's trust. Once Samantha went into another room, Leila turned away from the guests and stood by the open window. The fresh night air dispelled the weird smells in the room. Her nausea went away as swiftly as it had come on.

A car sounded on the driveway. It was about nine o'clock, too late for another guest to arrive. Leila looked out. It was Ashford's car. The garage door opened and closed behind him.

Suddenly, unexpectedly, a tingle ran all through her.

For the next half hour, she could barely pretend to socialize. Ashford's nearness was too much of a distraction. Soon, it became an irresistible temptation.

She had to see him. She craved his arms around her, his lips on hers, if only for a moment, and then she could come back.

The bathroom was down the hallway toward the stairs. If she returned quickly, everyone who did notice would think she had just gone to use it.

She dashed up the stairs. Her heartbeat quickened.

A light shone from beneath Ashford's closed bedroom door. She scratched the door gently. In a moment, he opened it and hurried her in. He didn't seem surprised. Her nearness must have tempted him too.

A single lamp lit the room. A dark gray curtain flapped in the night breeze from his open bedroom window, fanning a dozen small jars on the sill.

No words were spoken. They were unnecessary.

Leila folded herself into his embrace. Their lips met with the eagerness born of separation and haste. Leila pulled him toward her, with one arm around his shoulder and one hand on his hips. His lips explored her face and her neck. She pushed him backward to sit on his double bed, pulling his shirt up over his head and unzipping his jeans. When she entered his room, she hadn't intended to go this far. But she had to have him, all of him. She had to be quick about it.

He pulled her dress up over her head, then fumbled with her bra clasp. She laughed quietly, reaching back to help him with it, loving how excited he was. She couldn't stand to wait another second. As he touched her, every nerve of her body responded. Her pregnancy had heightened every sensation within her. She relished his lips and rough chin against her neck, his hands in her thick hair, his strong lower back clutched between her thighs. She urged him inside her, biting her lip hard to keep from crying out with pleasure.

When it was over, she fell against him, her head over his shoulder and the tingling skin of her breasts against his hot, thumping chest.

"I couldn't resist you."

He still said nothing. He didn't need to. She felt everything in his beating heart.

"Never let go."

But they had to. She had been gone too long. She got off of him, dressed, and cleaned herself up as best she could. She reapplied her lipstick, laughing as she wiped the evidence off of Ashford's face. He dressed too. They embraced for several long moments, then she opened his bedroom door.

"Well, isn't this interesting." Samantha stood in the hallway with her arms folded.

Leila gasped, then choked. Her knees briefly buckled from shock, and she had to grab onto the doorframe.

"I've suspected this for some time. Still, I'm disappointed. Why would you betray me like this, Leila?"

Ashford hurried out and stood beside her, facing his mother. "It's not her fault. If you want to blame anyone, blame me."

"Shut up. I'm talking to Leila."

"No, Mom, you're talking to me. Leila and I love each other."

"Aren't you gallant."

"I'm sorry we kept it from you, but it's time for you to know. We're together now."

"Don't be ridiculous. You've had your fun. Now, you can both move on."

Leila struggled to regain her composure. She couldn't breathe. She loved Ashford for standing up for her but hoped he wouldn't tell Samantha everything. It would be better to break it to her gradually.

"It's not that simple."

As soon as she heard Ashford say those words, Leila knew it was all coming out.

"It's incredibly simple. You're both young, attractive people who don't know a damn thing about love."

"Yes, we do."

"Bullshit."

Don't tell her. Don't tell her.

"Leila and I are having a baby together."

Samantha staggered back against the wall. "What do you mean? That's not possible, you careless idiots!"

Leila had never seen Samantha lose her composure before. It only lasted a moment before she steadied herself and returned her businesslike smile to her lips.

"Leila dear, I think you'd better go home. I need to talk with my son."

Leila couldn't move.

"You and I will talk on Monday at the office."

The surprise must have showed on Leila's face.

"No, you're not fired. I don't blame you for being young and getting swept off your feet. It's happened to so many of us women. You *will* come to work on Monday, and we will have a little talk."

Ashford squeezed her hand. She feared leaving him alone with Samantha. She knew his mother would try to turn him against her. But she had no choice. She had to trust in him. If he could be strong for her, he would have to prove it alone. She left down the staircase and out the back door, avoiding the party, which was growing louder.

24

SO, THIS WAS the day. No more secrets now.

Leila wasn't sure how she was supposed to act when she walked into the office on Monday, surely for the final time. Even though Samantha hadn't fired her . . . yet . . . she hardly felt like sticking around.

Samantha didn't make her wait. Even before Leila could put her purse down at her desk, she was called into her boss's office. To her surprise, Samantha greeted her with a hug.

"Dear, this must be so hard for you. So confusing."

Samantha's warm demeanor startled Leila, but she didn't let down her guard.

"You probably thought I would fire you this morning." Samantha closed the door and sat on the edge of her desk. Leila remained standing. "I hope it doesn't come to that. I'd rather help you."

Leila resisted the urge to fold her arms.

"I don't blame you for what happened. Ashford is persuasive—has been since he was a little boy. He's handsome. You're beautiful. You're both young. That doesn't mean I think you're a good match. I'm sure you understand that, even if my son doesn't. I've forbidden Ashford to see you again. But I'm not surprised by your attraction. It's natural."

"He's a grown man. He can make his own decisions."

"Not while I support him. It's my right to establish terms."

"Okay. So you forbid him from seeing me. But you can't forbid him from seeing his child."

"Now, you're making this more complicated than it needs to be. This can all be forgotten so easily."

"Don't even say it." Leila glared at her. "Don't make me hate you."

"Leila, Leila, use your head. Think of your career, your future. Things are stacked unfairly against women—in this business like so many others. It's especially stacked against an *immigrant* woman."

Yes, because of people like you.

"Everything is complicated by a child. Think of the man you will one day marry."

"I hope that man will be your son."

Samantha shuddered, unable to hide her horror at the thought that was for the first time put into words. Similar to the moment in her house, her lost composure only lasted a second before she resumed her cool, gentle smile, but Leila saw it and knew she had been right about Samantha. She would only allow Leila to be her subordinate or her enemy.

"You must realize that can never happen, and not just because of me."

"No, I don't realize that."

"You know how to live when life is tough; it's never been tough for Ashford. *I've* made sure of that, perhaps to his detriment. Right now, he's emotional. He thinks he's in love. But he doesn't want a baby. He wants to start a career and live a little. He and I have talked about it often. He wants to travel. He might still go to med school. He feels a sense of duty now, but do you really think he'd stick around? He's attracted to you now, but a baby will change your body. We both know that, but he hasn't thought about it."

In a flash, Leila understood Samantha's strategy. Rather than trying to turn Ashford against her, as she had feared, she was trying to turn *her* against *him*.

"He's my son, so my loyalty will always be with him, but I also feel sympathetic with you, as a woman. I don't want to see your career and your prospects ruined, forced to live as a single mother once he realizes that parenting is too hard."

"I believe he would stay. He's a good man. You know that, surely."

"Young people have such beautiful, naïve sentiments."

"Could you believe that Ashford really loves me?"

"I believe he really loves your big tits and your hot ass."

"Fuck you!"

Samantha smiled. "Just calling it like it is, my dear. Ashford's no different from any man. You can either listen to me or learn it the hard way like most women have to." Samantha took a deep breath, then walked around to the other side of her desk and sat in her office chair.

"It stuns me how ungrateful you are."

"What?"

"I don't mean toward me. I mean how ungrateful you are about the opportunities you have. Being in this country is not a right, and you shouldn't treat it so lightly. I'm so proud of you for what you've accomplished, but you're acting awfully cavalier about it. Success is a privilege for people like you. I'm all for equal opportunities, but have some common sense about it. Remember who you are and where you came from."

"Seriously, Samantha? *'People like you'*?"

"You don't need to decide anything right now. Take a few days. I know it's a tough thing to come to terms with, but you'll see it's for the best. More of us than you realize have had it done. You'll have plenty more chances with the right man at the right time."

"I'm not getting an abortion. I warned you not to go there."

"Then you're fired. Thank you for your contributions."

Leila threw her head back and laughed. It felt good. The veil of friendship had been ripped off of their meeting.

"Have an abortion or I'm fired? You can't do that. There are laws against that."

"Not that'll protect a beaner like you! You have no idea how fast I could have you sent back to Mexico."

"How dare you! I'm a legal resident, and for the hundredth fucking time, I'm not Mexican."

"Then I'll send you to hell. That's where you're really from, isn't it?"

The look in Samantha's eyes gave Leila a sudden wave of fear. Samantha saw her fear and grinned. She opened her desk drawer and pulled out a single folded sheet of paper.

"Remember this?"

Leila watched in horror as Samantha unfolded a piece of paper that she immediately recognized. It was the rescission document with Mrs. Collins's taped-on signature.

"You thought you shredded this, didn't you? You must learn to be more discreet."

Leila stared at the page, dumbfounded

"This is your career, right here, reduced to a single stupid piece of paper."

Leila felt the room swirling around her for a moment but steadied herself.

"You have three choices." Samantha leaned forward on her desk. "Give up the baby, come back to work, and we'll all pretend this never happened. Or you can disappear, have the baby if you must, but you will do it alone. You will never ask Ashford for a penny or else this little trick you played will come to light." Samantha put the sheet back into her desk and locked it. "I don't think you need to hear the third choice."

Leila stood on weakening knees, beginning to comprehend her total defeat. Samantha sat back down at her desk.

"Please leave me alone now. I have a lot of work to do."

Leila walked straight through the office to the elevator. She didn't make eye contact with anyone. She cried in her car. She couldn't drive yet. Her hands shook from anger. Once she managed to calm down, her anger turned into fear. What could Samantha really do to her? What had she said already to Ashford?

With shaking fingers, she pulled her phone out of her purse and tried to call him. He didn't answer. The same thing happened yesterday when she tried to call—straight to voicemail. It was strange. The few times before when she had called him and he didn't pick up, he always called right back. Usually, it was he who called, unable to get enough of her voice. Could Samantha have turned him against her this fast?

She wiped her eyes and started home. This was no time to feel sorry for herself.

It felt strange being on these familiar roads in midmorning.

She parked, then hurried toward the stairs. Halfway up, she stopped. A big smile spread across her face. Ashford was sitting on a suitcase in her doorway.

She ran to him, throwing her arms around him as he stood up.

"I've never been happier to see you."

"You know what this means, don't you?" He inclined his head, which she was still assaulting with kisses, toward the suitcase.

"I do. Your mother kicked you out, so you're moving in. It's wonderful."

She released him and stood beaming at him. All her worries, for a moment, had been washed away.

"Want to help me get the rest of my things out of my car?"

She skipped with him to where he had parked in the correct visitor parking area.

"Were you going to wait there all day?"

"I didn't expect you'd last long."

"You were right. She fired me. Now, we're both unemployed."

"I suppose you could say she fired me too. She even turned off my phone."

"Unbelievable."

They reached his car. Leila had expected to see more inside.

"Is this really all your stuff?"

"All I cared to pack in a hurry this morning."

"Where are all your potions and herbs?"

"Sacrificed to the cause. I'll let you get to know me a little better before I start stinking up your apartment with that stuff."

She laughed, tossing a backpack over her shoulder and picking up two paper grocery bags full of who knew what.

"I love you." She heard the words come out of her mouth. Was that the first time she had said it to him? She thought it was.

25

"DO YOU HAVE any idea how happy you've made me?" Leila rubbed her swollen belly.

"I'm beginning to understand. It didn't start out that way."

"Only because I didn't know what I could expect from you yet."

"Do you know now?"

"I knew when I came home and saw you at the door with all your things in that little suitcase. I trust you now." It had already been over two months since Ashford moved in with her. It was a strange time for Leila, not working, yet not feeling limited at all by her pregnancy. She tried not to be restless and to enjoy this time with Ashford, getting to know him and savoring his passion for her.

Ashford put the last of their dinner plates into the dishwasher, then walked over and sat beside her on the couch.

"Touch it."

He did. It was only a small baby bump.

"How does it make you feel, to know that's *your* child?"

"I'm still scared."

Leila smiled. "Of course you are. Boys don't dream about this the way girls do. You're an American boy, too, so that makes things different."

"What do you mean by that?"

"Latin men love a pregnant belly."

Ashford laughed.

"If you were Colombian you would want everyone in town to see that your girl was pregnant." Leila took Ashford's hand and put it back on her belly. "Latin cultures value family differently than they do here. Family life is a point of public pride, while in America it's more private. My father tried to explain it to me, but I never understood until now. As I feel this baby growing inside me, it makes me remember my roots. I thought I had put Colombia pretty well behind me, but a little bit of Colombia will be born in this child."

"Do you miss it?"

"Yes. It's my homeland. I could only deny that for so long."

"I'd love to see Cartagena."

"Oh dear, don't ever pronounce it that way again. Didn't you take three years of Spanish in high school? It's *Cartagena*, with a soft *g* and a soft *n*."

He laughed. "Sorry."

"I might forgive you." She winked at him.

"Do you think you'll ever go back?"

"I would love to go with you and our child. But it's difficult. It's more complicated than I've told you. I'll tell you everything in time. I promise."

"I know."

Ashford stood up, pulled the curtains, and threw open the windows behind them. There were no screens and the night air rushed in, still warm but pleasant now that the sun was down. Birds chattered in the mesquite trees.

"Mmm, that's nice," she said. "I love this time of year."

Ashford sat back down and put his arm around her. She nestled her head into his shoulder. Romeo made a show of walking in front of them but didn't hop up on the couch like he used to. He was warming up to Ashford but resented losing his exclusive cuddling rights with Leila.

"Are *you* happy, darling?"

He took a moment to answer, which told Leila all she needed to know.

"I'm happy to be with you. But it's hard for me. I wish I could do more for you."

"You've done so much."

He began to say something but hesitated. Leila turned her head to look at him.

"Don't be afraid to say what you feel. I think I already know."

"I would be a lot happier if I was working."

"But you are working. Your internship is important."

"An unpaid internship is a leftover luxury from my past life. A good partner, and a good father, provides. I haven't provided you with a thing. All I did was get you fired. Now, you're supporting me too."

Leila laughed. "I get it. Just be patient. Your time will come. After your internship, they'll offer you a full-time job."

Ashford hesitated again. Leila had grown to know him well enough to understand such clues.

"What is it?"

"I wasn't sure if I would tell you this, but I've already been offered a job when the internship ends."

Leila sat up straight. "That's wonderful. Why didn't you say anything?"

"Because it's not quite what I expected."

"Is it as an RN?"

"Yes. But not here. It's at a clinic in Santa Fe."

"What's so bad about that?"

"I didn't think you'd want to leave. You have your father here and your friends. If you want to go back to work after the baby's born, this is where you have connections. It seemed like it would be a selfish thing to suggest we pick up and move."

Leila grabbed Ashford's cheeks and kissed him on the lips.

"What's keeping us here? Why not? It would be a great start to your career. I won't be able to work again for at least a year. Let's do it. You can always apply for jobs back here later if we don't like it there. It will be easier once you have a job."

"Do you really mean it?"

"It will be an adventure. We're a little family now. We do things with each other. We do things *for* each other."

He pulled her toward him. "Let's stay together forever."

She smiled over his shoulder. She liked feeling the warmth of him against the life that grew in her. She hoped he could feel the baby too. "I like hearing you say that. I think it's the first time you've used a word like *forever*."

"I mean it. I've always wanted that with you. Things just started moving so fast that I got scared. But as soon as this happened, I've been committed to you and our baby . . . forever. I just didn't know how to say it."

She lifted her head off his shoulder, adjusting herself on the couch so she could look in his eyes. "Do you hear what you're saying?"

"Yes. I want to spend my whole life with you." He paused. "I want you to be my wife."

Only then did it really hit Leila what was happening, along with the realization that she had urged this on. She had welcomed him to move into her home and into her life. There hadn't been much choice. But was she ready to marry him? She was falling in love with him, and that frightened her. Even after she got pregnant, she had held something back from him, not sure if she was ready to love. There was no holding back now.

He was talking again, nervously. His fingers fidgeted. "I couldn't say anything at first, because I didn't want it to be about the pregnancy. That's sped things up, sure. But I dreamed of this even before we started dating. Now that we're living together, I love you more every day."

A few small beads of sweat formed on his forehead. Leila clutched his hand.

"I didn't exactly plan this out," he said. "But nothing with us has gone according to script, has it?"

She laughed and realized that she was crying.

"Let's get married. A wedding's not practical yet, but let's be engaged. I want to promise you that we'll be together forever."

"Yes." She drew him into her arms and held him tightly. "I would love nothing more than to be your wife."

She did want it. It would be wonderful to marry Ashford. But this all seemed a little too easy, and that made her nervous. Things had always come easily for Ashford, and this had been easy for him too, whether he realized it or not. How would he change over the years, and what would that mean for her and the baby? On the other hand, what choice did she really have but to say yes to him? The *yes* had been said that night at his house. She had nothing more to lose now and a lot to gain.

He held her for several long moments before they pulled back to look at each other—now in a new way.

"I suppose that wasn't the most romantic of proposals."

"It was as romantic as can be. *This* is romantic. I don't need a big show or a fancy ring. I need you with me. It's important that you let me take care of you now, so that you can take care of me later. I need us to know that if something happens in our lives, like your job in Santa Fe, it's always something we'll do together, as a family. That kind of trust is the most romantic thing in the world."

Leila watched as Ashford hopped up from the couch and walked into the kitchen. What was he up to now? Soon, he returned with a piece of cooking twine. He tied it loosely around her left ring finger. She burst out laughing.

"This will have to do for now, because your fiancé is broke. Give me some time, and I'll give you a beautiful ring . . . and a beautiful life."

"You already have." She kissed him eagerly.

"Wait. I have to call my dad and tell him."

Leila woke up early after trying to nap. She wasn't a good napper but had tried as her pregnancy began to sap more of her energy. It was the day before they planned to leave for Santa Fe. When she heard Ashford's voice in the other room, her ears perked up, but then she immediately regretted it.

"Mom, I called because I was worried about you. Will you stop about Leila for a second and tell me about yourself?"

A pause.

"Of course I didn't call you on Christmas. You turned off my phone, remember?"

Leila didn't like that he had called his mother, from *her* apartment no less, albeit on his own new cell phone. What was he going to tell her now? It felt like a small betrayal.

"I've seen some things in the news about the mortgage market that sound really scary. Are you going to be alright?"

His voice was muffled. Even awake, she shouldn't have been able to hear every word and she wished she couldn't. She didn't want to eavesdrop. That was a small betrayal too. But she could hear him clearly. She had always been so sensitive to sounds.

"Yes, I have thought about what it means to have a child."

Now that she had heard it, there was no way she could unhear it.

"A meltdown? Seriously, Mom. You worry about *my* stability?"

What sort of things was Samantha saying to him?

"What are you talking about?"

There was a much longer silence. Leila thought about putting in her earplugs and trying to sleep again, but that probably wouldn't help now.

"I saved your life that night. You've never once thanked me."

Leila's ears perked up. She couldn't help it.

"Mom, I can't believe you're turning this against me after all I did for you, after all those years of never telling what happened because I respected your pride. Do you actually believe I hallucinated the whole thing? I understand if you blacked out the night Stewart died—you drank half a bottle of vodka—but don't twist the facts to pretend it was all my fault."

Leila was dying to know what had happened, but she couldn't ask, not now.

"Now, I'm mentally fragile? Mom, the reason I stayed at home for so long was to keep my eye on you, so you wouldn't try to hurt yourself again. I never expected gratitude. I knew it would have been hard to talk about. I guess I assumed it was a silent understanding between us. Why do you have to turn it all against me?"

Leila was on the verge of tears listening to this. She didn't know what happened when Ashford's brother died, but many things were suddenly clear. Ashford had been a lot more than a spoiled rich boy living with his mother into his mid-twenties. By the sound of things, he let himself be seen that way for a very mature reason.

"I need to go, Mom. You have my new cell number now. You can get in touch with me if you need to."

He had probably planned to tell Samantha about their move, maybe even about their engagement, before Samantha took the conversation off the rails. Leila was glad he hadn't told her those things.

She waited in bed, wondering if Ashford would come back into the room. She decided to admit to having overheard. She wanted him to know. She didn't want to hold a secret from him and wanted to know this new side to his history . . . as much of it as he would tell. Maybe she already knew enough.

26

THE MOVE TO Santa Fe went smoothly. They pulled a small U-Haul trailer behind Leila's Toyota. Ashford had sold his car the week before. Leila had also sold the diamond and sapphire necklace with only a hint of spite—one final commission check.

It was a long drive, but they made it in a single day. In retrospect, Leila thought they should have split it up over two days. It surprised her how tired she got and how many little things made her uncomfortable now. Even Romeo handled the trip better than her.

The clinic in Santa Fe helped them find an apartment and set up a one-year lease in Ashford's name. That was the length of time he committed to remain in Santa Fe before trying to find something back in Phoenix. Theirs was a north-facing unit in a tan stucco building. The full branch of a sturdy pine tree framed the top of their living-room window from outside, casing the view of the mountains beyond the quaint city. The air was pleasant and cool, a refreshment as summer began. Still, Leila expected she would miss Phoenix come winter.

Right away, Ashford made a positive impression at his job. Leila saw how the work invigorated him.

He had changed since Leila first met him. She once questioned his motives for going into nursing, but there was no doubting him anymore. He had learned to love, and it came through in his work. Leila could see how happy it made him, both to serve the patients at the clinic and to feel like he was providing for her. There was still no practical need, as her savings could have supported them for another year or so, but she understood why it was important to him. It allowed him to hold his head high as he got a crash course in adulthood.

In time, Leila knew she'd want to work again, but it was nice to have a break. Based on what she saw in the news, it was clearly a good time to be away from the mortgage business.

She had worried she would be lonely in Santa Fe, away from her father, her friends, and everything she knew. But the people were so welcoming. Ashford's coworkers befriended them right away, as did several of the neighbors in their apartment complex. Santa Fe was small compared to Phoenix. Everyone was less anonymous.

How could she have ever pictured this, just a year before? How could she have imagined how completely her life would change for the better? She had been so afraid—first to give her heart, then of the broken condom and what it would mean, then of Samantha's wrath. All those fears had turned into joy.

Yet, in the back of her mind, she couldn't help remembering the three choices that Samantha had threatened her with that morning in December. It was the third choice that Samantha wouldn't even tell—and Leila chose it. What could Samantha really do to her? How far would her spite go? Surely, in time, Samantha would give up her pride for the sake of a relationship with her only surviving son and grandchild.

Leila was thankful for the gentle summer in the high desert as the baby grew. She could still go outside and have the windows open at night. In Phoenix, she never would have wanted to leave the apartment.

Their daughter was born in July—*Cristina*. Leila always knew it would be a girl. One day, she would tell Ashford the full meaning behind that name.

She had wondered if she would miss the feeling of having the baby inside her—that closest of all physical intimacies. But once the little girl was free and held to her breast for the first time, that first intimacy was replaced by one even more wonderful. This child was still a part of her but was her own little person too: real, unique, with a vibrant personality that showed itself in her first days of life.

Manny and Carmen visited. Leila made them promise to take two days for the drive, for the sake of Manny's knees. He was scheduled for double knee replacement surgery at the beginning of December.

On the second day of their visit, Leila asked Manny to go for a short walk with her while Cristina was asleep. Ashford was at work, and Carmen stayed to watch the baby. They stopped at a little park across the block from her apartment and sat down on a bench. Neither of them were in much condition to walk far.

"Am I being very foolish?" Leila asked him.

"What do you mean?"

"I still barely know Ashford, and here I've moved to another state with him. I agreed to marry him."

"What else would you have done?"

"I don't know. It's all happened so fast."

"Don't overthink your blessings, my dear. You love him, he's the father of your child, and you know he has a good heart. That's all you need. No man is perfect, and Ashford will have his faults just like any man would. You have your own faults. But God threw the two of you together, so let it be the blessing it's meant to be."

Leila smiled. Manny had such a simple, beautiful way of looking at life. This was exactly why she needed to talk to him.

"I've never been happier for you than I am right now," he said. "Seeing you with a good man and a new child, it's the culmination of everything. Cherish the blessing. Don't think your life could be perfect, or you'll ruin the fact that it's *good*."

He was right. She couldn't ask for a better man than Ashford. He was young and had much to learn. But he would grow and she with him.

She had been with him long enough now to know his true character. It was not only manifested in the way he treated her, even through the most difficult phases of her pregnancy, but in the way he treated other people too. He was genuinely kind. He always treated women with respect. Maybe at first she had thought him a little dull. There was not much about Ashford that seemed mysterious. But she had been attracted to mysterious before, and it was usually a mask for danger. The dangerous men ultimately either broke her heart or made her afraid. Ashford was a man a lot like Manny, who had walked away from the fight and was a better man for it.

"You've got everything figured out, *Papá*."

Manny grunted in protest. "I've learned some lessons, sure. I'm hoping to spare you from learning them the hard way like I had to." He paused. "I've told you before that love is the only thing worth living for. I really believe that, but it's hard for anyone, including me. Contentment isn't something that's in my nature. Why do you think I joined the revolution as a young man?"

"But you're content now."

"No, I'm old. It's different."

Leila laughed.

"Contentment, like love, is a choice more than a feeling. You'll need to learn to make that choice in your marriage. I've been married to Carmen for a long time now, and it isn't always easy. To be honest, she and I are more different than I imagined when we first met. We've become more different over the years. That happens with some people. But I've chosen to love her no matter what, and our lives are *good.*"

Leila thought back across the years. "If we were to go back to when we were staying in that little inn in Cartagena, and both imagine the life we have now, with the partners we have now, neither of us would have complained or worried whether we had made the right decisions."

"Exactly. That's the way you should always look at it. I try to, but it can be hard. Because of my nature, it's hard for me to accept a life that's *good enough* or a marriage that's *good enough,* but I've been more blessed than a lot of men. I've been more blessed than I deserve. So, I choose to be content with it."

Leila looked out at the trees that lined the park against the bright blue of the afternoon sky. She wanted to believe that her dream of a good life for herself and her child was coming true. This *was* the life she had wanted, even though it had come about faster than she expected, and not in the manner she expected.

After Manny and Carmen left, Leila watched as fatherhood changed Ashford. For Leila, the reality hit as soon as she knew she was pregnant. Ashford took longer to process it; because he didn't carry the baby, it didn't truly become his reality until she was born. Now, Ashford wanted nothing but to serve Leila and take care of Cristina. It brought her joy to see his love. This was no man to be put off by the daily challenges of parenting. Samantha had tried to make her believe Ashford was a different type of man—one who would grow weary of responsibility. Leila didn't see that trait in him at all. Did Samantha really not understand her own son, or had she just been trying to scare her?

Maybe living with her and the baby really did change him, just like it had changed her. How could it do otherwise, for a good man with a heart full of love?

Leila had never been religious like her father. Her childhood taught her to trust herself, not God. She believed that her hard work made everything possible. But now, when Cristina slept in her arms or nursed at her breast, Leila understood more what the idea of God really was. Manny was proved right in telling her that all her hard work was only worth it if done for love. He also told her God *is* love. Those had always seemed like two separate thoughts. Now, she knew their connection.

In the past, God hadn't made sense to her from the literal descriptions in the Bible. But God was here in their Santa Fe apartment, alive in this love that flowed between herself, Ashford, and Cristina. This was what Manny had tried to explain to her, even though he was too conditioned by his Catholic vocabulary to describe it in a way she really grasped.

There was no way for her to tell herself that her hard work had earned *this*. Cristina was a gift. No other word could describe it. Hard work had made the birth more comfortable and given them the luxury to make slow rather than desperate transitions in their lives. But the child herself was a gift. *Life* was something that could not be earned, bought, or borrowed. Life was a free gift of love.

Autumn came to Santa Fe on a gentle north wind out of the Rocky Mountains, scented with pine and juniper. The blanket of aspen trees on the hillside turned bright yellow. Leila would stand by the open window, breathing in the cool breeze, welcoming the new scents. But that wind also carried a reminder of high mountains, glaciers, and icy streams. What would it be like to pass a winter in a place where it snowed? She had never been in snow for more than a day's excursion. This would be another new experience in a year full of so many. They began to keep their windows shut at night.

Leila relished this time to bond with Cristina. She also made a point to focus on Ashford—to serve him while he worked so hard for them, to still look beautiful for him when he came home, despite the exhaustion of motherhood and her self-consciousness about her postpartum body. She made sure to leave room in their interrupted nights to make love. He had given up more than she had for this life—to be a family. She never wanted him to doubt his sacrifice.

She was fortunate. She had become entangled with Ashford before she knew much of anything about him. It was hard to honestly judge someone's character when he was desperately in love with you. But with each month that passed, she grew to believe that Ashford was a truly good man. It could have turned out many different ways. It still could.

These thoughts were why she kept the ambition to work again alive through that wonderful time. Much as she *did* trust Ashford, she still wanted to know she could take care of herself and her daughter if she needed to. She'd still only known the man a year. She stayed patient with the feeling—why rush this special time?

She wasn't restless yet, but she felt it stirring. As the years passed, Cristina would start school and become more self-sufficient. Leila didn't want the world to leave her behind. She had always dreamed of motherhood, but that should be a component in a full life, not the result of her dreams. She wanted to give Ashford and Cristina so much more. Perhaps there would be other children too, but it was too soon to broach that topic. She decided that once they returned to Phoenix next year, she would look into options for returning to the mortgage business, ideally working from home.

But for the present, she relished the wonderful moments and the bonds she was making with her fiancé and daughter. Her heart nearly burst with gratitude for all the love she had received.

27

"WHY THE LONG face, Sam?" Cox leaned against the doorframe to her office.

"Shut up, and get on your phone."

"Nothing I love better than getting sworn at all day long."

"Since when do you bitch about making calls?"

"I know when I'm spinning my wheels," Cox said. "After Lehman went down, no one will even talk to us."

"Try harder."

Cox took one step back toward his desk before turning around. "Are we cooked, Sam?"

"You'll be cooked if you don't lock a loan soon."

Samantha pressed her back against her high office chair, her hands flat on the arms. Cox wasn't stupid. Her bluster was all for show, and he knew it. If he had come around to her side of the desk, he would have noticed that she hadn't even bothered to log into her computer this morning. She'd been going through the motions all week.

It had been a bad year. As soon as the subprime mortgage meltdown started, Samantha knew it would be bad, but each time she thought it couldn't get worse, somehow it did. It didn't surprise her when Countrywide went under, followed by IndyMac. They had been leaders in the subprime market. When Bear Stearns went bankrupt, it freaked people out a little more. They had not originated subprime mortgages, but a review of their books showed how heavily leveraged they were in mortgage-backed securities. Rumor had it that Washington Mutual was next on the feds' list. Who would have thought that a year or two ago? Alamo Trust Bank tried to change to an A-paper lender, but their clientele couldn't qualify for prime mortgages.

She knew Cox was out there calling subprime qualified people with only Fannie Mae or FHA loans to sell to them. No wonder he was getting sworn at all day. It was clear where this would lead, with home values declining and subprime mortgages having been banned by Congress conveniently late in an election year. Maybe subprime lending was a bad idea from the start, but by turning off the faucet so suddenly, Samantha blamed Congress for the foreclosure crisis looming a year or two down the road.

As bad as it had been all year, no one was prepared for this. It had been less than a week since the collapse of Lehman Brothers, one of the most respected investment banks on Wall Street. If even Lehman was neck deep in subprime mortgage securities, nothing was safe. Credit markets had seized up around the globe. The stock market was in free fall. No one knew when light would appear at the end of the tunnel. If it did, most of the financial world would assume it was another train.

Cox was right. It was impossible to sell a loan in this environment. If by some miracle he did, Samantha would have nowhere to place it.

Samantha sat in her chair, reliving the memories of her years in this office—nine years that had passed in a flash. She was sad that it would end with such indignity.

So much success, yet what did she have to show for it: a

couple of rental properties that now sat vacant with underwater mortgages, a stock portfolio that had been sliced in half almost overnight, and a big house in the North Scottsdale hills, but no one to share it with.

She went to lunch by herself and drank two martinis. She reapplied her makeup in the restaurant restroom before returning to the office. She wanted to look her best. She would go out the way she lived every day in this profession.

Was it that stubbornness that had gotten her here, to the brink of ruin? Or were the events of this year so far beyond her control that she need not blame herself?

Samantha *did* blame herself—for so much. She should have had better foresight and diversified her business before it was too late. She should have spent more time on the relationships than the money. It would be relationships she would need to get back on her feet once the dust settled. After this desk was gone, she would be completely alone.

No office, no friends, no sons.

When Stewart left home—almost twelve years ago now—he was rebelling against the limits of his own body as much as he was rebelling against her as a mother. She couldn't help but blame herself a little, and especially blamed herself after he died four years later. But in retrospect, it all seemed a little more inevitable than it had at the time.

But Ashford—she never imagined he would desert her too. How could he throw all she had given him back in her face? Should she have raised him differently? Was this her fault? She missed him and seethed with resentment for the girl who had taken him from her—a girl she might have loved but instead was forced to hate.

She was a grandmother now. The thought was surreal.

The afternoon hours ticked by. More than once, Samantha asked herself if her premonition was wrong. Perhaps she read too much into the signs all around her. She didn't know whether to wish to be wrong or not. What did it matter? Whether their doors stayed open, they had lost the ability to do business. They might as well get it over with.

At about three thirty, the elevator doors opened. Samantha's heartbeat quickened for a moment, and then her heart sank. She had been waiting for it all day, but it didn't help. She was overcome with sadness and a sense of failure. Much as she had expected it, she didn't start to grieve until that moment.

Six people stepped off the elevator, four men and two women, all wearing black suits. The feds had come. She saw the reactions of her people on the floor. Mona's head fell. Tommy sat back and folded his arms. Cox cast his eyes back toward her with a forlorn expression. Her last loyal soldiers were lost.

The seizure didn't take long. With few words exchanged, Samantha handed over the keys. The feds didn't want any help nor to be told where things could be found. They had this process down; they certainly had enough practice. Each employee was given a banker's box and instructed only to take personal belongings. The boxes would be inspected for sensitive customer information.

She knew this was only the beginning. Later would come inquests, hearings, possibly even charges for financial misconduct and fraud. She had her plan for everything she could think of, but what if they found something she wasn't prepared for? She hated to think what might turn up in a decade of careless loan files. Her late nights this week at the shredder could only protect her so much.

Samantha boxed up her things. She had been prepared for everything but the indignity. The humiliation of it nearly reduced her to tears.

By the time she stepped out of her office, Tommy, Vicky, and Mona were already gone, as were the two new loan officers Alamo

Trust had placed there after the merger.

Cox waited for her in front of the elevator, his banker's box tucked under one arm. She carried hers with both hands and met him there. Neither pushed the button right away.

"It's been a good run, boss."

Samantha allowed herself a smile. Together, they looked back at their office for the final time. The feds had already rearranged the desks and started pouring files out of the boxes that had sat neglected for so long.

"It sure has."

Cox put his hand on her back. She couldn't tell if the gesture was one of compassion or if he was coming onto her; classic Cox. She pushed the elevator button.

"Let's go get a drink."

28

LEILA WOULD ALWAYS remember Santa Fe as one of the most wonderful chapters of her life. There was something dreamlike about it, making it feel less than real. But it was only an interlude. Even during that beautiful year, which brought her daughter into the world and saw her love for Ashford grow, she knew the escape couldn't last.

She had been protected in a cocoon of peace, as if the mother, not the daughter, had been in a womb. Soon, the real world would call back to her, just like it had called to Cristina. But unlike the child, Leila knew from experience how cruel the world could be. Only now as it neared its end did she realize how much she had needed this respite. She figured she was strong enough to face whatever the world had for her next.

Leila looked out the airplane window as the Valley of the Sun came into view. She had brought Cristina with her on the short flight. Ashford stayed in Santa Fe to work.

As the plane touched down, she looked at the silver ring with a small diamond on her finger. It wasn't fancy and didn't catch people's eyes, but it was better than the piece of kitchen string.

Ashford said he would buy her a bigger diamond in time, but she didn't want him to. This little ring was symbolic of this time in their lives. It meant a lot to her because it was one of the first things Ashford bought with money *he* had earned. It was special to her just as it was.

She thought April or May would be a good time to have the wedding. It wouldn't be large, but there was still a lot to plan—the venue, the dress. She knew what sort of dress she wanted to wear. Now, the question was where to find it and how hard did she want to work to lose the rest of the baby fat that still clung to her sides.

The air outside baggage claim was cool, and Leila could tell it had rained. She unzipped her bag and pulled out the sweater she had worn to the airport that morning.

Carmen drove up.

"Leila, you look great!" Her stepmother got out of the car and hugged her. "I'd never believe you had a baby a few months ago. Look how big she is already."

Leila slid into the passenger seat next to Carmen, Cristina secure in her car seat behind her.

"How's my dad?" She would see him in half an hour, but she wanted to hear Carmen's perspective first.

"Complains all the time. I can't keep him sitting down. He almost insisted on coming with me today."

Leila laughed, glad to hear Manny still had his spirit only a few days since his surgery.

"I bet he can't wait to put those new knees to use."

She looked out the car windows at the familiar hills of the Phoenix valley. Everything looked lush and tropical today. The rain had turned the hillsides from their usual dry olive color into a deep, rich green. The palm trees were wet and happy.

Manny tried to leap up from his chair as soon as they walked into the house, but Carmen and Leila were too quick for him, pushing him back down. Leila handed the baby to Carmen and bent down to hug his shoulders.

"Three weeks I have to stay home! Can you imagine?"

"You'll have to get used to it when you retire," said Carmen.

"I'm never retiring. I've decided now."

"I've been staying home for almost a year now," Leila said. "It's been great."

"I bet you're itching to get back to work though." Manny knew her well.

"Can you really only stay three days?" Carmen rocked the baby in her arms. "I wish you could stay for Christmas."

"I can't keep Cristina away from her daddy too long."

"I wish he could have come visit too," said Manny. "I like him. You found yourself a good man."

"Yes. Yes, I did."

Once Cristina was fed and asleep, Leila slipped across the yard to see Jen. Considering the economy, she wasn't surprised Jen still lived at home, a year and a half after graduating college. She hadn't found a permanent job and was now thinking about going to grad school.

Leila's visit had a dual purpose. She wanted to be with her father after his surgery, but she also needed to start planning the wedding and Jen was eager to help. Over the next three days, the two of them dove into the task in earnest. They visited a half-dozen potential venues and narrowed it down to two. Dress shopping was a tougher task. Leila knew what she wanted her dress to look like, but the path from vision to reality was fraught with obstacles. She didn't have an "off-the-rack" body, nor did she feel comfortable with the expense of a custom dress.

Something would have to be tailored. Should she tailor it to fit her right now, or account for the ten to fifteen pounds she hoped to lose before the wedding? She would have given up if not for Jen, whose determination kept her going through the frustrating search.

Meanwhile, one of the final two venues she identified was managed by a company connected to Paul Weidman. She felt nervous about contacting him. Last time they spoke, he was losing tens of thousands on the disastrous Desert Villas project. She wasn't sure if he would forgive her for her involvement or if he was even still in the real estate business. Counting on the good rapport they had always shared, she gave him a call. To her relief, he was thrilled to hear from her. He agreed to work out a deal for her on the venue. She told him he and Clary were invited to the wedding.

She was glad he had managed to survive in real estate. He would be a good connection for her if she decided to return to the business. It didn't surprise her when he told her Samantha's office had been seized by the Federal Reserve, but it was still sobering news.

On her final day in Phoenix, she and Jen stopped for lunch at the mall in Scottsdale after another fruitless visit to a bridal shop. No sooner were they seated than she heard a familiar voice behind her.

"Leila! Where you been all this time?"

She jumped from her seat and hugged Cox. She laughed, surprised by how glad she was to see him.

Without waiting for an invitation, he pulled a chair up to their table.

"You seem no worse for wear, after all that's happened," she said.

"I guess you heard."

"Yeah."

"It was crazy, man. The day the feds showed up was just the start. The inquisition that followed was awful. There were a few days there I thought I was heading to jail."

"Justice. I always tried to tell you it would bite your ass one day."

"Yeah, our loan files were a steaming pile of shit. Fraud all over the place. But Samantha's good. Everything they found she managed to pass the blame elsewhere. Ultimately, I think the feds didn't have time for small-time players like us. They'd rather go after big fish like Killinger and Mozillo."

"They're just as good at covering their tracks as Samantha."

"Yep. That's the irony of it. The mortgage business brought down the whole fucking economy, but everyone seems to be wriggling out of any real consequences."

"Somehow, I don't sense any remorse in your tone. If anyone deserves to go to jail, it's you. You were the worst of the bunch."

He shrugged, grinning. He was the same old Cox. As they talked, Jen pretended to look at the menu, but Leila could tell she was listening.

"But seriously, where were you?" he asked. "Samantha looked everywhere for you."

"I moved to Santa Fe. Why would Samantha want me?"

"For the hearings. I'm surprised she didn't have you subpoenaed."

A chill passed up Leila's spine. "Maybe she did." She didn't want to dwell on the thought. "What happened to Samantha?"

"Oh, she came out of it on both feet. Declared bankruptcy, let her rental properties go but kept her house. She'll have another job as soon as she wants one."

"And you?"

Cox cackled. "I locked four loans last week."

"No way!"

"Haven't you heard about the HARP refinance bill they passed?"

"No."

"So, you're literally living under a rock up in the mountains?"

"Pretty much."

"It's this new program where people can refinance even if

they don't qualify, even if their house is underwater, as long as their loan is with Fannie or Freddie."

"Whose bright idea was that?"

"Who do you think? Congress."

"Will those guys ever get a clue?"

"The hell if I care. Rates are down, and my phone's ringing all day. No income, no assets, no problem!"

Leila glanced at Jen, who had put down the menu, no longer pretending she wasn't enjoying the conversation.

"There's money to be made if you want back in."

"I have been thinking about it. I'd like to find a way to start slowly, maybe working from home. I had a baby, you know."

"Got knocked up! You know that could have been my baby. I gave you every opportunity."

She hit at him across the table as he leaned away from her swing.

"But you had to go for the scandal with the boss's son. Samantha was *so* pissed at you."

"We're getting married at the end of April. After that, I'd like to work again."

"Dammit, don't get married. I haven't had my shot with you yet."

Jen snickered.

Cox stood up and handed Leila a business card.

"Give me a call when you're ready. I can get you a job working from home. You're good. It's a new refi boom. You'll do great."

She looked at the card. She had never heard of the brokerage it listed.

"One other thing you should know—starting next year, you'll need to be licensed to originate mortgage loans. You have to go through this asinine twenty-hour course and then take a stupid test, do background checks, get fingerprinted, and all sorts of shit. They might even ask for that firstborn of yours. You can do the clock hours online. You should start banging that out."

"Thanks. I'll look into it." She extended her hand. "It was good to see you, Cox. We'll be in touch."

The waiter was at their table as soon as Cox left. Leila glanced at the menu and ordered the first thing she saw. Cox had given her much to think about, but those were thoughts for another time.

She was tired of shopping. After lunch, she wanted to go back to her dad's. After only a few hours apart, she already missed her baby, but Jen insisted they go to one more store.

"You're leaving in the morning. This is your last shot to find a dress before you have to order one online. Then you'd really be taking your chances."

The store Jen had in mind was right here in the mall. She could stand one more hour. Arriving at the boutique dress shop, Leila attempted to describe what she was looking for to the proprietor. Jen chimed in, clarifying as best as she could. The woman at the counter listened as she looked over Leila's figure.

"I think I have the dress for you. It's not precisely what you described, but when you put it on, you'll see what I mean."

She walked to the back and emerged a moment later holding the wedding gown. Leila and Jen looked at each other hopefully. Neither was willing to get too excited until Leila tried it on. Even before tailoring, how it wore would tell the story. Leila hurried to the dressing room and slipped it on, stepping out for the shop owner to zip up the back. She turned and faced Jen, trying to hide her smile.

"That's the dress," Jen said.

"This *is* the dress."

"You look like a vision," said the shopkeeper. She reached for measuring tape and pins, sizing Leila up and making her marks.

Leila moved back and forth, listening to the beautiful *swish, swish* of the dress brushing against itself.

"Hold still."

Leila was so excited. Maybe it wasn't perfect, but it was pretty close. She avoided asking about the price. Manny wanted to pay for the whole wedding. She would save him money on the venue, even if she gave it all back on the dress.

"Err on the snug side. I'm going to lose ten pounds before the wedding."

"Of course you will, sweetie."

On a plane again in the morning, she looked forward to her last few months in Santa Fe. She would savor each day, but she also looked forward to coming back. She would start the mortgage licensing program as Cox suggested. No harm in taking the course; it didn't commit her to anything. She did want to work again, and it was easy to think of getting back into the old career.

Was that really what she wanted?

29

"I DON'T KNOW how to explain it," said Ashford. "I just don't like it." He wished he had kept his mouth shut.

"And you only tell me now, the night before my test? Don't do this. I need to stay focused."

"But why do you have to get back into mortgages so soon?" Ashford fidgeted. He hadn't understood his own feelings in these months since Leila's return from Phoenix. Now that he had finally voiced his thoughts, he knew he'd said it all wrong.

"Do you feel threatened?" Leila folded her arms, looking at him. He could tell she was trying not to get angry.

"No, I would love for you to get back to work and feel satisfied. It's just mortgages. The business makes me uneasy. My mother."

"I thought we'd decided not to worry about her. Mortgages are my career. This is the way I can support us."

"Haven't I supported us just fine?"

"So, you *are* threatened."

"No." Ashford was frustrated, more at his own inability to communicate than at her.

"What do you expect me to do if I'm not going to work again?"

"I didn't say you shouldn't work."

"It sure sounds like that's what you're saying."

"Don't make it about that. I'm not trying to tell you how to live. I'm not that kind of guy."

"Well, I'm not a stay-at-home wife and mother. That's not the girl you fell in love with."

"Forget it. I wish I didn't bring it up."

Ashford turned to leave the room. Leila reached out and grabbed his hand, turning him back toward her. She looked him in the eyes.

"Tell me what this is really about. I can't just forget it. *You* brought it up. Now I need to know what's going on. We're going to be married in a month. We have to be able to communicate."

Ashford took a deep breath, trying to think. When Leila started doing the coursework for the mortgage exam, he had felt a strange discomfort in the pit of his stomach. As the test drew nearer, the feeling had grown stronger. It wasn't exactly fear; he didn't know how to put it into words.

"Just be careful. I don't like the thought of you going back into that world—my mother's world."

"She has no power left to wield."

"You don't know that."

Now, he heard her take a deep breath.

"You can trust me. You *have* to trust me."

Ashford nodded. He could think of nothing to say that wouldn't make him sound like a man looking to crush his woman's career, or at least a man feeling threatened by her success. Proud as he felt to have been able to support her this year—as much as it empowered him—this wasn't about him. How could he make her realize that?

Instead, he screwed it all up. They'd had their first argument.

He kissed her. "Good luck tomorrow. I do trust you."

"Everything will be okay. It will change. It has to. I understand if you feel resistant to that. I do too, a little. But this fantasy we've been living can't last. Our lives have to develop and grow. I need to know our relationship can too."

She still didn't understand. He hadn't been able to communicate his unease at all, but trying again now would only make things worse.

He slept poorly that night and felt distracted at work in the morning. As planned, he left at lunchtime, having requested the afternoon off to watch Cristina while Leila took her exam.

They kissed when he got home as if nothing had happened, but Ashford felt a coolness in her lips. She was focused on her task, and his words yesterday probably made her feel like she was going into it alone. It saddened him. Until now, they always went through things together, good or bad.

She paused in the doorway before leaving. "Does this T-shirt make my arms look fat?"

He looked toward her with surprise. She was wearing a gray T-shirt with short sleeves over jeans and held her light leather jacket, about to put it on. Ashford laughed. "You look beautiful. You always do, and I'm not just saying that."

She smiled. "Are we in love again?"

He rushed to the door and kissed her.

He closed the door behind her, then looked around the room, feeling better. A few open boxes sat on the living room floor, but they had barely begun packing. They didn't have much stuff, and what they did have they used most every day. The bulk of the packing would happen next week, leading up to Ashford's final day at the clinic. He already had a job waiting for him near Phoenix, ironically at the same hospital in Glendale that had turned him down a year and a half ago.

It was time. They were both ready.

Ashford had sensed the change in Leila in the three months

since her trip to Phoenix. Preparing for today's test, as well as planning for the wedding, gave her a sense of purpose. He hadn't been aware of her previous loss of energy until it came surging back. He wished he had commented on *that* yesterday. It was good for her to have goals and would be good for her to work again. He agreed. But did it have to be this? So soon?

He looked down at the baby in his arms, surprised to see her looking back up at him with intrigued eyes. He smiled. Until he had one of his own, Ashford always thought one baby was more or less like the next. But this little girl was so full of personality and surprises. Her look toward him was filled with wonder and trust. *She* would not believe he'd been afraid to be a father. She thought he was the perfect father. It felt good to be depended on so completely by someone and to know that he could handle it. He would do anything for Leila, and he would do anything for this little girl.

Leila had called their year in Santa Fe a dreamy break from the real world. For him, it meant something quite different. It wasn't a respite from real life. It was his first real taste of it. He now knew what kind of man he was capable of being. He knew he could support not only himself but a family. He had grown to love his new identity as a dad—first so frightening, now unimaginably fun, even if it was a lot of work. In a month, he would have another identity still. He would be a husband.

He put Cristina into her crib and sat at the kitchen table, trying to study for the job he would start in a few weeks' time. The afternoon passed. About five o'clock, Cristina cried to be fed. Ashford took her on his lap and fed her from a bottle. At eight months, Leila was slowly weaning Cristina off of breastfeeding, having cut back to once or twice a day. With her little head against his arm, holding the bottle with the other hand, Ashford felt intimately connected to his daughter. She took the food offered from his hand with perfect trust.

He knew that, as a man, there was no possible way for him to understand the intimacy of a mother's connection to her child, first from the womb, then at the breast. A father's bond was slower but no less profound. It lacked the physicality, which Leila told him she felt from the moment of conception. But this little girl was as much a part of his flesh and blood as she was of her mother's.

After Cristina was satisfied, Ashford began to prepare his and Leila's dinner. When would her exam be over? He couldn't remember if she had said. It was a timed test, so it couldn't be *that* long. The testing center was only a couple of miles away, in downtown Santa Fe. It did seem like she had been gone a long time. He started to call her, then remembered that she told him they made the testers put their cell phones in lockers to keep them from cheating.

He returned his attention to dinner. He enjoyed cooking for Leila on his days off. Just as little Cristina showed her trust in him while he held her bottle, he wanted to show Leila she could trust him by caring for her. She prepared dinner most of the time, since she was home while he worked. But tonight was an opportunity to flip the script. He hoped to surprise her with a nice meal, to celebrate her success and show her his support, despite his bungled comments yesterday. She had said they gave the results of the test right away.

His mind raced back to that first night he cooked for Leila, almost a year and a half ago. How excited and nervous he had been that whole day, arranging the house for her visit while being careful not to do anything that would tip off his mother when she returned from her conference. That night was like a dream—the way Leila glowed when she walked up with a smile on her full lips, her long legs lit by the waning sun. When he first kissed her that night, it was different than before. That kiss prefaced what would happen. The ecstasy of making love to her that first time was something he would never forget. Through everything that followed—the next morning and in the weeks and months afterward—while Ashford may have wished that things had happened differently, he never once wished he had not met Leila or wished they had not dared to love each other. He glanced at the baby and was even more convinced of his feelings.

Ashford wasn't sure when he started glancing at the clock. By seven, his eyes were glued to it. Surely, the testing center wouldn't even be open anymore. Where was she? Had she run an errand after her test?

He called. No answer. Straight to voicemail. He forced himself to be patient. Either the test was much longer than he realized, or she forgot to turn her phone on afterward.

Another possibility came to him. What if she failed the test? Perhaps she decided she needed time by herself before she talked to him. She might blame him for failing, after what he said yesterday. She might not have wanted to come home right away. Whatever the case, there was no reason for him to worry.

But he *was* worried. This didn't feel right.

He Googled the local testing center. There was only one in town. He called, but they were closed. What should he do next? He could think of nothing but the police and that seemed extreme. Especially if she was avoiding him on purpose, he would infuriate her by taking drastic measures.

Ashford took a deep breath and looked toward the crib. Cristina slept peacefully. She wasn't worried; why should he be? Leila could take care of herself. She had done so for years. There was surely some obvious explanation for her tardiness. Any action on his part would seem foolish once everything became clear. He called again. Straight to voicemail.

What could have happened? It was hard for him to picture her being in danger. It seemed impossible that she could have been abducted or something horrible like that. Leila would be a match for any potential kidnapper. In bustling downtown Santa Fe, she wouldn't go quietly against her will. Had there been an accident? Surely the police would have come or at least called him.

He tried not to entertain the thought, but it drifted in anyway, playing on his insecurities: What if yesterday's argument had unmasked a deeper discontent? Could it be that she was not as happy with him as she seemed? He tried to force the thought out of his mind.

From the beginning, Leila was slower to come into love than he was. Ashford was always aware of that. It was hard to say now what course their relationship would have taken had she not become pregnant. But what about now? Did she love him as much as he loved her, or was she with him for the sake of the baby? With a new job, and Cristina a little older, would she still need him? Every indication, every spark he saw in her eyes and felt in her body, told him that her love was growing stronger each month. They were developing new, special intimacies that could only come with the time they had spent together. But what if that was all an illusion born of his own infatuation with her?

Maybe tonight she didn't want him to reach her.

There was nothing to do but go to bed and try to get some rest. He lay in bed but couldn't sleep. Neither could the baby, restless without her mother in the room.

Ashford didn't get to sleep until it was almost dawn, then overslept, waking up at almost nine a.m. When he saw her vacant side of the bed, the gravity of the situation hit him, and he wished he'd done more the night before. Leila wouldn't stay away by choice. Even if she was angry at him, even if she no longer wanted to be with him, she wouldn't leave her baby daughter. How could he have thought her capable of that? He tried calling her one more time, then called the clinic and said he wouldn't be coming in. Next, he called a taxi to take him to the testing center.

He brought Cristina, strapped to his front. Leila's car was still parked in the lot. He didn't know if that was a good or bad sign.

The testing center had just opened. The girl working the front desk said she hadn't been working the night before. Ashford asked if she could call whoever had been working the previous night, which earned him a scowl. Could she look to see if Leila had checked in for the test, if her cell phone was still in the locker? Who was he? Her boyfriend? Oh, her fiancé. Another skeptical scowl and a repeated line about confidentiality.

Deflated, Ashford walked out to the parking lot. Unsure what to do next, he called Manny. He hadn't heard from Leila either. Manny had no hesitation in declaring that something was wrong and chided Ashford for failing to report Leila missing last night.

Next, he called the police. He waited by the car for half an hour until two officers arrived. They didn't seem very concerned as Ashford told the story, but they agreed to investigate.

They went inside and the girl at the desk, suddenly cooperative at the sight of the police officers, checked her computer and confirmed that Leila had checked in for the test the previous afternoon, but there was no record of her having completed it. Her purse, with cell phone and car keys, was still in the locker.

Up until then, Ashford had tried to believe there was an easy explanation. Now, his heart tightened with dread. Leila was in real danger, and he had stood by for a whole night doing nothing. So much for all his promises to take care of her.

The police called the employee who had worked the testing desk when Leila checked in the previous afternoon. He told them he remembered seeing her check in but didn't remember seeing her leave. She could have left during his break, or after his shift ended, he added noncommittally.

Ashford urged the officers to pursue it. Something had obviously gone wrong during her visit to the testing center. They reminded him that this was *their* job and he ought to let them do it. It didn't help when Cristina started to wail. They sent Ashford home.

Back at the apartment, he felt sick to his stomach. Cristina didn't know what was going on, but she knew her mother wasn't there. She gazed at her daddy with confused but trusting eyes. He bit his lips to keep his tears at bay. He had to stay strong for her. He had to keep his mind sharp too.

Leila was gone—unfathomably, inexplicably. He felt crushed by his helplessness and the fear that he would never see his beloved again.

PART IV

EL MAR

30

MANNY HURRIED AHEAD on the Cartagena street in the darkness of night. The lights in the houses were all off, but there was just enough light to see his way. Gunfire sounded in the distance. He wasn't sure if it was growing farther away or if it had always been that far. Even at such a distance, after all the fights he'd been in, gunfire still made him afraid.

After walking for uncounted blocks, Manny paused. Yes, this was the place. He recognized the houses, the flickering lampposts, and the rough stones of the street, but it didn't look right. Something was not as it should be. He wanted to keep going, away from here, but his feet were rooted in their spot.

"This way, *hermano*. Hurry!"

He looked toward the voice. A woman he had seen before was urgently beckoning him through a doorway across the street. His feet compelled him that way.

Through the door and down a steep staircase he followed, behind a single lighted candle carried by his guide. The basement passage turned to the left and led into a wider chamber. The distant gunfire was more muffled from down here, but it still persisted.

A dim lightbulb hung from the ceiling. Manny paused to allow his eyes to acclimate. On one wall was a window. The glass was dingy, and once he got a better look he saw that it was only a window into another room. A figure loomed on the other side. He hurried over and saw that it was Leila.

He slapped his hands against the thick glass and called her name. She should not have been here. She was in danger. She saw him and ran to the other side of the glass, her eyes wild with fear. She wasn't looking at him, but past him.

Manny turned around.

Inches away from him stood Paulo, his frame towering, his eyes gleaming, his face caked with dry blood from the cut below his eye. The room swirled around Manny. A sharp ringing sounded persistently in his ears. He wanted to cry out but could not. He could see that Leila was shouting, but no sound came from beyond the thick glass.

Manny awoke, jolting upward in bed, drenched in sweat.

It had been several years since he'd had this dream. Always before, the woman behind the glass was Marissa. Sometimes he saw her face, sometimes not, but he always knew it was her. The dream took different forms but often started with the woman who had guided him to safety that day in Bogotá. Paulo was usually there too, sometimes seen, sometimes merely sensed in the shadows. This was the first time the woman in the dream had been Leila.

He looked down at the sideboard and the buzzing cell phone, which had awakened him. The ringing stopped briefly, then started again. It was Ashford, calling repeatedly. Taking a moment to steady his nerves—to bring himself out of the nightmare of sleep into the nightmare that real life had become— he answered the phone.

"Manny, I'm sorry to call so early. I finally found out what happened. Leila was picked up by ICE—immigration enforcement."

"What? Why?"

"They wouldn't tell me why or where she is, since I'm not technically related. It's obscene when I'm here with our own child! It can't be right."

Manny's head swirled with horrible possibilities.

"Why would immigration want to arrest her?"

"I don't know." Manny caught his automatic answer—the trained lie—and a knot tied up in his stomach. Because he *did* know. He had gotten so used to hiding the truth for Leila's own protection. But wasn't it time to tell Ashford? The lie hadn't protected Leila at all.

"Let me give you the number. You're her father, so they should tell you more."

Manny wrote the number down on a notepad Carmen kept by their bedside. "I'll try, but I'm not sure they'll tell me anything either."

"Why not?"

He took a deep breath. "Ashford, come back to Phoenix . . . as soon as you can. The immigration detention centers are here, south of the city. That's where they'd take her." He paused. "There are things you need to know . . . about me, about Leila, about your daughter. Leila may be in more danger than you think, and if so, we don't have a lot of time."

"The car's packed. I'm leaving now."

Manny got up. He ran his hands along his face, then walked into the kitchen to make coffee. His new knees clashed painfully against the old muscles that held them in place. He glanced at the clock. Yes, it was early, too early to call the number Ashford had given him. What was there to do but go into the motions of another day? He would go to work again, come home and try to sleep, then do it again, even though it all seemed like such a waste.

Could Leila really have been picked up by ICE? Surely, she hadn't committed a crime to endanger her legal status. Could they have found out who she really was, or more accurately, who she *was not*? This had always been a possibility. He and Leila had known it from the start, even though they never spoke of it.

Everything he did was for his daughter. His whole life had become an expression of his love for her. For twenty years, even before he met her, his own life had been lived toward the purpose of making a good life for her. Now, she had vanished. Everything seemed lost.

His mind returned to his dream. All these years, his inability to save Marissa had haunted him. What sinister force had brought Leila's face into that recurrent nightmare? The thought of losing her too was more than his tired heart could bear.

All the failings of his life pressed down on him. Leila had been his one success—the one good thing he had done to earn the right to be proud of his life. If he could no longer give her anything, or worse, if his very gift of a new life had turned itself against her, then what use had he to go on? Was his life's work, all his love, all *her* work, about to disappear?

He was growing old. He craved the peace of a life well lived and the love of the family he had worked for. Ah, but peace was not the reward for men such as him.

31

EXHAUSTION STUNG ASHFORD'S senses. His eyes resisted the urge to close. His back muscles ached. His right foot was stiff from driving for too long. He sat in the hot car, at a loss for what to do next.

He looked out at the grim detention center: a low, tan building, rising from the desert, the same color as the barren hills behind it. Even the twisting barbed wire fence faded into the colorless landscape. It was a prison, and the girl he was supposed to marry had been caged here.

That she had been here, so recently, was poor consolation now. He tried to summon a sense of her into his heart, but it was no use. There was nothing about this place that echoed her presence.

The car, *her* car, was packed with as many of their belongings as it would fit: two empty coffee cups, a water bottle, and a crumpled fast food bag littered the passenger-side floor. Driving straight in from Santa Fe, he had dropped off a confused Cristina and an angry Romeo with Carmen in Phoenix before continuing south to find this place.

He was too late. By how long, he couldn't know. Now, the search started over. Another day would end with Leila still missing.

Exhaustion tempted him. He wanted to rest. He wanted to hope that everything would work itself out. He leaned his head back against the headrest, his eyes open, fixed on the detention center across the empty parking lot and wire fence. With the ignition off, the car was starting to heat up.

It used to be that way for him. Things *did* work themselves out. His mother always made sure of it. Even the risks of his adolescence, in hindsight, weren't risks at all because of the huge landing pad of a safety net she always had for him. But everything was different now. He was on his own, and now he was *alone*. He had wanted that, in order to take care of Leila.

Some care. He'd utterly failed her.

He couldn't allow himself to rest, not even for a minute. Manny's words on the phone this morning haunted him: *We don't have a lot of time.* He started the car and drove onto the highway back toward Phoenix.

All the memories of his time with Leila rushed back at him, but they had lost their joy. How could he forget that their last day together saw their first argument? Would she know he was looking for her, desperately trying anything to find her? Would she trust that he *could* find and save her? He wasn't sure he believed it himself.

Ashford had never been a hero. Even the single heroic moment in his life had been turned against him by his mother's pride. Now, when he needed to be a hero, he wasn't sure if he had it in him.

Almost as soon as the doubt crept into his mind, he remembered Cristina's little face and the way she had looked at him this afternoon when he left her in Carmen's arms. He already missed his daughter after only a few hours apart. He had to do this for her too, not only for Leila, not only for himself. *She* didn't doubt that he had it in him. There was nothing like being a daddy to make a hero of a man.

As he drove, Ashford's tired mind struggled for focus. The people at the detention center had told him that Leila's case had been processed and then she had been moved. They didn't even know where. He needed to find out *why* she'd been arrested. That would give him clues about the next step in her case.

Manny would have some answers. But for others, Ashford had to talk to his mother.

The familiar outline of Camelback Mountain came into view as he drove into Scottsdale. His emotions roiled as he turned off the highway toward his old home in the North Scottsdale hills. He missed his mother, despite all that had been lost between them. But he suspected that she was somehow behind Leila's disappearance. If that was true—the cruelty of wrenching a mother away from her infant daughter—he would never forgive her.

He drove up the long ascending driveway and parked in front of the house. The sun was low against the western mountains. Being here felt so familiar in every way, but his heart wasn't fooled. This wasn't home anymore.

Samantha ran out the front door as soon as Ashford got out of his car. He was aware of how he must have looked—unshaven, hair unkempt, clothes wrinkled. This was no time for vanity.

"The prodigal son has returned!" She embraced him.

Ashford held his tongue but wanted to call out her hypocrisy. She was no prodigal's parent meeting the wayward son on the road. *She* had sent him away.

"Mom, I need some answers."

She took a step back from him and pushed her blond hair behind her ear. "Is that the only greeting I get after all this time? After all these months dying for a word from you?"

"Do you know what's happened to Leila? Do you know why?"

"What do I care?" Her tone gave her away. She may have been able to fool her clients, but she couldn't fool him. *She knew.*

"Tell me what happened. Why did immigration pick her up?"

Samantha sighed. She turned and took a step toward the house but turned back when she saw he wasn't going to follow her inside. "Oh, honey, if you could know what I've been through this last year." She wouldn't look into his eyes. "Without you, I've endured it all alone. They closed down my company. I went bankrupt. Did you know that? All those years I worked to build it, and now it's gone. I lost everything I worked for just like I lost you. It's been horrible."

Ashford did feel for her. He could see how she'd changed. The year really had worn her down. Much as he would have wanted to be there for her through it all, their severance was her choice, not his.

"What happened to Leila?"

Samantha looked down at the ground, cowed by his persistence. "There was a hearing. We all had to testify, but she couldn't be found. Where did you take her?"

"So you had her subpoenaed?"

Samantha turned away again. When she turned back, her eyes had changed. She finally looked at him directly. "What do you want from me? Are you looking for someone to blame for throwing your own life away? Yes, I had her subpoenaed. The investigators found forged papers in her loan files. When she failed to appear, the court drew the obvious conclusions. It never became a criminal trial, which I assume is why they didn't try harder to find her. But naturally it would catch up to her in time."

"I see."

However his mother wanted to frame it, Ashford understood that she had made Leila take the fall for her own indiscretions in the mortgage business. It was almost too easy. Samantha got to keep her house and resume her career with a different bank, while Leila, the one who always tried to do business right, sat in an immigration prison. Anger boiled up in his chest.

"How does it feel to have taken a mother away from her infant daughter?" Ashford regretted the words as soon as they came out of his mouth. His mother had lost a child too.

"Me? You're blaming me? How do you think I feel? That bitch took my last son away. You were all I had. I hope they deport her ass. She never belonged here."

"Why do you hate her so much?"

"Come back to me." She extended her arms toward him. "Look at you. You need me. I'll help you get back on your feet. I'll help you take care of your child."

"I can take care of myself and my daughter."

"Where's the baby? I want to see her."

"I'm not bringing her here. You'll need to earn the right to see your granddaughter." He opened the car door.

"That's not fair. After all I've done for you."

"Goodbye, Mom."

32

"SO, NOW YOU know the truth. Leila is not my natural daughter. Neither she nor I have told this to anyone, until today."

Ashford sat stunned in Manny and Carmen's living room, trying to process the amazing story he'd just heard.

"I know she wanted to tell you, but she was afraid because of your mother."

Ashford nodded. It made sense, but it stung that she wouldn't trust him with her deepest secret.

"I'm sorry I kept it from you as well." Manny turned to Carmen, who sat with disbelief written across her face. "For her protection, we had to turn the lie into the truth we lived every day. She couldn't afford the smallest slip into an old habit—a remembered name. You see how quickly things can unravel for even the most well-established immigrant in this country. They might come for me next."

So many thoughts raced through Ashford's head.

"But how did anyone find out now?" Manny broke the silence. "That's the part I don't understand."

"I don't think it was her identity that got her into trouble."

Ashford had recovered from the initial shock of Manny's story and was beginning to think through possibilities again. "I saw my mother this afternoon. She was definitely behind Leila's arrest, but I don't think she knows what you just told me. If she knew, she wouldn't have been able to help telling me."

"Then what was the reason?"

"I believe my mother had Leila framed for mortgage fraud."

Manny put his hands to his face. "People will be eager to prosecute a case like that. It may give us a little more time, but it would be hard to save her."

"But Leila did nothing wrong. I'm sure of it. We were away. She never got the subpoena. My mom framed her. Once they realize that, they'll have another hearing or a trial and she can clear her name."

Silence hovered in the room. Manny and Carmen looked at him as if he had said something wrong. He was confused.

"My boy, you have *no idea* how it works for people like us in this country. I love you, and I don't blame you for your ignorance. But please, open your eyes. A hearing, a fair trial . . . those are the privileges of US citizens. A handsome white boy like you can live your life, take a few risks, knowing if you slip up you can always make it right in court, maybe hire a good lawyer. It doesn't work that way for us."

Manny continued, "All these years, as 'American' as I seem to be, I've stayed vigilant every day. One slip and it could be the end of this life. It doesn't even matter that I'm 'legal,' with all the right paperwork. That status can be revoked so easily. One too many beers one night or one time losing my temper in an argument, that's all it would take. ICE is *looking* for chances to deport Latinos. With something like mortgage fraud, the processing of the case is expedited. Any hearing would be quick and one-sided."

Ashford heard Manny's words and began to feel the weight of the horrible possibilities, along with the guilt of his own privilege.

"Now, think about what would have happened in this hearing. Who are they going to blame? On one side, you have your mother: white, beautiful, articulate, with a team of lawyers ready to lay out her case. On the other side, you have a Hispanic immigrant who left the state and didn't show up for the hearing. You think she'll have a chance to clear her name now?"

Manny paused. "But as dire a picture of her chances as I just painted, if they found out that she isn't really my daughter, things would move even faster. She'd have no name and no rights. She might have already been deported to Colombia. She would be in some *real* danger there."

"That can't be possible. It's not right! She has a child here. They can't really do that, can they?"

"They can do whatever they want. Noncitizen mothers are taken away from their children every day."

Ashford stood up and looked out the dark window. His legs were weak from fear and exhaustion. Tears hovered in his tired eyes. The nightmare grew more terrible by the day.

Through the window, Ashford could only see the shadows in the small yard. Leila's spirit was still there, in memories of happy afternoons and evenings filled with laughter and music.

Through all the worries of their first year together, something like this had never even entered his mind. Could it have been in Leila's thoughts as a vague terror? He had worried about their finances, about his severed relationship with his mother, about his fitness to raise a child. But their togetherness had never been in doubt. As long as they were together, they had told each other so often, the world could do its worst. He had never imagined the possibility that Leila would be taken away from him.

"What was her name . . . before?"

"Cristina."

He smiled. Of course. While *Leila* had become her identity, she wanted to let her hidden identity live on in another.

How heartbroken she must be on this night, perhaps in a prison cell, perhaps abandoned in a country where she knew no one, with no resources and no future. How could a mother— with a heart brimming over with love—live without her infant daughter? That child was part of Leila's soul from the moment of her conception. Ashford understood now. Even this afternoon, separated from Cristina for half a day while he drove to the detention center, he missed his little girl. Losing her would crush everything in him. How could Leila live with that bond severed?

His own mother had started this, out of jealousy and injured pride; one mother taking what was most precious from another.

Ashford was angry at his mother, at the immigration authorities, at his country. How could they do such a thing? Even a violent criminal should have the right to a fair trial, to see her family. Yet a mother had been wrenched away from her infant child because she was born in the wrong place. The injustice of it stunned him into rage.

He had to find her. Their own love was secondary. He had to reunite mother and daughter if it cost him everything . . . if it was the last thing he did.

Ashford turned back toward Manny and Carmen. "What can we do?"

"Tonight, we can pray. There's nothing else to be done right now. Try to get some rest. You look exhausted. Save your strength. Tomorrow, we'll call every immigration court in the state if we have to. I know a couple of immigration attorneys too. We'll call them. If Leila's still in the country, we'll find her."

"And if not?"

Manny didn't answer. Ashford saw his gaze grow distant for a moment, perhaps with a memory he didn't want to voice.

"Pray, my boy. And rest. It's all you can do right now."

Late that night, Ashford lay awake in Manny and Carmen's spare bedroom—Leila's old room. Cristina slept soundly on her back between his arm and his torso. He had the sheet and the Aztec-patterned quilt folded down under her chin and across his chest. The baby was comforted by her father's presence, but she also comforted him. A short time ago, he was terrified of the fatherhood thrust so unexpectedly upon him. Now, it was all he had, his only identity.

Ashford felt the baby's breath rise and fall beside him, with a rhythm that mimicked his own. In sleep, her breath was marked by other noises—a gurgle, now a little coo in a tone that anticipated how her childhood voice might sound. Each new moment of expressive cognizance he saw or heard in her gave him a tingling anticipation of the future. With each moment so filled with promise, he didn't want to miss a single one. But he wanted to share these moments with Leila. He wanted her to hear each new sound and see each new expression on their daughter's young face. She had already missed too much time with their baby.

He leaned his face forward to smell the top of the baby's head. Her scent was fresh, new, and unblemished. It relaxed him and would soon ease him into sleep.

Ashford loved this little girl with every fiber of his body. It was a different kind of love than what he had for Leila, in ways he never could have understood if it had been explained to him before. He clung to Cristina as the only thing in his world that made sense and as his only connection to the woman he loved. The baby clung to him for the same reasons, missing her mother, comprehending with her primitive senses that something was amiss in their world.

"I'll find Mama," he whispered. "I promise you, I'll bring Mama home."

33

LEILA FINISHED HER simple breakfast, savoring the last of the strong Colombian coffee.

"*Muchas gracias, Padre*. You've helped so much."

"I wish there was more we could do. But the church is poor in Colombia."

"*Lo sé.*"

She glanced around and listened in amazement. There was a shocking familiarity to the morning sounds of the city outside the stone walls of the rectory. She was really here in Cartagena. Even after this long and horrible ordeal, culminating in yesterday's terrifying plane trip, she still half-expected to wake up at home next to Ashford.

The room was sparse but inviting. Either the priest or perhaps a nun kept the whitewashed walls and blue tile counters of the kitchen clean. The wood table, where they ate off tin plates, looked like it could have been made of the same boards as the floor. An ancient tin kettle, now quiet on the stove, still filled the room with the smell of coffee. On the wall hung two icons, one of St. Louis Bertrand, the other of the Blessed Mother cradling her child. Looking at them almost made Leila cry.

She tried to count the days since she had seen her daughter—a couple of weeks, maybe more. It already seemed like an eternity. The separation might drive her insane. Sorrow tore at her heart, but she knew she had to stay sharp.

She had slept last night on a cot in the chapel, together with two other women who had been on her flight. Relatives had picked up one of them early that morning. The other sat with Leila now in the rectory kitchen. This wasn't the first time Leila had slept in a church. As a young girl, she sometimes snuck into one or another of the many small churches of Cartagena to pass a night, usually during rainy season. The churches weren't comfortable, but they were safe. Last night in this church stirred many unexpected memories.

"Do you know anyone in the country?" the priest asked her. "Any family or friends from your childhood?"

"No. There's no one."

"Do you want to try calling again? Surely, someone in the US could send you a little money."

"No, there's no use calling again."

She would have loved nothing more than to call Ashford or Manny and Carmen. The irony was that she didn't remember any of their phone numbers due to the convenience of cell phones. She was embarrassed to admit it to the priest. The one number she would have remembered, Manny and Carmen's home phone, had recently been disconnected as they both transitioned to cell phones.

Last night, she did the only thing she could think of and tried calling her own phone in hopes that Ashford had picked it up at the testing center. But the call went straight to voicemail. For all she knew, it was still in that locker.

"I could email them. Do you have a computer here?"

The priest smiled. "You've been in the United States too long. We are a simple parish. I do know that there's an internet café about a mile east on the transversal."

"Thank you. I'll try that this morning." She was desperate to get in touch with Ashford and Manny. She needed to hear their voices, but email would be a start. She still found it hard to believe that she had not been allowed a realistic chance to contact them while at the immigration detention center. When you no longer had a name, neither did you have any rights, apparently.

She saw the priest look away with a strange expression.

"What is it?"

"You don't seem like someone who is here with anything to hide, but you are beautiful, and that is reason enough to be careful. You should know that the internet café in this neighborhood is often watched."

"What do you mean?"

"It's a common first destination for deportees. Some people are interested in knowing who comes back. A beautiful woman with no family—no one to miss her if she disappeared—would be particularly interesting. Be aware of your surroundings."

The only thing Leila could be aware of was that she was here and her daughter wasn't. Now that she was free, she *had* to find a way back to Cristina. Her heart yearned for her. Her hands ached to hold her. Her breasts still swelled with milk for the baby who was gone. She could have only so many regrets for herself. She had done the best she knew how with the hand she was dealt. But for Cristina, she deserved more from a mother than this.

Despite the hopelessness of it all, Leila felt better after her first night out of a prison cell. The rest, the shower, the food, and the coffee had helped so much.

But the biggest help of all was the humanity shown to her and the other women by this priest who had sought them out and brought them here. It meant so much to be treated with compassion. It helped her feel strong again. For the first time in weeks, she was looked at as a human being, after being an anonymous case file in the immigration detention center and a mystery at airport reception—a girl who was supposed to be dead.

"I'll pray for you," said the priest as she prepared to leave.

"Pray for my daughter, not me. Pray for the little baby who's without her mother."

Leila hesitated for a moment on the street outside the white stucco church. The day had already grown hot. She carried her leather jacket; it was too warm to wear it.

She had no money, no identification, no phone. After spending half her life away from here, she was back on the streets of Cartagena, completely alone.

There were some services available to help people in her situation, but not many. Colombia had too many of its own poor to worry much about the poor the United States deposited here.

She had to find a way back, a way to reverse this nightmare. But she also had to survive. That was her first duty to Cristina. Her instincts brought her back to childhood as she calculated how long her breakfast might need to sustain her. That thought used to temper the enjoyment of every meal.

The gift of a new life, which Manny gave her so long ago, had been snatched away. But not all of his gifts were lost. She returned today as a much different person than the girl who used to roam these same streets. Thanks to Manny, she was educated and skilled. Surely, that would help her find work.

First, she would email Ashford, then find a job.

She had never been to an internet café before—they didn't exist when she was a child, and she had no need for them in the US. But she instinctively knew her strategy for using one without money. It wasn't too different from other hustles she'd learned as a girl. All she had to do was find someone leaving before their time was up, forgetting to sign off. It might be tricky, but she was good at that kind of thing.

She walked out into the familiar city. Only a few blocks away from the church, she knew where she was and followed the major street toward the center of town. Every sound stirred her nostalgia. This city bustled in its own unique way. White and brown apartment buildings with cluttered balconies lined the street on each side of her. Lush, tropical trees grew up from breaks in the pavement.

Down the narrow side streets, with the apartment buildings closer together, a web of electrical and phone wires, sometimes tangled with clothing lines, crisscrossed above the broken-up stone streets. Some of the smaller alleys were only made of packed dirt. Others doubled as storm drains for the flashfloods of the rainy season. Beat-up cars and motorcycles jostled through the street, with only a passing attempt at the concept of lanes. Loose bricks clattered from beneath the speeding tires. Up on the hills to the south, dilapidated but brightly colored houses were packed together in the dark-green rim of the jungle—blue, yellow, green, and tan were the colors that painted the houses beneath wide leaves of palm and banana trees.

Cartagena hadn't changed much. Oh, it was beautiful! Nostalgia might have comforted Leila, if not for the gaping hole of loneliness in her heart.

She forced focus upon her mind. She had been a survivor and a fighter since her earliest memories. If she could take care of herself on the streets as a child, she could do it again as an adult, for however long it took. She didn't want to take care of herself, though. She wanted to care for the people she loved.

The tears she had forced back so many times crept up again, and again she choked them away. The situation was hopeless. Deep down she knew that. How could she ever be allowed to return to the United States? But hopeless as it was, she *had* to hope, because without hope, she would lose the will to survive.

As she walked, Leila grew more aware of her surroundings. Long dormant sensory memories returned. The familiar sights, smells, and sounds sparked strange emotions. Strangest of all, she realized that she felt afraid. It was an acute fear for her safety, not the general fear of life that came from her arrest and deportation. This fear was more immediate. The sense was tied to these very streets. It was something she hadn't felt for many years.

Almost as soon as she recognized her fear, she spotted the internet café on the next corner.

She stopped, remembering the priest's warning. She had told him she knew no one in Cartagena, but that wasn't entirely true. The only people she knew were not people she wanted to meet. Could *he* have already found out she was back in Colombia? Would he really care after all these years?

There was no way. She was being paranoid. She wasn't thinking straight. It was the priest's words that made her wary and her hormones that whipped her into a ridiculous paranoia. She suppressed her fear and walked on toward the internet café. She had to try this. Even if her fear *was* based in something real, she would risk her life to connect with her family.

She looked through the window. It didn't take long to find someone leaving carelessly. She slipped in and got on the computer. A teenage boy was working the café counter, but he had his head buried in a magazine and she doubted he saw her slip in.

She got online, opened her email account, and took a deep breath.

There were a dozen emails from Ashford and several from Manny. She read them quickly. They were both confused and frightened. None of the other emails would matter now. But one more name caught her eye. She had an email from Samantha. She didn't open it. She didn't want to know anything Samantha might have to say.

She emailed Ashford and Manny separately. There wasn't

much she could say, except that she loved them and missed them. She promised to email them again tomorrow. Hopefully by then she would have a job and a place to stay. Then she could tell them where to call her.

She decided to log into her online banking and see if perhaps she still had access to her savings and credit accounts. A message popped up as soon as she entered her password.

THIS ACCOUNT HAS BEEN FROZEN DUE TO AN OFAC ALERT. PLEASE CALL THE NUMBER BELOW FOR MORE INFORMATION

Of course. She knew enough about banking laws that she should have guessed that would happen.

She was about to close the browser, but her eyes fell back on Samantha's name in her inbox. She couldn't help it. She opened the email.

"Leila, I promise to make sure your daughter always has everything she needs. But only if you never try to get Ashford to follow you to wherever they sent you. Ashford understands this too. You're a tough girl. You'll be fine."

Leila closed the browser and stood up. *Bitch! She still can't leave me alone.*

She walked toward the door. The teenager at the desk looked up at her. A flip cell phone whipped up in his hand and he snapped a picture of her.

Panic rose in her chest.

She rushed out and hurried down the street.

She became dizzy and nauseous. Samantha, then another kid with a cell phone camera, just like at the airport. What was happening? This was beginning to feel like some weird nightmare. It couldn't be real. Her mind wasn't right after everything she had gone through.

As she walked, the fear stayed. She sensed she was being

followed. She tried to figure out exactly where she was. She paused at an intersection, then turned left. If her memory served her right, there was a shopping mall a few blocks this way. She had to get off the street for a moment to steady herself.

There it was—a clothing store entrance at the edge of the mall, with a short white lattice fence in front of a bright-pink door.

She slipped inside, pausing to catch her breath. There weren't many shoppers inside this early. A quick look around confirmed that no one had followed her into the store. The cheap clothes on the racks reminded her how badly she would love a change of clothes. She had been in these same jeans and gray T-shirt for too long. But she had no money even for fresh underwear. She lingered between the racks, taking several deep breaths, then made her way across to an exit at the other side.

Leila stepped out the other side of the store, back to the open street. She gasped. Two policemen stood waiting for her.

"*Señorita*, please come with us."

"*¿Por qué? No he hecho nada.*"

"*El jefe te ha pedido.*"

"*¿El jefe?*"

One of them grabbed her arm, not maliciously, but firmly enough that his point was clear. Before she had a chance to think if she should try to escape, she was shoved into the back of a police car.

Had they been watching her since the airport? Were they waiting at the church this morning? The priest had alluded to that, and she should have been more careful. She'd be a profitable piece of ass in the wrong hands. The teenagers taking pictures at the airport, and again the one at the café, could be working for traffickers. These cops might be working for them too.

They didn't drive far. She recognized the precinct police headquarters that she and her friends had always avoided as children. She was ushered up three concrete steps between the two policemen, then seated alone in an office.

The room was a mess, with three piled desks and chairs strewn at random. Pictures and certificates hung on almost every inch of the walls. A fan whirred in the corner, kicking up corners of paper. There was something stuck in the fan; it clattered at every rotation. The room smelled of stale coffee, flat Coke, and cigarettes. It was a workroom for men who lacked the civil budget to hire regular cleaners.

Being brought here rather than to some remote place should have been a good sign. But something was wrong.

She started to look around the clutter of the room, wondering if there was anything that could be useful—some money perhaps or a weapon. Before she could get her bearings, she heard a click and her eyes darted back to the door. The knob was turning. She cowered in her seat.

The door opened. She muffled the cry that nearly burst out of her mouth. There he was—Paulo Varga—dressed in the uniform of the precinct chief.

"*Bueno, La Alta. Volviste.* I knew this day would come. You've changed a great deal. *¡Qué linda!*"

He closed the door, leaned against the wall, and licked his lips. She remembered when he licked the dripping blood she'd drawn off of those lips years ago. All the terror from that night returned tenfold.

"What do you want?" Her own voice sounded weak to her, full of dismay and defeat. "I've suffered enough. Why won't you just let me be?"

"I want to help you. Manny tried, but he was always a coward. Now, you see how badly he failed. You need a real man."

"Why are you doing this to me?"

"You have no cause to fear me. I've never done you any harm."

"You tried to rape me when I was a little girl. Are you going to rape me now?"

"That's an ugly word. I don't want to hurt you, but you do owe me."

Leila's heart raced. What could she do? This was no longer a mere street thug. He was the chief of police.

He took a few steps closer to her and grinned. "You have a debt to pay. You and Manny both. You took his name, after all. Now, his sins are yours."

"If revenge is what you're after, then stop being polite. I can't stand it."

"Why so hostile?"

"Because you fucking arrested me. Are you going to sell me off as a whore or just keep me locked here for yourself?"

"You're better than that."

Leila tried to judge what her chances of escaping him would be. He was a lot older, but he looked stronger and more imposing than she remembered.

"I want to paint a picture of you," he said. Considering everything that had happened, it sounded too bizarre. "I've wanted to paint you for years. Ever since you came to my house that night. I tried several times, but it's hard to paint someone from memory."

She remembered how his paintings had looked. In retrospect, it surprised her that they had been so sexless, his models so lacking in femininity. But worst of all, they lacked *life*. The women had looked like painted corpses. She remembered the dream she used to have, with her face dead in one of those pictures. Now, here Paulo was wanting to paint her. The thought of him doing that horrified her almost as much as the thought of him raping her.

"I want to help you and care for you. It would be stupid of you to refuse. The girl I met on the streets long ago took her chances when they were offered."

Leila tried to think quick. She wanted to fight, preferring even death to the degradation of submitting to such a man. But through everything, Cristina never left her mind. Her goal was to find a way back to her daughter. Dying here would do Cristina no good; neither would rotting in a Colombian prison or being forced into captive prostitution. Was there a way to play this to get Paulo to help move her closer toward her goal without doing something that would make her want to die instead of live?

"*Así que*, Paulo, can you help me get back to the people I love?"

His expression changed. Even a man as conniving as Paulo was not immune to the plea of a beautiful woman. His lust, she knew, could blind him in other ways. If nothing else, she could buy herself a few more moments before he raped her out of spite.

He was clearly thinking about it. She could see his erection in his tight police pants. She wanted to vomit.

"I'd love nothing more than a glass of water right now," she said. "I'm parched. I don't even know how many days I was in prison before they flew me here yesterday."

"Relax here. I'll send my secretary in with some water and lemon." He didn't move. "You people the United States deports need someone to help you get started. Luckily for you, you have me. Tonight, I'll take you out and show you that life in Cartagena will not be so bad. Then you can sit for me while I paint. I'll find a pretty dress for you."

His eyes scanned up and down her body, which made her skin crawl.

"Yes, I think I know what will fit that beautiful body you've grown into. So sexy." He licked his lips again. "I'm not as bad a man as you think. You'll soon learn to enjoy spending time with me."

He left the room, not forgetting to lock the door behind him.

34

THE DOORKNOB TURNED again. A different man walked into her makeshift prison cell, carrying the lemon water.

He wasn't dressed in a police uniform, but he wore a name badge of the department. This must have been Paulo's secretary. He had a sad, oddly youthful face. His round midsection and slouched shoulders gave away his years, probably mid-forties. He was younger than Paulo but had none of his athleticism. His dark hair was pulled back into a ponytail. He handed her the glass, observing her with curiosity.

Leila read his badge out loud. "San Juan el Bautista Velasquez. That's quite a name. I think I've heard it before." She recalled Manny's stories of the revolution. "You were my father's friend."

"That was many years ago."

She heard the remorse in his tone and guessed that he knew who she was too. "Is there anything you can do to help me? Would you do that for Manny?"

"Manny left. Paulo gave me work when I got out of prison."

"Please help me. I have to get home."

He turned, clearly uncomfortable, and left the room. This man was no fighter anymore. She saw it in how he carried himself. He was a defeated man who had lost his hope for life. He wouldn't be any help to her even if he wanted to be.

The lock sounded in the door behind him.

What did she need help for, anyway? She would do better on her own. Paulo was nothing but a bully, and if she couldn't fight him, then she could outsmart him.

Leila took a large drink of water, then got up and rummaged around the room. She didn't even know what she was looking for—a key perhaps. The clattering fan seemed to grow louder, making it difficult for her to concentrate. She had an urge to find and extract whatever was stuck in it. What a stupid thing to be distracted by at a moment like this.

She had to escape before Paulo returned. She might not get another chance. In a drawer she found a pile of coins, which she stuffed into the pocket of her jeans. In another cabinet she found a knife in a leather sheath. She slid it into the inner pocket of her jacket, which she put back on, despite the thick, hot air of the room.

There was one high window on the wall across from the door. The iron latch was rusted, hanging loose from its catch. She couldn't escape through the door, but the window was worth a try.

She slid one of the desks beneath the window. It scraped roughly and loudly on the concrete floor. She climbed up on it. Opening the pane, she stood on tiptoes to get her head through. The office was on the second floor. A lump rose in her throat as she looked down a flat concrete wall to the pavement of the alley below. How far was that—fifteen feet, twenty? It would be quite a fall.

She forced herself to be brave. She took off her heeled sandals and dropped them out the window, then hoisted herself up and through. She lowered her legs, hanging onto the window frame, stretching her body downward, shortening the drop as much as she could. Her arms began to hurt. She squeezed her eyes shut and let go.

Her feet hit with a thud. She let her knees bend and her butt hit down. She waited for a moment to catch her breath, then stood up. She was fine. Nothing was broken or sprained. Her soles would be a little sore, as would her rear end.

She ran, carrying her sandals, which fortunately hadn't broken. These streets were filthy, but she had run barefoot on them many times before.

If there was a favor Paulo did her, it was to bring her back to the neighborhood she knew so well and to leave out enough coins for a bus. She found one, bound for the Old Town harbor, a good destination. In the touristy areas, things worked differently. A barrio thug of a police captain wouldn't have much influence there.

A half hour on the bus helped her calm down. She focused on breathing, trying not to think too much . . . about any of it. She got off the bus amongst the multicolored colonial buildings and cobbled streets. She heard English and French mixed with Spanish on the sidewalks and coming through open shopfronts. Not far from here stood the little inn where she and Manny had waited for their plane tickets and visas. That time didn't seem so long ago anymore.

It now must have been past noon. If she was going to make use of this day, time was running out. She walked toward the shore and began making inquiries at the hotels.

There were several new ones around the neighborhood of Getsemaní, where new urbanity mixed with the colonial and the decrepit. The high stone walls that separated fancy houses from the street were splashed with colorful graffiti.

Soon, her legs were aching, but she kept her focus, smiling methodically through each conversation, trusting she still looked pretty, though she had no makeup on and her hair was matted into a ponytail. She should have started out by going to the makeup sample counters at the department stores, pretending to be an American tourist.

Late in the afternoon, she got lucky. One of the smaller hotels found their restaurant short-staffed with a large party of Australian tourists reserved for dinner. The hotel manager told Leila she was a godsend, with her serving experience and perfect English. He didn't seem to notice her hesitation before saying her name was Marissa Montero. She knew he needed a waitress and trusted he was smart enough not to ask her too many questions.

The best part of the job was that they gave her a uniform, getting her out of her dirty clothes. Counting on tips, she could at least buy fresh underwear and new shoes in the morning.

As she left the office, she realized that she should have used a different name. She wanted to have a name in which she felt love, which was why she chose the name of Manny's first wife. But Paulo would remember that name if he tried to look for her here.

She walked across the stone courtyard. Cartagena harbor came right up to the edge of the hotel grounds. Fragrant vines lined the upper balconies. She walked through the open-walled restaurant, behind the kitchen, to the servers' bathroom. She washed her face and changed into her uniform. *Hotel Caribe* it said across the left side of the black shirt. The pants were also black. The uniform didn't fit her great, but this wasn't the time to care. Some safety pins and needle and thread would also be on tomorrow's shopping list. One of the other waitresses let Leila use her makeup to freshen up before their shift.

"Where did you come from?" The girl stood beside her at the bathroom sink. She was dark and petite, with big brown eyes.

Leila sighed. Surely, it wouldn't hurt to tell someone. "I got deported from the United States yesterday."

"¡Dios mío, pobre mujer!"

"At least I have a job now. It's a start."

"Do you have any place to stay?"

Leila shrugged.

"Stay with me tonight after our shift. I live close by."

"Are you sure?"

"*Por supuesto*. What are you going to do, sleep in the street or spend more than you earn for a room here?"

"Thank you. You're very generous." She handed back the makeup. It wasn't quite her color, but it would do.

"Marissa, right?"

Leila remembered to nod. The false name was safer, even with this girl who could be a friend.

"I'm Alejandra. That's a beautiful ring on your finger. Are you married to an American?"

Leila looked down at her ring—the little diamond Ashford got for her as soon as he could afford to. "It's hard to remember, but I think our wedding was supposed to be next weekend. It seems like something from another lifetime now."

"Can't you stay there if you get married? That's what I always thought."

"It doesn't work that way anymore. Ten years ago, maybe, but not now. Not if they really want you gone."

Alejandra blotted her lips and buttoned up her purse. "My apartment is small, but you're welcome to stay as long as you need to. I live with my grandmother and my baby daughter. You won't mind?"

Leila smiled. "I have a baby girl too."

"Still in the United States?"

"Yes."

Leila saw the horror that filled Alejandra's eyes. Another question seemed to hover on her lips, but the two young mothers just looked at each other. The moment was filled with more confusion than understanding.

"*Vamos, chica,*" Leila said. "We'd better get to work."

Late that night, with her body throbbing in pain, Leila lay on the couch in Alejandra's small apartment. Despite her exhaustion, she couldn't sleep. The city noises beyond the thin walls were cacophonous. Her mind raced, spurred by all the sounds that pounded against her inner ears.

She couldn't even begin to process everything that had happened. But for the first time since she had left Ashford in their apartment in Santa Fe, she felt a little progress. She had made a start.

She ached for her daughter. She longed to feel Ashford's arms around her. Would she ever see them again? Was there any way back? Was there even any way she could contact them without putting herself in danger?

Leila even missed Romeo. What she wouldn't give to have her kitty plopped heavily on her legs right now.

She closed her eyes and tried to picture where Ashford might be, what he might be feeling. Was he back in Phoenix? Would he even know where she was, what had happened to her? It comforted her to picture Cristina with her father. At least the baby wouldn't lack love.

Leila didn't realize she was crying until the first teardrops released from her cheeks and fell onto the scratchy couch cushion beneath her head. It was the first time since boarding the plane that she had let herself cry.

Her last night with Ashford, they had argued. She hated to think about it. It seemed so petty now. She wished she had been more loving to him. She had been afraid to get too close. Even after everything that happened . . . after everything they sacrificed for each other, she had still held something back from him. It broke her heart to think how she wouldn't allow herself to love him as much as he had loved her. How many chances did you get at a love like that? Now, her chance was gone.

She hummed a lullaby, hoping by some magic to reach them through the intensity of her longing.

"I love you, Cristina. I love you, Ashford." She willed the words across uncounted miles. She pressed the engagement ring on her finger to her lips. "Find me, my darlings."

35

LEILA WAS SURPRISED by how late into the morning she slept. It had been hard to fall asleep, with everything that weighed on her mind and heart. But once she did, her body welcomed the time to recover. Alejandra and her grandmother were not early risers, so the apartment was just coming to life when Leila rose. She showered and put on the new, ill-fitting restaurant uniform.

Alejandra met her in the apartment kitchen, wearing short-shorts and a loose tank top with a dim blue star and letters so faded that Leila could barely read *Dallas Cowboys* across the gray of the shirt.

"Is there a computer at the hotel we can use?" she asked Alejandra while they ate corn cakes and drank coffee with coarse sugar.

"We're not supposed to, not for personal things."

"Are there no exceptions?"

Alejandra considered for a moment. "Let's go over a little early today. I can get you online before our shift."

"Thank you. I have to tell my family where I am."

"Is there anything they can do to help you?"

"I don't know. But they'll want to try if they know where I am."

"I'll write down our phone number here. We can't call out to the United States, but they could call you here."

"That would be wonderful. You've been so kind to me."

Leila felt grateful to be eating a second breakfast on her second day in Cartagena. It was lucky. As badly as things had gone, it could have been worse. Alejandra's grandmother's kitchen couldn't have been more different than yesterday's clean, white kitchen in the rectory. Pots and dishes were everywhere. Various photographs and trinkets hung on the yellow walls. The pipes in the ceiling clattered as water washed through from the apartments above. The one similarity to yesterday was the ancient tin coffee kettle on the stove, emitting the same wonderful smell.

Leila felt Alejandra's eyes on her as she sipped her coffee. She was examining her with curiosity and wonder.

"I've heard stories about people deported from the United States," she said, "but you're the first person I've met who actually has been. Are all the stories true?"

Leila sighed. "I'd heard the stories too and never really believed it. Living in the United States all those years, it was always in the back of my mind, but I never believed it could happen to me."

She remembered everything, back to the day she left her home here in Cartagena. Once Manny gave her a new identity, she had been so trusting of the new life. She really became this new person. But she always should have been more cautious, knowing her danger. It was still tough to know exactly what had happened after her arrest, but her false identity didn't seem to have been too tough for the authorities to unravel.

"Yeah," she said, "now that I've been through it, I have to say the stories *are* true. It was awful. It happened so fast. I barely remember the time in the detention center. I must have been delirious, maybe even sedated. I do remember being afraid. Any of those guards might have tried to have their way with me, and there would have been nothing I could have done, no one I could have told. They said I waived my right to an attorney, which I can't imagine having done unless I'd lost my head. They told me I had a right to a phone call, but I couldn't remember the phone numbers and email wasn't given as an option. So, I was completely alone and at the mercy of the people who just wanted me out of the country as fast as possible."

"Why would anyone want you out of their country? Look at you. You're beautiful."

"I don't even know what I can say. I was successful, too, until I made one little mistake. Then it was all over."

"It just doesn't make sense to me."

How could she explain it to Alejandra, who had never been to the United States? She had never imagined before moving there how resentful some people were toward Hispanic immigrants. It took years before she felt like she could almost understand the root causes of those feelings. What she never gave enough thought to was the *danger* that arose from that prejudice.

"Most Americans are wonderful people, but there are a few who have such hatred. No, hatred's not a nice thing to say. It's *fear*. Some people there are so afraid of losing what they have, so they lash out against anyone who they think might take it from them. They perceive that Latinos want what they have. Maybe we do, but there's enough prosperity in the United States for anyone who's willing to work for it. One person's success doesn't take away another's opportunity. The fear is persistent. The fear looks like hatred, but that's not the heart of it."

Even Samantha was only afraid. She was afraid of losing control—of her son's destiny, of her career, of her fortune. It came out as prejudice and hatred, but it was rooted in fear. Realizing this made Leila feel a little less bitter toward her.

"There are frightened people everywhere. In the United

States, it's the frightened people who have all the power." She didn't want to dwell on it. She wanted to focus on what was ahead—getting as settled as possible and getting in touch with Manny and Ashford to devise a plan. What that plan would be she didn't know. What path was there to getting reunited with her daughter? There had to be some way.

She tried not to worry about Samantha's cruel offer and especially tried not to think about Paulo. It was yesterday's nightmare that would hopefully just go away. Now, she was with caring people. She had a job and a fresh start. This part of town was far from Paulo's jurisdiction.

Leila finished her breakfast and stood up. "I want to go buy some things before work. You know, makeup, shampoo, underwear . . . I have nothing. Thankfully, those Aussies tipped good last night. I'll meet you back at the hotel this afternoon."

The restaurant was empty when Leila arrived at Hotel Caribe that afternoon. Last night, the whole bayside of the restaurant had been open, with a nice breeze coming off the water. Now, the glass doors were shut and the drapes were pulled. It was a newer restaurant, catering to tourists, so air-conditioning was a must. It was being protected now from the hot afternoon. She sat in the shade of the awning, looking out toward the lapping shore of the bay until Alejandra arrived. She hopped up and followed her new friend in.

"Good," said Alejandra, "the night manager hasn't arrived yet, but I have a key. Let's hurry so we don't get in trouble."

She logged on to the restaurant computer, then turned it over to Leila, who opened her email. There was only one, from Manny.

"Leila, do not email again from this account. Do not tell us where you are yet. You are in more danger than you know.

Wherever you emailed from yesterday was not secure. A few hours after you wrote, Paulo Varga emailed me too. He knows you are there, and somehow he got into your email."

As Leila read the words, her head swirled. She felt nauseous. It wasn't possible, except that of course it was and she realized how careless she had been yesterday at the internet café. Reading Samantha's email had shaken her up and she had left too quickly, forgetting to log out and leaving herself open to the very trick she had pulled to get online in the first place. That teenager with the flip phone must have gone over as soon as she walked out.

Stupid. Stupid.

She changed the password on her email account, then logged out and shut the browser. This place was surely not secure either.

How far would Paulo go to find her? How many places did he have eyes and ears?

"Are you okay?" Alejandra was watching her from a stool nearby.

Leila looked up at her. Those big brown eyes in a head too small for them accentuated the girl's curiosity. Alejandra had been nothing but kind to her. How careful did she need to be? Was there no one she could trust?

"Yeah, it just all makes me so sad. I get overwhelmed."

"I bet. Are you done?"

Leila nodded.

Alejandra stood up and reached for her arm. "Let's take a short walk by the harbor. We have some time before our shift. The air will do you good."

Leila took Alejandra's arm and allowed herself to be led out of the restaurant.

So, not even email was safe. How horrible. She certainly couldn't ask Manny and Ashford to call at Alejandra's grandmother's apartment. Paulo might end up calling instead. She was completely alone and isolated now. Would she ever see her daughter again?

36

"ASHFORD, MANNY, A letter from Colombia!"

Ashford leaped up as Carmen ran in, holding an envelope. She handed it to him. Manny stepped up behind him, placing a hand on his shoulder as he opened the envelope with trembling fingers and pulled out the two sheets of paper. The three read it silently together.

My Dear Ashford, Manny, and Carmen,

What is there for me to say after all that has happened except that I love each of you so much. I long for the day when we will be together again though right now I feel hopeless.

As you know, I was arrested and deported to Colombia. Samantha threatened me with this the day I told her I would not give you up, Ashford, or give up our child. I didn't believe she would be able to carry through with the threat. I should have been more careful. When I went in for the mortgage exam, they tracked me down. I'm not entirely sure whether I was deported for the mortgage case or if it had to do with my ambiguous identity. I know that my name raised questions. How much they found out about my past I don't know. My case was processed and closed so fast.

It was so confusing at the detention center. Florescent lights blasted down in the shared cells the whole time, so even when I slept I awoke delirious. I suspect I was given some sort of sedative. I've heard about these things happening to other people who went through it, but I always assumed it was an exaggeration.

I wish I could console you by telling you I am safe, but you already know that is not true. I am hiding and I am afraid. Here I don't even have a name. Manny, the people from your past want revenge. I have a place to stay and a job at a restaurant in a hotel. But I don't know how long it will be before I'm forced to move on. I don't know how badly they want to find me.

Worst of all, I don't know any way I can get back to you, whom I love so much. I think about Cristina every second of every day. Ashford, I dream of you every night. I imagine a future where we can be a happy family again. I need your love and am dying without you.

I cannot tell you how to contact me, as I don't have a phone and I would not feel safe having you call or write me here. Even email is unsafe. Nothing is secure and the cafés are watched. I'm scared to try again after what happened last time. I will write again as soon as I think of a way for us to safely connect.

Kiss our daughter and tell Cristina every day how much her mother loves her. Each moment I spend apart from her cuts wider the gaping hole inside me. I dread that she will forget me. I am no longer in captivity, but my loneliness and hopelessness has built a new prison around me. I am a mother in exile. I am a mother with a broken heart.

Sending all my love,

Leila

Ashford took the letter, once he was sure that the others had also finished reading it, and sat down on the couch. Manny took the envelope and went to his own chair.

Ashford didn't know what to say. He didn't even know what to feel. Leila's letter was dark, but somehow it gave him hope. This was the first contact since that initial email almost a week ago. He knew what he needed to do.

"So, he hasn't found her yet," Manny said. "That's good. She's being careful. She hasn't forgotten how. But it will be hard for us to find her too."

"Why wouldn't she tell us where she is?" asked Carmen.

"She's afraid if we wrote back the letter would be intercepted."

"Would that really happen?" asked Ashford.

"You don't know Colombia. Look how easily they intercepted her email."

It was difficult for Ashford to believe.

"Look at this postmark." Manny pointed at the corner of the envelope. "She mailed it from Cartagena harbor, but put no other identifying mark on the envelope. It's hard to feel hopeful, but this letter does encourage me. When that man emailed me last week, I didn't know what to think, especially after Leila went silent. I didn't know if she knew he was looking for her or not. But now we know she does."

He went on, "I did some research too. I found out that Paulo Varga is the police chief of the neighborhood in Cartagena where I used to live. He is an evil and powerful man, with ties to the old Pablo Escobar drug cartel, as well as the worst human trafficking rings in Northern Colombia. Men like him have arms and eyes everywhere. He clearly has informants at immigration. That's why she wouldn't say where she's working. That's why she has been too afraid to email again. I'm sure the network at her hotel isn't secure."

"But why? Why does he care about her?"

"She escaped from him years ago, and men like that can never forgive being beaten. I escaped from him too, so this is also tied into his revenge against me. He has a legitimate grievance against me. I can't deny that even after all these years. That's why he threatened me as soon as he found out how to email me."

"What would he do to her?"

"Everything you don't want to imagine. He's an evil man, Ashford. You will have to be extremely careful not to stumble into any of his traps."

Ashford looked up and caught Manny's eyes. It startled him that Manny already knew what he had in mind. It was what had to be done. Manny understood.

"I wish I could go with you," Manny said. "But with my weak legs and a face Paulo knows, I'd be a burden to you. This is something you have to do alone."

"What are you two talking about?" asked Carmen. "I don't understand."

Ashford took a deep breath and turned toward Carmen. "I'm going to Colombia as soon as possible. Leila can't return here. I have to go to her."

"How will you find her?"

"I don't know, but I have to try. She said she can't live without me. Well, I can't live without her either. And Cristina can't live without us both."

"You're not thinking of taking the baby with you?" Carmen looked aghast. "It might be dangerous. You don't know anyone there, and you barely understand Spanish. Leave Cristina with us until you find Leila."

Ashford looked from Carmen to Manny, then back at Carmen. "If I go, Cristina may not be safe with you here either. Leila implied in her letter that her identity was discovered. That's probably why we were never contacted. In a legal sense, we're not even technically family. That discovery puts you in danger too, Manny. I don't think you want anyone finding out that you lied on your visa application all those years ago."

"It's something I've worried about many times. But as long as I don't make any waves, I think I'll be safe."

"There's a danger you haven't thought of. It's my mother."

"What could she do now?"

"She could take Cristina. She's been emailing me every day. She calls too, but I haven't answered. I'll admit I'm afraid to. Her words all sound kind. She promises to take care of Cristina and provide for her. She wants to help raise her. She doesn't know that Leila isn't your blood daughter, but *someone* in the US knows. If my mother tries to, she *will* find out. If I'm in Colombia, alone, when she does, then she would come after Cristina. As her only blood relative in the country, she would win custody easily."

Manny ran his hands along his face. Ashford could see beads of sweat on his forehead.

"I have to take Cristina with me. It may be dangerous, but there's no other way. If I find Leila, *when* I find her, I won't be able to bring her back. They won't let her come back to the country, at least not right away. So, Cristina and I won't be coming back either.

We'll have to stay in Colombia. That's what it means to be a family."

Ashford felt excited and hopeful. Yes, he was also afraid. He looked back at Manny, encouraged by how Manny seemed to understand what he himself was only just beginning to wrap his head around. Ashford's life was about to change forever. Once he took this step, there was no undoing it. He looked over at Carmen, who nodded.

"You'll take care of Romeo though, won't you?" Ashford smiled, trying to lighten the moment.

"Yes. We'll give her kitty a good home."

"I'm proud of you," said Manny. "I believe you can find her. We know she's working in a hotel restaurant. We'll put together a list of all the hotels in the city that have restaurants, but my guess is that she's in either Bocagrande or Getsemaní. That's a good place to start. There are a lot of tourists around there, so you should feel more comfortable and bring less attention to yourself than you would in the center of the city. Still, you must be careful. A young man traveling alone with a baby is unusual. I'll tell you everything I know about Paulo Varga, because you must avoid him at all costs.

"But even more important than you avoiding him yourself, you *must* keep him from knowing about Cristina. If he can't get to Leila, he'll go after the people she loves. The only reason he went after her in the first place was to hurt me. You're right that you have to bring Cristina with you. But you also have to understand that having the baby in Colombia puts all of you in more danger."

Ashford nodded. Manny stood up and walked toward Ashford, who also stood up. Manny placed his hands on Ashford's shoulders. "My son . . . may I call you that, even though you haven't had the chance to marry my daughter?"

Ashford nodded again. Manny's eyes welled up with tears.

"I feel closer to you, my son, in this sorrow we're sharing. Leila's disappearance has been a pain I never thought I would have to endure again. I lost an infant daughter. I watched my first wife get shot and die before my eyes. I didn't think I'd have to go through something like this again."

Manny looked down for a moment. With effort, he brought his teary eyes back up to face Ashford's. "Even though those two losses were painful, losing Leila would break my heart the worst of all. My first wife had lost her hope. My infant daughter hadn't yet developed hope. But Leila's hope was something I had worked for many years to be able to give to someone. Seeing how hard she worked for her success allowed me to forget all the old sorrow and believe that my value as a man would be realized though her. She was my daughter in every way that mattered. She was my joy."

Manny took a deep breath. "I was never prouder of you than when I saw in your eyes—before you said it—what you are prepared to do for Leila. You restore my faith and my hope. I see too that you understand the cost. You understand that you will leave behind everything you know, love, and have worked for in this country."

"Leila is all I know, love, and have worked for. I would give up anything to be with her. That was true since the moment I met her."

Ashford looked from Manny to Carmen, then toward the crib where Cristina slept, with no comprehension of the great adventure she would soon take to find her mother. He did feel afraid. He had never viewed himself as a brave man. This would take more courage than he had ever needed before. It was time to learn if he had that kind of courage within him.

37

ASHFORD LOOKED OUT the window of the crowded bus at the bustling city of Cartagena. He held Cristina close on his lap, his other hand clutching his suitcase handle. Even though the bus was coming from the airport, it didn't look like there were any tourists on board.

Everything looked strange and foreign. The traveling he had done outside of the US was always in a setting carefully planned by his mother. They were either in cities where English was prevalent—London, Rome, Singapore—or in a bubble of American safety with minimal contact with the destination, such as on that well-planned and comically comfortable hike in Nepal when he was fifteen. He had always wanted to actually touch and experience the places he traveled to. Now, he would have his chance. He was terrified of having to use his inadequate Spanish.

As the bus neared the port, the architecture changed into a surprising mix of tall high-rises and ancient brick and adobe buildings from colonial times. These two styles were crammed anachronistically onto the same city blocks. The high-rises were mostly white, shimmering in the bright noon sun, while the old structures were yellow, dark green, blue, or pink. Lush greenery sprouted everywhere, healthy in the moist heat. Trees grew from the small parks and patches of earth between the street corners. Flowered vines hung from pots on balconies. It was elegant but decrepit at the same time.

What was he doing here? How would he even start this crazy search? He and Manny had written out a detailed plan, mapping out his strategy to search for Leila. If she was working at a hotel near the harbor, he should find her in time. But even that was uncertain. She wouldn't be using her real name. He would have to be careful how he asked his questions so as not to put her in increased danger.

Sweat drenched his shirt despite the open windows of the bus. He was used to the dry heat of Arizona, but this humidity was different. Besides, buses in Arizona were always air-conditioned. Cristina didn't seem to mind. He supposed this place was in her blood. Maybe he could learn a thing or two from her.

The bus stopped in a square in the middle of Old Town. Ashford stepped off with the baby strapped to his front, pulling the suitcase behind him. Traffic buzzed around the perimeter of the plaza. A tall monument rose from a patch of grass in the middle. A salty breeze reminded him of how close he was to the south Caribbean Sea. He looked around to gather his bearings, trying to remember all the pointers Manny had given him. He reached for the city map in his pocket.

"*¿Amigo, necesita un taxi? ¡Qué bonita bebé!*"

Ashford jumped. The voice was close by him, almost shouting. He turned and saw a curly-haired man in a short-sleeved yellow shirt, bursting with enthusiasm.

"Uh, *no, gracias.*"

"You are American! I have English. May I help you today?"

"I don't need help." Ashford began to walk.

The man fell in beside him. "A hotel perhaps? I have friends so you will get fair price."

"I said no thank you." Ashford stopped and looked the man squarely in the eyes. "Please."

"Okay, *amigo*. You have a nice day." The man turned and hurried away.

The encounter threw him off, meaningless as it was. His nerves were on edge.

He consulted his map as people buzzed about him, then figured out the correct direction, toward the inn Manny had suggested. It was the same inn that Manny and Leila had stayed in years ago while awaiting their visas and plane tickets to America. Manny thought the familiarity and nostalgia might draw Leila to that place, especially if she knew they were looking for her.

He arrived at the inn: *Casa Azul*. True to its name, the outside was painted sky blue with yellow trim. Going inside, the woman working the desk smiled as she looked at his baby.

"*Sí*, we have your reservation, *Señor* Cohen." She struggled with his unfamiliar last name. "May I have a credit card for the room?"

"*Por supuesto.*" He reached toward his back pocket, but it was empty. "My wallet. It's gone. That man picked my pocket." He had slipped into English, but the woman clearly understood.

"Oh no! Cartagena is awful with pickpockets."

Ashford wanted to run after the curly-haired man, but it was hopeless now. He had been gone for ten minutes or longer, and here was Ashford with a baby and a suitcase. He was such a fool, leaving his wallet in his back pocket in a place like this.

"I'll call the police," said the woman.

He watched while she picked up the phone, then he came to his senses. "No. There's nothing they can do. Please don't." He wouldn't be a fool about this twice. The last thing he needed was to be known by the police after only an hour in the city. But what would he do, with no money and no credit cards? He sat down in the lobby to think.

He had to call Manny, even though he was embarrassed. He wanted Manny to be confident in him, to believe he could really handle himself down here. Right now, Ashford wasn't so sure he could. If he couldn't even take care of his own wallet, how was he going to outsmart the men pursuing Leila?

Before leaving Phoenix, he'd added an international calling plan to his cell phone. He swallowed his pride and called Manny, who gave the inn his own credit card to secure Ashford's room as well as made a cash advance for him through Western Union. They had already agreed to pool resources for his trip. Ashford promised he would be more careful going forward. Maybe he only imagined the disappointment he thought he heard in Manny's voice.

The hotel clerk showed him to his room. Her name was Elena, and she was very curious about him, as were the people he had passed earlier on the street. Even the people on the bus had all been watching him. He stood out like a sore thumb.

"If ever you need me to watch your baby, let me know."

"Thank you." But Ashford had resolved to take Cristina with him everywhere. If this police chief found out about them, Cristina would be in danger. If she got kidnapped, he could never live with himself. His own love for Leila was secondary now. His primary duty was to reunite Cristina with her mother. He wouldn't let her out of his sight for a single moment. He would protect her with his life if it came to that.

While unpacking in his room, he called his bank, which canceled his cards and arranged to mail a new credit and debit card to him at the hotel. He still had his passport, and losing his US driver's license was a small hardship here. He might never need it again.

It was that easy. In a few days, his lost wallet would be forgotten. How different—how unjust, really—that he arrived here, like Leila, with no money and no credit. But as a privileged son of the American system, all was made right for him. Leila, on the other hand, had been spit out and rejected by that system and left with nothing to fall back on.

After the calls were made and Cristina was changed, Ashford sat down on the bed and looked around the room. The window was open. He took a deep breath, familiarizing himself with the air of this new place. Being here felt right. He knew Leila was close, and that knowledge stirred not only his hope but his *desire*. He longed for her now like in the early days of his passion for her, before their relationship began. It was a desire that took control of everything inside him: a passion in his heart and an urge in his body. This search was about the love of a severed family, the need to reunite a mother with her child. But it was also about a man's longing for a woman. Ashford wanted to be near her and melt into the delight of her essence. He wanted to hold her, kiss her, tear her clothes off, and make love to her. Being here, knowing she was close, awakened his obsession for her.

He wanted to begin his search. But first he had to make sure he had everything he needed for Cristina. Traveling with an infant was complicated. He went back downstairs. Elena pointed him toward the stores he needed, and he ventured out with the baby strapped to his front.

Ashford was grateful that she had not cried once since they landed. The flight was difficult. He'd had to apologize repeatedly to the other passengers, first flying from Phoenix to Houston and then across the Gulf of Mexico to Cartagena. He remembered Leila saying how good she was on the flight to and from Phoenix back in December. No such luck this time. But since landing, and especially now, her eyes were open wide with wonder at the unfamiliar city.

"This is your mother's city. This is where she's from. Even better, she's here now. We'll see Mama again very soon."

After the terror of his first few conversations, his high school Spanish began flooding back to him. Leila always bragged that Colombians spoke the cleanest Spanish in all of Latin America. Ashford didn't know if that was true, but he did find that he could understand people better than he'd expected.

His legs and shoulders were worn out by the time he returned to Casa Azul late that afternoon. His arms were weighed down by two grocery bags full of diapers, formula, food for himself, powder, and various sundries—hardly the supplies of a daring rescue mission.

Back in the room, Cristina fell asleep, and he needed to rest too. He lay down on his back and sighed.

So here he was. Now what?

38

IF ONLY IT had been another time—even another girl's life—this would not be so bad. For *La Alta* perhaps, but not for Leila del Sol.

A job in just this kind of hotel had been her childhood dream. Before Manny gave her a new life and grander hopes, what she had now would have seemed like the pinnacle of her ambition.

But Leila could not spend a single moment of her day forgetting the void that the separation from her daughter carved out in her heart.

She stepped down the stone embankment and sat on the final step above the water. A grove of palms to her right protected her against the hot afternoon sun. The water here on the inner side of the harbor was calm. She saw only a handful of boats in the bay. It was too hot to fish, and the tourists had all returned from their morning adventures. Soon, she would be serving them cocktails in the bar after their *siesta* and then dinner in the restaurant where she had now been working for almost two weeks.

With the help of some pins and a needle and thread, she had improved the fit of her restaurant uniform. These clothes, along with a new T-shirt and pair of shorts she had bought, were her only clothes other than what she came in.

She looked across at the familiar outline of the city—her city. Where she sat was close to the middle of the round horseshoe of the bay, with the Bocagrande peninsula stretched to her right and the main part of the city sprawled out on her left. The lush Isla de Manzanillo poked out into the water. She did love Cartagena. Deep in her heart, she had always hoped to come back one day, but not like this, not alone.

Still, being here now felt oddly natural. Was this how complacency set in?

As the time began to pass, she had to wonder if this was her life now: serving at this restaurant, sleeping in the working women's dormitory, which she had moved into after the first few nights on Alejandra's couch. Maybe there was no way back. Maybe this was the life she would have to get used to.

A few days after her arrival, she had seriously thought about sneaking onto a cruise ship docked in the harbor. She had scoped it out all through a morning, strategically noting the possible ways on, the way she and her friends used to sneak into football matches or into hotels as children. They were never bold enough to try a ship.

In the end, she was too afraid to try it. The stakes were too high now. As a child, she would have gotten shouted at, whipped at worst if caught. Now, who knew what a man who discovered her hiding on a ship might do. She'd given up and gone into the restaurant to work. She hadn't even been sure it was an American ship. Even if she had succeeded in getting aboard, she might have ended up in Buenos Aires or someplace else.

Maybe she could get a legitimate job on a cruise ship. Would they let her work on one without identification? That could be her way back. She could slip ashore at a US harbor—illegally, of course, but people did it all the time. She had to stay sharp and look for a chance.

Until then, she mustered the energy for her shift each day, pushing aside the pain in her heart. Serving was hard work, but it was work she knew and was good at. She'd landed at a good restaurant. The people who dined there were the right kinds of people. Perhaps, though she could not yet envision how, she might meet someone who could help her find a way back home.

Because Cartagena was *not* home. Home was wherever Ashford and Cristina were.

Alejandra kept trying to draw her out, to get her to come out with her on one of their nights off. Leila wouldn't go that far, but she found herself enjoying being drawn into the jokes and the girls' gossip. It made her feel human again. Last night, she and Alejandra had danced a cumbia together in the kitchen, to the sound of the band out in the bar. Leila found herself laughing harder than she had in weeks but felt guilty about it afterward. Work was something she could enjoy because it had a purpose. But play—dancing, going out with other girls—she couldn't do that.

But why not? Why should she feel guilty for laughing last night? A moment or two of enjoyment during a heartbroken existence was no sin. She had done nothing wrong to deserve this. She never hurt anyone in her life. Why did people want to hurt her? Why, even now, after all she had suffered, did she have to go into hiding with a false name? Must she live in fear as well as loss? She seethed with resentment toward the people who had done this to her—Samantha first and now Paulo.

Her eyes followed a pair of gulls flying low over the calm water of the harbor. A couple of boats pushed out, braving the afternoon heat.

Her anger, sadness, and fear had worked her up to the point that it was now hard to think straight sometimes. But the routine of the job helped her feel more grounded. Quiet moments like this helped too. She wondered if her confusion had made her read too much into things, particularly that encounter with Paulo. Maybe he wasn't as malicious as she remembered, not as powerful as he seemed. Maybe she was being overly cautious in trying so desperately to avoid him.

That first day was now a blur in her memory. Paulo had probably given up looking for her. He could find other girls to paint. After trying once to see if he could get her to submit to him, he would have moved on. Surely, he had better things to worry about as a police chief. Why waste his time?

She recalled the extreme caution of her letter home. Why couldn't she let her loved ones know where she was and how to contact her? They must be dying of worry, when really, she was okay. She would email them again tomorrow. She had gotten herself too scared by what happened the first time, but there were ways to do it that would be safe. She could open up a brand new email account on Hotmail or something. Paulo wasn't that sophisticated, and he surely didn't care *that* much. She had simply been careless that first day.

After emailing, she could arrange a phone call. It would be so good to hear Ashford's voice. The isolation was killing her.

She couldn't go back to America, but perhaps Ashford could visit her here, bringing Cristina. Maybe, even though it seemed too much to dream of, they could start a new life with her in Colombia.

She shook her head. She had slipped into dreams again.

That would be too much to ask from Ashford. She had already asked much more from him than he was ready for. He had a good start to his career now. Why would he want to leave America? She knew he loved her, but how long would it take for him to forget? And then Samantha really would have won.

Stop it, Leila. These were horrible thoughts, worse than the unrealistic dreams. Theirs was not a family that had any business being broken up. These were the thoughts Samantha wanted her to think. Ashford was a good man. He loved her, and he took his responsibility as a father seriously. She could no more take Cristina away from her father than he would be able to rest knowing she had been taken from her mother.

Those thoughts she'd had in the early days of her pregnancy were before she fell in love with Ashford. Now, she could no more give him up than bear the thought of being forever separated from Cristina.

Time would give them a chance to be together again. She had to keep hoping. If anyone knew dreams sometimes did come true, it was her.

She stood up, stretching her tired back and sighing. It was time to start her shift in the restaurant. One more day and night. One day closer, she had to believe, to being reunited with her daughter. She slung her bag over her shoulder—a makeshift purse filled with all her possessions. She didn't have much besides the clothes she came here in, but she couldn't leave anything at the dormitory. A woman roughly her size would not be above stealing her nice jeans or leather jacket.

She turned away from the sea and walked up to the hotel grounds.

It was Saturday. The restaurant would be busy tonight. Tomorrow was her day off, which she usually dreaded. This time, she looked forward to it a little with the thought of sending another email.

Nearing the hotel office to sign in for her shift, Leila heard an unexpected voice. It was familiar, but she couldn't place it.

"Yes, I've seen her." That was the hotel manager's voice. "She works here."

Leila froze, then slid behind the wall and crouched beneath the back window of the office. She carefully set her knee down on the gravel.

"How long?" Now, Leila placed the voice. It was Paulo's secretary and Manny's former friend, San Juan el Bautista Velasquez. Panic rose in her chest.

How did they find her? Her caution had *not* been unwarranted. She hadn't been paranoid. She hadn't been careful *enough*!

She heard another voice through the window: Alejandra—her *friend*.

"Yes, I know her. She stayed at my apartment the first few nights because she literally had nothing. She told me she was deported from the United States."

"How did she seem to you?"

"Really sad . . . upset. I would be too. She has a baby daughter they took her away from."

Leila clenched her fist. Now, Paulo would know about Cristina.

"Has she done something wrong? Is she in trouble?"

"No. But there's someone who wants to meet her."

"She should be here any minute." It was the manager again. "Her shift starts soon if you'd like to wait."

"No. I'll go. And please, don't tell her I was here."

"Whatever you say."

She heard San Juan el Bautista leaving and had a rash impulse to confront him. What harm could it do now that he knew she was here? Maybe now, away from the police station, she could convince him to help her, not to give her up to Paulo. Wasn't he once her father's friend?

But she stayed where she was behind the window. Thinking she could trust him would be more foolish than having trusted Alejandra. She would be better off acting like she knew nothing of his visit. Let them think they had her. She would work her shift, then disappear. There was no reason to go back to the dormitory. With her upcoming day off, she would have a two-day head start. One more night of Saturday tips would help too.

She touched the inside seam of her uniform pants. The bad fit was a bit of a blessing because she had space to sew in all the money she'd earned so far, as well as the knife she stole from the police headquarters. She would have to work tonight with extreme alertness, ready to dash away at the first sign of danger—ready to fight if she wasn't fast enough.

And after tonight, what then? The easiest thing would be to find a job in another hotel, but how long would it be before Paulo tracked her down again? Perhaps she should leave Cartagena, but she didn't have enough money to get far, and there would be no work outside of the city. What if Ashford and Manny were looking for her? She had to hope they were. But how would they find her before Paulo did?

She mentally counted the money she had sewn into her pants as well as tonight's expected tips. It could last her a couple of weeks, paying for daily food and the cheapest bed. By then, she would have to work again. She couldn't survive long without working. But first, she had to make herself disappear. That part she was good at. She had learned how to disappear at a very young age.

What had she done to deserve this exile? Now, not only to be taken away from her beloved, to have her own baby wrenched from her breast, but also to be hunted so that she couldn't even take the time to grieve? Had she not suffered enough as a child to earn a chance at joy?

39

"*UNA CERVEZA MAS. Este es la última.*"

San Juan el Bautista knew he should have stopped two beers ago. But he still wasn't ready to go back and face Paulo. He'd rather be a little drunk.

He didn't go far after making his discovery at the hotel. He only drove a few blocks before deciding to stay in the Getsemaní neighborhood. It would be a long drive back to the headquarters on the opposite side of the city. The open-air bar grew crowded as the Saturday evening livened up, but Juan felt his solitude as he sat alone at the end of the bar. A man like him didn't fit in around here. The beer made him less uncomfortable about it, even though each one cost twice what a beer cost in El Centro.

Paulo had been sending him to Old Town almost daily for this search. He complained about it every time. But Paulo had been right—the girl did come here for work. Paulo would be giddy when he learned what Juan had found, yet Juan was in no hurry to tell him. He would be helping Paulo ruin another person's life—just as Paulo had ruined Juan's.

Juan knew why Paulo cared so much about this girl. It was ridiculous, but after all these years, Juan understood his boss. Paulo couldn't stand to be beaten, not by anyone. He had worked so hard to track Manny and never stopped resenting Manny for escaping him. To make it worse, Manny took a girl Paulo had set his eyes on. Her falling back in his lap was more than Paulo could have dreamed of. Now that she was so close, he wouldn't rest until he found her, paying back Manny after all these years.

Juan sipped at his beer, his shoulders slouching over the bar top.

His heart burned with resentment. He hated Paulo but also needed him. He was oddly comforted by the control. Knowing this made him hate himself too.

Juan often wished he'd died that day at the Palace of Justice in Bogotá. He had dreamed of a better Colombia back then. Now, he worked for the kind of man who made it a corrupt and evil place. It was hard to remember that boy he'd been—full of vitality and hope. It changed when he started killing. With each bullet he fired, it was a little piece of himself that he killed.

Manny told him that day would make him a man. But he never said what kind of man. It turned out Manny, who ran away, became the better man, while Juan, who stood and fought, had nothing at all to be proud of.

He touched the gun under his shirt. In his youth, it felt good to carry a gun. Now, it felt ridiculous. Not being official police, he couldn't carry it openly, but Paulo had supplied him with a department-issued weapon anyway. He must have known how much Juan would have liked to kill him every day, also knowing that he would never dare.

There wasn't much to hope for anymore. Things would never change. Even simpler dreams of other men were beyond him now. He would never marry and have children. Even if he had not become unattractive—out of shape and uninteresting—he had nothing to make a woman think twice about him. There was no story about himself he could tell, no sense of humor to draw on, no talents or interests. After being a handsome boy, he doubted any woman had taken a second glance at him in the years since he got out of prison.

Juan glanced up as a group of young people came into the bar, laughing and hanging on to each other's arms. A man and a woman leaned over right beside him to order their drinks but didn't seem to notice that he was there. Anonymous as always.

All he had now were his comforts, like this warm sensation from his beer. He hated the comforts too, but he couldn't give them up. His work for Paulo allowed him to have a nice little apartment and never go wanting for food and drink. He consumed more of both every day than he should. These comforts meant something after the poverty of his youth—the poverty that drove him toward revolution to begin with. These simple comforts should have been enough to make some poor woman want to be his wife, if only there was something compelling about him.

Juan turned around on his stool, savoring the last few drops of his beer. There wasn't much to distinguish the bar from the street outside as passersby mingled briefly with the people spilling out of the crowded bar. He more intently watched the people on the sidewalk, on this side and across the street, in anticipation of the one he hoped might pass.

Because now, depressed by his thoughts and emboldened by alcohol, he didn't really want to let Paulo win. He didn't care what happened to the girl. He didn't even care about her father. Manny deserted him, after all. He had no loyalty left for Manny. But he would enjoy seeing Paulo outsmarted for once. He would like to see Paulo have to suffer with his desires just as Juan suffered with his own. It wasn't fair that Paulo always got the girl.

Getting in Paulo's way would be incredibly foolish. If he weren't drinking, it never would have crossed his mind. He wasn't smart enough to do anything without getting caught. Better to go home and suffer his loneliness in peace.

San Juan el Bautista finished his beer and stood up on wobbly knees. He stepped through the bar crowd into the street. His eyes latched on to a figure coming toward him from the other side of the street.

Even if he hadn't been watching for him, it would have been hard to miss the man with the baby strapped to his chest, who walked with tired sadness toward his lodging at the end of another fruitless day. He looked so out of place.

He had been watching this man too while searching for the girl. The blond father with bad Spanish was the newest neighborhood character. Juan had suspected a connection and now he was pretty sure of that suspicion after learning this afternoon that she had a child. He wondered if the poor man knew how everyone in Getsemaní was talking about him. Everyone knew he had been asking questions in the local hotels and restaurants. It was a wonder the girl hadn't heard about him by now.

Juan crossed the busy street and fell into step beside the man. "I often see mothers looking for their baby's father in Cartagena." He trusted that the stranger understood Spanish well enough. He himself would not have been able to say more than a word or two of English. "But you're the first father I've seen going to seek the mother."

The American looked sideways at him, surprised, maybe even afraid. "Who are you?"

San Juan el Bautista smiled. It had been a long time since someone had looked at him with fear. He savored it.

"One with open eyes."

"Stop playing around. Who are you, and what do you know? If you're trying to get money out of me, it won't work."

Juan snorted. *Typical American.* "I bet you'd pay to know where your girl is."

"What do you know about Leila?"

The man stopped and examined him. Juan stopped too. The baby looked from one to the other in confusion.

"She's here in Getsemaní."

"You've seen her!"

"Not here. Weeks ago I saw her, after she arrived in Cartagena."

"Tell me where she is."

"Why should I?"

The American grabbed his arm. The fear in his eyes had disappeared. Now, he looked angry and annoyed. Juan knew he had been foolish and was now desperate to get away. He may have been the one with the concealed gun, but he had little doubt this man could hurt him, even kill him if he wanted to, despite the baby in his arms. Such was the strength of his grip and the passion in his eyes.

"Let me go," Juan pled. Having lost his moment of power over the man, he now began to hate him. "I'm not the one who wants to hurt your *novia*. She's working in the restaurant at Hotel Caribe."

The man released his arm.

"You'd better hurry and find her before Paulo Varga does."

"That name!" Fear returned to the man's face.

Juan laughed. *"Sí. Ese nombre.* You'd better not let him find *you* either."

Juan scampered away, relieved to be free of the crazed father. It was time he told the chief what he'd discovered.

40

ASHFORD'S HEART BEAT wildly. Could Leila really be this close? After a week without hope, might his search end tonight?

He wanted to run straight to the shoreline, to find the Hotel Caribe. He remembered the name. It was on his list, but he hadn't gotten to it yet. But Cristina had started to cry, reminding him that she had needs too. Her diaper was full, and her stomach was empty. His own inn was close. He needed to take care of Cristina first.

Ashford was frustrated to be slowed down by the baby when his goal could be so close. His first week in Cartagena had been a series of frustrations. Soon, everything would prove to have been worth it.

At the front desk, Elena gave him precise directions to Hotel Caribe. "You're not thinking of leaving us, are you? They'll charge you much more."

"No. Don't worry."

And if he found Leila tonight, what would he do then? Would he bring her back here? They couldn't go home. She would still be in danger and he and the baby too. Those were not thoughts he'd taken the time to work through in his rush to find her.

Who was that drunkard tonight, and how did he know where Leila was and who *he* was? He knew about Paulo Varga too—the man Manny told him to avoid at all costs. He recalled the pickpocket and that his driver's license might still be floating out there somewhere. There was no way to know if the two encounters were connected, but he had to be more careful, even in his excitement.

With Cristina cleaned and fed, Ashford set out again. Elena looked up with intrigue as they passed the desk. Soon, Cristina was asleep against his chest, soothed by food and the steady rhythm of her father's gait.

"Sleep well, *niña*. You'll awake in your mother's arms."

The streets were still busy, loud with shouts and honks. But when he came to the hotels at the waterfront, the night was beginning to calm down. Most guests had retired to their rooms.

There it was, the sign lit against the night sky: *Hotel Caribe*.

It was a chic, modern hotel. He could see that the restaurant opened up in back. Cumbia music rang from the beach side of the hotel. It sounded like a radio instead of live musicians. He avoided the front entrance of the hotel and walked around back to the open restaurant. All the guests were gone, and the staff was cleaning up, ready to close for the night.

Ashford's breath quickened as he approached. His heart thumped. Even Cristina woke up and looked intently at the scene, sensing perhaps that something important was nigh.

About half a dozen workers were in the empty restaurant, and he saw that Leila wasn't there.

"*Hola, señor.*" A man in kitchen garb paused from his task of stacking chairs upside down on top of freshly scrubbed tables. "Do you need a room? I can take you to the hotel desk. Oh, *qué linda bebé.*"

"No. I don't need a room. I'm looking for someone who works here. Leila's her name." He paused. "Or maybe Cristina."

Ashford wished he had thought of a better way to ask his question. Still, the man was not impolite or impatient with him.

"Nobody here by either of those names. Are you sure?"

"No. She might have another name." He wondered if he should pull up a picture on his phone.

"Wait." It was a girl's voice. "I think I know who you're looking for."

Ashford looked across the restaurant as a girl in a waitress's uniform, dark and petite, with large brown eyes, walked toward them. She stopped in front of him, looking him in the eyes, then down at the baby.

"This is her child, isn't it?"

He nodded.

"I knew it had to be. She looks just like her."

"Do you know her?" Ashford's breaths came faster.

"Yes. I know her as Marissa. But that doesn't really matter. You must be her *novio*."

He nodded impatiently.

"It makes me so happy that it's you. *¡Qué romántico!* When the man came asking this afternoon . . ." She trailed off. Ashford wasn't sure he understood her Spanish correctly. "She's in the back. Follow me."

They hurried across the restaurant, through to the back of the kitchen, where a few clothes racks stood mostly empty.

No one was there. The clatter and splash of dishwashing sounded close by.

"Let me check the ladies' room." The girl disappeared through a door and reappeared a moment later. "How strange. I just saw her back here a few minutes ago."

Ashford froze. Yes, she *had* been here. There was an unmistakable sense of her in the air. It couldn't really be her scent, with the heavy odors of old food, dish soap, and the sea hovering in the air. Still, he did sense something that was unmistakably *her,* like she had just left the area. She was still close. He knew it.

"Which way would she have gone?"

"To the bus stop. I'll walk you there."

"We'd better hurry."

They came toward the front of the kitchen, where the full restaurant was in view.

"Ah, there's your friend. The one you sent this afternoon to ask about her. Perhaps he's seen her."

"What?" Ashford stopped. "I didn't send anyone."

"Yes, you did. Who else . . ." The girl seemed to realize the truth just as Ashford looked across and saw the drunk from earlier tonight entering the restaurant, trailed by another man. She grabbed his arm and pulled him down behind a sink counter.

"Where can I hide?"

"There's no good place. I can't sneak you out the back from this way either. Stay here. I'll try to send them away." She paused. "Tell her I'm sorry. I'm so sorry for telling that man about her. I didn't know."

Ashford nodded, hoping this would be over quick. Each moment lost would take Leila farther way.

But the moments ticked on and on. He heard voices from the men out front, then heard the voice of the girl who had hidden him. He knew she would not expose him, but the man from the kitchen, whom he first spoke to, wasn't as cautious. A voice thundered over the others.

"*¡Un bebé!* A baby here in Cartagena!" Then he laughed. Once he started, he couldn't stop. It was a cruel, wicked laugh that chilled Ashford to the bone. Cristina gasped and looked like she would cry.

"No, Cristina," he whispered. "Please don't cry." He rocked her close to his face. He could see the fear in her eyes.

"Is he still here? Where did he go?"

The voice was closer now—at the edge of the kitchen. This had to be Paulo Varga.

Ashford held Cristina close and knew from the look in her wide, terrified eyes that she wouldn't cry. Even the smallest children know the look and sound of evil. Her infant instincts knew better than to cry out in the nightmare, when the monster still didn't know she was there.

Ashford heard the man's breath now, across the wide double sink. He listened. They were both there, the second man's breath coming quicker and, with it, the scent of beer. Then they passed, and across the gap he saw them on the other side of the kitchen, walking toward the back. This was his chance.

Cradling Cristina in front of him, he ran low through the restaurant and out into the darkness as the remaining waitstaff looked on in surprise. He heard the waitress's voice once more as he hurried away.

"I told you he had already gone."

Back in his room at Casa Azul, Cristina fell asleep almost immediately, having forgotten her waking nightmare. Ashford wept. It was the first time since Leila's disappearance that he gave in to his tears. He had tried so hard to stay strong for Cristina, but his strength had reached its limit.

Leila had been so close, but now she was truly gone. After tonight, she would hide better. He didn't have the remotest idea where he would start searching next. How could he hope to outsmart Paulo Varga and his men? He would even have to outsmart Leila herself, since she had no idea he was looking for her.

He missed her with every bone in his body and every beat of his heart. He couldn't bear the thought that she might be lost to him forever.

41

THE LIGHT OF dawn filtered into the church. A glow lit the high windows above the white arches of the nave and the four long, narrow windows behind the altar.

Leila awoke, her body aching after sleeping on the hardwood pew. She had changed into the jeans, gray T-shirt, and leather jacket that she had arrived. Her uniform from the restaurant at Hotel Caribe made a pillow beneath her head. She had saved it only for this and would now discard it.

The light began to illuminate the features of the church—dark pews against bright-white columns, walls, and ceiling. The beginning of a new day.

Another day without hope. Another day without love.

As her eyes blinked open, she looked up at the statue of the Blessed Virgin Mary that she had slept under after leaving the restaurant in the middle of the night. The face of the statue had gentle, sad eyes, but the plaster made them look glazed over.

Leila felt that way now. She was growing numb to the endless parade of sadness. She couldn't cry anymore. She wanted to. She wanted to feel the viscerality that tears could give to her sorrow.

Her eyes remained on the statue of the sad mother. *Stabat mater, doloroso.* That was her life now, a mother whose sorrow was becoming her identity.

Leila thought of her own mother, who died before Leila could make many memories of her. Paulo had told her once that her mother died of AIDS, and that was possible, even probable, although her death occurred long before the disease had a name in the slums.

A legacy of sadness had been passed down from one young mother to another. Leila had often longed to talk to her mother in her quiet hours. She ached to feel a spiritual connection with her now. She would have liked to try to pray with Mother Mary, here at this beautiful statue, as so many others did. Her father told her that kind of communion with the dead was not only possible, but essential. She knew it comforted Manny to think of his lost loved ones in the communion of saints. Leila longed to believe it, now more than ever.

It grew ever more likely that her own daughter would also grow up with no memory of her mother. Leila's heartache would be passed on to Cristina more easily than her love. Of all her worries during the early days of her pregnancy, *this* never once crossed her mind: to bring a child into the world with so much love, only for the bond to be severed. It would take a miracle to bring their family back together now.

Leila had survived without a mother. So would Cristina. But it shouldn't have had to be that way. Everything she ever did, all her work and plans and goals, had been toward one thing only: to give her child a good life. That was why she chose loneliness for so long, trying not to love until she was ready.

She always knew her opportunities were not to be taken for granted for a single moment. Her own mother had lacked those chances. The gift of life was all she could hope to give Leila. But

Leila's daughter should have gotten so much more. They were *that close* to having a wonderful life together.

Everything was lost. Everything was wasted.

She couldn't even bring herself to cry about it.

Yes, Cristina would be okay. Ashford would be a good father and give her all the opportunities an American girl should have. She had no doubt Ashford's heart was broken for her now, but years would pass instead of weeks. One day he would marry again . . . no . . . he would marry for the *first* time. He deserved that— another woman who would be a good replacement mother for Cristina. There would always be a hint of sorrow in her, but she would not know everything she had missed out on from losing her real mother. She would never feel the great love her mother had for her.

While Cristina would be fine in the end, Leila would never recover. She knew that for a fact. Perhaps she would continue to escape from Paulo, but she was starting to feel like it wasn't worth being afraid of him anymore. She was already beaten. The people who hated her—Samantha, Paulo—had won. Her life might as well end now.

She once asked her father how he managed to go on, after losing his wife and child. How did he ever learn to love again? The difference for Manny was that death had forced him to start over. It wasn't that way for her. While Ashford and Cristina lived, she would never be able to move past her love for them.

Manny said love was always worth it. He must have been wrong. Yet as she tried to imagine her life before meeting Ashford—tried to wish she was still in her comfortable apartment in Phoenix, with a lonely, simple, and prosperous life—she couldn't bring herself to wish none of this had happened. She had many regrets. So many little things drove her crazy wondering if she could have done this or that differently to avoid starting down the road that had led her here. But she could not wish she had never met Ashford and known his love. She could not wish to not have brought Cristina into the world. Those were bonds she could only regret in their loss.

So, was love worth it?

Leila remembered a night, only two years ago, though it could have been from a different lifetime. That night she went home from work late, after unexpectedly catching Ashford's eyes in the parking lot while he waited for his mother. That was the night she dared to ask herself if life could mean more. In many ways, that question was the start of all this. She didn't want to go back to loneliness now that she knew how much life could mean. But how could there be meaning anymore without *them*?

She stood up, stretched, then found the restroom to wash her hair and tie it back as best she could. The old uniform went into the wastebasket. She returned to sit in the same pew.

Somehow, today, she would go on. This day would pass and so would the next. The instinct to survive and protect herself would drive her to find another place to live and another place to work. The smart thing would be to leave the city, to take a bus up the coast to Barranquilla or even Santa Marta. She could start over someplace where Paulo would never look for her. But what sort of life would she be starting? What would be the point? How would she grasp for hope? Survival alone wasn't enough.

She heard the doors around the church starting to open. A man's footfall sounded on the stones, and then a fan was switched on. She turned and watched as he turned on eight or ten more fans around the sanctuary. An old woman with black lace covering her head puttered down the center aisle and sat near the front of the church. Soon, people in groups began to enter, and in half an hour the church was about a third full. A few of the men gave Leila a second glance, even though she knew she must have looked like a mess. But for the most part, she went unnoticed—the first one there for the first Sunday Mass, no one suspecting she had been there all night. Her anonymity was her disguise, but she was weary of it. She craved identity, a name, people to love.

A family of five filled up the rest of her pew. The mother looked at Leila, smiled, and offered a friendly *"Buenos días. Paz de Cristo."* Leila smiled. The small gesture was a little drop of salve for her parched and chafing heart.

She hadn't planned on staying for the Mass, but after the greeting from the woman in her pew, she wanted to. The liturgy was familiar and comforting. The Scripture readings were full of hope. Most comforting of all was the community that surrounded her with a spirit of companionship and love. Maybe in time she could become part of something like that again. She imagined coming here and being known: smiles, kisses on the cheek, *'Paz de Cristo,' 'Y con tu espíritu.'* It was in such small ways that one learned to build their life again after everything had been lost.

42

THE DAYS WERE beginning to run together for Ashford. The monotony was unbearable. It felt like he had been in Cartagena far longer than three weeks.

His Spanish grew better, and his skin grew darker. It was a different kind of sun here, so close to the equator, and he noticed how different his tan was than in Arizona.

Since the night at Hotel Caribe, there had been no trace of Leila, not even a clue to point him in the right direction. Before that night, he had been methodical in his search, checking off likely hotels and restaurants from his list, narrowing down the places where she might have found work. That plan had now been thrown out the window. His search had expanded to other parts of the city. He had talked to social workers and immigration officers, but nobody had seen her or heard anything about her— at least, not that they were willing to admit to him.

He couldn't help questioning the usefulness of what he was doing. How long could he keep going on like this, spinning his wheels? His money was almost gone. Soon, he would have to ask Manny to send more if he was going to stay.

That was the question he hadn't wanted to ask. How long *should* he stay? The question was necessary now, for Cristina's sake more than his own. He took good care of her but knew this was difficult for a baby in such a key time of her development. Was it time to go home and regroup?

Today, Cristina was stuffy. She seemed sensitive to the recent shift in the weather. According to Elena, the summer rains would start soon. Neither of them were used to this humidity after the dry heat of Arizona. Ashford reached his handkerchief up to dab the baby's nose as they walked back toward the hotel. It was nothing more than a cold but another reminder that this wasn't a suitable way to raise a child.

A few days before, he had contacted the local hospital to ask about work. He could stay for ninety days without a visa; after that, he would need a work permit. He had meant the hospital call merely as an exploration of options, but they were eager to bring him in for an interview. He declined.

He also emailed an agent from Doctors Without Borders, who responded with equal eagerness. There was a pressing need for qualified nurses at the city hospital and in the fieldwork going on in the poor barrios in the southern part of the city. The thought of working was enticing, especially here, where he knew his abilities would be put to good use. But how would that help him find Leila? The purpose of his being here wasn't to carve out a life for himself in Cartagena. It was to find Leila. After weeks of failure, the singlemindedness of his task became exhausting. His search had lost its focus.

There was another problem with the idea of working. It would force him to find childcare for Cristina. He wasn't willing to do that. In all these weeks, he hadn't let her out of his sight for a second.

Returning through the lobby of Casa Azul, Elena looked up from the desk but didn't greet him. After all this time, Ashford and his baby had ceased to be interesting to those who saw them every day.

He had almost left this little inn twice: first out of fear for his own and Cristina's safety, then because he thought it was time for cheaper lodging. He had talked himself out of the first fear. After the night at Hotel Caribe, Ashford realized how useless it would be to hide. The drunk had made that clear to him earlier that same night. Everyone around here knew who he was. He couldn't search for Leila from the shadows.

If Paulo Varga had wanted to hurt him, he would have done it already. He didn't dare. Ashford and Cristina were American citizens with all the protections that came from that status. Technically, they were tourists. He knew where the embassy was if there was danger. He was safe out in the open, and Cristina was safe as long as she was with him. They knew who he was and where he was. There was nothing he could do about it. But there was nothing much they could do to him either.

How ironic that he relied on his American status for protection, when the only reason for being here was because those protections had been taken away from the woman he loved.

He had also put off the question of cheaper lodging. After mentioning to Elena that he was looking to move, she had talked to the owner and they offered him a cheaper rate because of his long-term stay. He couldn't have done much better in this part of town. Short of renting an apartment, he was better off staying here.

Back in the room, Ashford set Cristina in the middle of the big bed. She was smart enough not to fall off, but if she got too close to the edge, Ashford had rapid instincts to protect her. When he first arrived, he had intended to buy a crib for her, but after one, then another night of her sleeping in the bed with him, he never did. After a while, it only seemed like something he was *supposed* to do. She always slept in the space between his arm and his body. He invariably awoke the moment she did, and even in sleep, he never let her roll away from him or over onto her stomach. Eventually, it would be hard for her to learn to sleep on her own, but that was a worry for another time. They had enough worries now, and both needed the comfort the other gave.

It was hard to believe that she was nearly ten months old.

Ashford had grown used to this little room, with its creamy yellow walls, the big colorful quilt, the wood desk that needed a new coat of stain, the simple wood chair that was surprisingly comfortable. On the walls hung a few black-and-white pictures of people; he had no idea if they were historical figures or family pictures of the hotel's owners. There was a sink in the room, under the window. The toilets were right outside their room, shared by the rest of the floor. For what it was, it was as comfortable as could be.

With one eye on Cristina, Ashford opened the curtain and looked down at the street. Early evening traffic buzzed around. Nothing looked out of the ordinary. It was instinctual to look for people watching him, even though he had never seen anyone around here. If they were monitoring him, they knew how to keep out of sight. They were professionals, after all. He was in this way over his head.

What could be worse than finding Leila, only to lead these wicked men straight to her and not be man enough to protect her? Flying down here had felt brave and valiant. Nothing about this felt that way anymore.

Through it all, he tried to remember things Leila would have said to encourage him. She would have known something to say now.

How he longed for the music of her voice. How he longed for her touch, the smell of her hair, the taste of her lips, the smoothness of her skin against his.

Last night, he dreamed about her. They were together

somewhere, but he couldn't remember if it was their apartment in Santa Fe or an unknown place. It didn't matter. What mattered was how real it felt to be together. Every detail about her was crystal clear. The dream was romantic and sensual. He woke up just as they were about to make love.

What if he never found her? It was a thought he'd never wanted to consider, but it had begun to force itself on him. How many weeks, months, or even years would it be until his memories of her were not so clear, first lost in waking, then not even clear in his dreams?

What about Cristina? How much had she already lost of her memories of her mother?

Ashford set some water to boil in the electric kettle he kept in the room, then took a clump of leaves out of his pocket. It was *yerba santa,* or "bear's weed," which he first spotted in a nearby park soon after arriving in Cartagena. It was a moment of rare pleasure to spot a plant he remembered from his studies on herbal medicine. Today, he had gone back there, knowing the plant could help break up mucus in the respiratory system. While the water boiled, he chopped up the leaves and put a little into a cup and the rest into a jar.

"Daddy's going to make you feel better, okay?"

He made the tea, not too hot, then strained it into her sippy cup and mixed it with a bit of lemon and agave. He placed the jar with the rest of the chopped leaves on the windowsill. It was the third one, next to some aloe he had saved and a handful of palm berries.

Ashford shook his head. So, his collection was already starting here too. If only Leila could see this.

He took the cup of medicinal tea over to the bed and propped the baby's head up on his arm, helping her swallow it. She enjoyed the warm, soothing drink and tried to drink it faster until some of it dribbled down her chin. Ashford laughed.

"Okay, that's enough. I'll make you more later."

Soon, she breathed without sniffling.

"Daddy will always take care of you. I love you. Do you know that, *niña*?"

Here in Colombia, it may not have been a creative nickname for a baby, but it had become Ashford's favorite for her.

"Your mama loves you too. More than you can imagine. Never forget that. She's thinking about you right now. Cristina, never forget your mama."

"Mama," said the baby so clearly that Ashford jumped.

His heart was broken and filled with joy in the same moment. She had not forgotten . . . not yet. But oh, how much longer did the mother and the child have to live apart?

The next day, Ashford called Manny. At the start, their calls had happened daily. Now, they happened maybe once or twice a week. Ashford knew why. He was embarrassed to have nothing to report to Manny for his time here, no good news to encourage the heartbroken father.

He didn't tell Manny about Cristina's first word. That was a moment he needed to share with Leila or with no one. After admitting to Manny that he was out of ideas, he was surprised to hear something like resignation in Manny's tone.

"Maybe it's time to take a step back and think this all through. I wonder if we're going about this the wrong way?"

"What other way is there?" Ashford asked.

"Maybe it's time to let *her* come looking for *us* . . . when she's ready."

After hanging up, Ashford thought long and hard about Manny's choice of words. He had been thinking the same thing but couldn't admit it, even to himself. But after all this time, wasn't he just being stubborn? His chance to find Leila was that night at Hotel Caribe, and he hadn't been quick enough. That sort of chance wouldn't come again. Now, what was he even hoping for: To outsmart Paulo Varga and his men? To uncover whatever hiding place Leila had found, only to put her back in danger?

Manny understood all of this. Ashford was beginning to. The facts were hard to face but couldn't be ignored forever.

He and Cristina had only left the room briefly this morning, to buy a little food. Now, she slept while he sat next to her on the bed. After another cup of yerba santa tea, her congestion was pretty well gone.

If only he could let Leila know he was here. If only she knew how hard he was trying to find her. Perhaps it could give her the hope she needed. How could he give up, when she might be mere blocks away? But on the other hand, she might not even be in Cartagena anymore. It would have been smart for her to leave.

It wouldn't be giving up. It would be waiting until the right time. At least in Arizona, Leila would know how to contact him if she chose.

He looked down and stroked his baby's sleeping head. She would be better off there. After all, his duty was to his child. Even Leila would agree. He couldn't live this way forever. It had already gone on too long.

"What do you think, *niña*? Do you want to go home?"

43

MANNY WAS ALONE when the letter arrived. It was only the second letter since Leila's deportation, and the first since Ashford went down to Cartagena. Since the incident at Hotel Caribe, Ashford had had no new leads and Manny had run out of things to suggest to him or ways to encourage him. In the last few days, they had started to plan for Ashford's return. Neither of them liked it, but there hardly seemed to be a choice.

Manny tore into the envelope, wondering if this would change things.

Dear Ashford, Manny, and Carmen,

I had hoped to write you again much sooner, but my ordeal in Colombia has made it impossible. It has been all I can do to survive and avoid the people who are looking for me. Yet it feels worthless to stay alive without you, the people I love.

I nearly emailed you several times, but while in the city, I always stopped myself out of fear. I left Cartagena for a while and while it was safer for me out of the city, it was difficult to find work. There were only a few odd jobs. I plan to return to Cartagena in a few days. I am almost out of money and need consistent work again, despite the danger I feel there. I try to stay optimistic. At the bus station, I saw an advertisement for talent acquisition on the cruise lines. I am going to attend the event next Saturday. Perhaps if I can get work on a cruise ship I can find my way back to America.

There is still no address that I can give you to write back to me, but I think a call would be safe. I would love nothing more than to hear your voices and say some words to Cristina. There is a church, Santa Cruz de Marga, where I went to Mass once before leaving the city. I will go back next Sunday. That should give enough time for you to receive this. If you call after the morning Mass and ask for Sylvia Nuñez, I will be waiting for the call.

I love you all so much and cannot describe how much my heart yearns to be with you. Perhaps hearing your voices will bring back a portion of my hope.

With all my love,

Leila

Manny checked the postmark date. It was already Saturday. He could call her at the church tomorrow. Better yet, Ashford could go there in person and find her at last. But he hesitated to call Ashford right away. Sending him there might be the most foolish thing in the world. If Paulo was watching him, it would lead him right to Leila, and their desire to see each other could lead both of them into a trap.

A trap.

Something didn't feel right. Manny read the letter again.

Talent acquisition. The phrase jumped out at him. His mind raced back over fifteen years as he repeated the words.

It came to him—why the words were so familiar and haunting. He remembered Paulo sitting on his couch, with that toothy smirk on his face, leaning forward, handing Manny a business card. What was it that it said? Manny racked his brain until his memory brought it back. *Estrella de Indias: Ascenso de Talento.* A horrified thought began to play in his mind. The trap was not set for Sunday at the church, it was at the talent event. Could it be that she was walking into Paulo's trap a day earlier, Saturday . . . *today*?

Manny got online and did a Google search, but Paulo's business had no website or online advertising. That was to be expected. He changed it to an image search, and then he found something. Someone had posted a photograph of a poster hanging in Cartagena last week. It was an advertisement for a talent event. On it he saw the dreaded words again: *Estrella de Indias.* There were pictures of smiling girls in uniforms, with a drawing of a palm-lined beach and a cruise ship in the background. "Find the job of your dreams," read the photographed flyer. It looked just like that old business card—Paulo's trap to lure poor young girls in search of a legitimate job, only to find it was something very different. Leila was about to become his next victim.

He zoomed in on the picture to read the date of the event. Yes, it was happening today.

"No, no, no," he said out loud. He lurched for his phone and dialed Ashford. There was no answer.

He dialed again. "Pick up, boy, pick up!"

44

SHE HAD TO come back, despite the danger here. The city of her childhood comforted her. Cartagena was all she had left.

Even if today proved fruitless, she would be able to find work again. She would have to; her money was just about gone.

She had spent almost two weeks between three small towns on the Caribbean Coast. They weren't much more than fishing villages. The people she met were kind, but there was little they could do to help her. There was no work and little contact with the outside world, certainly no internet cafés. In one of the villages, the only phone was at the courthouse. When someone received a call, the entire town knew about it. She couldn't stay anonymous in a place like that. Paulo would hear about her eventually. It was better to be back in Cartagena.

The trip back had taken longer than Leila expected—repairs on the main road into the city had sent the bus on a reroute through the hill country, delaying it two hours. She walked from the bus stop toward the inner-harbor docks. According to the address on the flyer, she needed to go to Isla de Manzanillo, across the transversal bridge. She could have taken another bus, but she hesitated to pay a second fare. Every coin was precious now. She could walk the rest of the way and still get there before the end of the event. The afternoon sky was dark; it smelled like rain would come on fast. She wore the same jeans and heeled sandals that had come to Colombia with her and a new black blouse that was already showing signs of wear. Her few spare clothes and possessions were light in the bag on her shoulder.

After more than a month in Colombia, she was beginning to feel like a native again. She remembered old phrases and mannerisms from her childhood and picked up more current ones from the people around her. Nobody would have guessed she had been away for so long.

As she neared the inlet, she saw an American cruise ship docked to the north. It would probably be sailing back to Galveston or Fort Lauderdale. Maybe . . . if only . . .

That was what she was coming here today to find out.

A glimmer of hope stirred in Leila's heart. Today could be the start of something. And tomorrow, if Manny and Ashford called her at the church, perhaps she could give them some good news. If her father had received her latest letter, he would surely call. She hoped Ashford was there in Phoenix too. She would love to hear his voice. She needed the assurance of his love. She knew he loved her, but it was lonely not to hear him say it. What was the name she had told them to ask for again—Sylvia? It all felt so ridiculous. She should have arranged a phone call sooner. It couldn't be that dangerous. Her paranoia had clouded her senses.

On the bridge, she saw a group of girls coming toward her.

"Have you come from the talent fair?" she asked them. "Is it still going on?"

"Don't waste your time, *muchacha*. Those idiots don't know what they're looking for."

"Is it that bad?"

"Not worth waiting for the rain that's coming. That's not the type of place where you find legitimate work."

She was surprised to hear a man's voice close behind her.

"Go on," he said. She turned around. The man was tall and lean, with curly hair and a short beard. He had appeared on the bridge out of nowhere. "You're just the kind of girl they're looking for."

"What does that mean?"

"Go if you want, but you'll see," said the other girl, and the group moved on down the bridge.

Leila walked a few steps farther, then looked back. The man waved at her, motioning her to continue. Then he lit a cigarette and leaned against the railing.

Memories of her childhood stirred as she walked onto the urban island. She and her friends used to come here to swim at the beach on hot days. This was where the locals came, to a beach lined with trees instead of the gleaming white hotels on the peninsula. No one would be here swimming today. A sharp wind off the water reminded her that it would be pouring rain any minute. She reached into her bag and put on her leather jacket, then hurried toward her destination. The girl on the bridge was right. It was a surprising place for a talent search or a job fair—unless it was for *that* kind of job.

She reached the destination, feeling suddenly wary. It was a simple single-story, aluminum-front building with a jungle park creeping right up to the back of it. Two barred windows framed the front door. There was no signage except for a crudely hung poster reading *Estrella de Indias* and the same picture she had seen on the flyer at the bus station. A few girls milled around in front, but not as many as she had expected to see. Was she too late? Had the talent event already happened? Or did the impending storm scare everyone away?

She crossed the street as the first raindrops began to fall. This really didn't feel right. The front door opened just as Leila reached the group at the side of the house. A girl walked out.

"What's going on in there?" Leila asked her.

"It's very disorganized. I don't know if those guys are *legítimo* or just a couple of pimps, but it seems safe enough. They took my number and said they might have a modeling job for me. That's not what I came here for." The girl looked up at the sky. "It's only an art studio in there. Give it a try and see if they like you—if you don't mind the rain." She walked away.

An art studio.

She walked up to the window and looked through the iron bars. She didn't see anyone at first, only some pictures on the walls. Portraits of women.

Terror seized her and froze her where she stood. She knew those portraits. Every face looked lifeless, awful, like the one she had seen of herself in her nightmares. She couldn't tear her eyes away. Her feet were rooted to the ground as if it *was* a nightmare.

A man walked into the room. It was San Juan el Bautista Velasquez. For a moment, their eyes held. He looked afraid too. He turned.

"She's here!"

In her panic, Leila didn't know which way to run.

The front door opened again.

"The rest of the auditions are canceled. Go home before the rain starts."

Girls began to disperse around her. *No, girls, don't go.* Her paralysis broke, and she hurried away from the front door, around the side of the building. She turned straight into Paulo Varga.

She gasped. She tried to cry, but the shock knocked the breath out of her lungs. In one motion, Paulo wrapped his long arm around her and ushered her through the side door into the house.

She was standing in the center of the bare room, with Paulo at the side door and his secretary now guarding the front door.

Raindrops thundered onto the aluminum roof. Ghastly women's faces looked down at her from the walls. She would have cried to the girls for help, but no one would have heard through the pounding rain. They were surely all running away from the place now.

"*La Alta,* I knew you'd come."

She'd been such a fool, walking right into his trap. She took a deep breath. Her knees started to steady. She clenched her fists.

"You've been so cruel to me, running away, hiding." He began to pull paints and brushes out of a crate. "I never wanted to hurt you. You were wrong to be afraid of me."

She still had the knife in the inner pocket of her jacket. But he probably had a weapon too and would know better how to use it.

"But what's past is past. I can forgive. Now, you're here and we can finally start. I've actually started already." He propped a mounted canvas on the crate against the wall. It had a blue background and the shape of a woman's shoulders and bust in a colorful dress—some old-fashioned folkloric costume. But where the head should have been, the canvas was blank. It looked grotesque.

"Put this on." Paulo thrust a colorful mass of coarse fabric into her hands. It was obviously the dress in the picture. Was this the kind of clothing he thought made a girl look pretty?

The idea of her face filling that hole horrified her.

"I'm not putting on your fucking dress." She threw it down. He could rape her, he could kill her, but she wasn't going to indulge his fetish. She would not stand here and let the nightmare come true.

Paulo grabbed her wrist. She let him and looked him in the eyes, refusing to grimace from the pain of his clutch.

"You are the daughter of a whore. How dare you."

"I am the daughter of Manuel del Sol."

"The daughter of a coward, a traitor. That's even worse."

She resisted the urge to hit him with her free hand. That was what he would expect her to do. He was too strong for her. Her wrist was being crushed, but she would not show him her pain. She kept staring at him, matching the hatred in his eyes with her own. She doubted any woman had looked at him like this before.

He would let go of her wrist and that would be her chance, maybe her only chance.

She knew he had let go when the blood rushed back into her hand through the bruised veins. He was still inches away from her. She lifted her knee as hard as she could into his crotch. He wailed and crumpled to the floor.

She rushed toward San Juan el Bautista at the door. He instinctively stepped out of her way.

"You're fucking useless," she heard Paulo say to him as she fled out into the rain.

She ran away from the house. She wouldn't have much time. She had to get across the bridge into the main part of town where there might be safety in crowds. The girls were long gone. The streets, busy half an hour before, were empty now as the rain pounded down.

Leila reached the edge of the bridge and saw that the bearded man who had sent her on was still there, standing in the downpour as if he didn't care. He saw her coming and started walking her way.

She stopped, panting. What a trap Paulo had set for her. That was the only bridge off the island. She turned and ran toward the beach. It was probably half a mile to the jungle park where she could hide. That might be too far. If only she had started that way first.

Paulo shouted her name behind her. His voice sounded far away, but when she heard footsteps splashing on the pavement, she knew he was gaining on her. Her lungs burned.

Fear and pain worked to cloud her thoughts. She forced herself to think, calling up the instincts of her childhood. If she could not outrun him, she had to hide. If she could not hide, she would have to fight. He may have been faster and stronger, but desperation was a powerful equalizer.

She reached the sand of the deserted beach. She couldn't hear the steps behind her through the rain and her own sharp, painful breaths. But she knew he had to catch her soon. The storm clouds had turned the afternoon as dark as evening. The rain plastered her hair to her cheeks and her jeans to her aching legs. There was nowhere to escape. She would never make it to the darkness of the jungle park. He was too close behind her.

Leila reached for the knife inside her coat. She pulled it out and whipped around in the same motion. Paulo crashed into her. She fell to the sand as she worked the blade out of its sheath, too slow to swing at him before he realized what she was doing.

He lunged for her arm, but she was able to twist away. From the ground, she slashed back at him with the knife, but he hopped away from her, then kicked, knocking her down into the sand. The knife slipped out of her hand.

"I know that knife, you thief!" Paulo jerked her up to her feet, then threw her down toward the water. She landed in the windswept surf, feeling her head submerge briefly as it fell back against the packed sand. He splashed in toward her, lifting her up by the shoulders as she tried to kick and swing at him.

"I only wanted to love you!"

With her wrists in his grasp, she tried to swing an elbow at his cheek, but it only tapped him meekly. He responded by punching her in the stomach. She buckled over, the wind knocked out of her. Her hands and knees hit the wet sand.

"Please, Paulo. For the love of God!"

He grabbed her waist from behind, then slapped the back of her head. "I'll forgive everything if you just let me love you." He pulled her up close against him, then threw her face first into the water and crashed in after her.

His weight came down on top of her. He grabbed her arms but then released one of them as his hand groped and tugged at the buttons at the front of her jeans. She threw her free elbow back but missed.

Noises blared in her ears: his shouts, her cries, the waves, the rain, thunder.

She never heard the shot.

Then his grip was no longer as tight. He fell onto her, but his weight was without force. She flipped him off of her and he lay in the surf, his face cast in confusion and hate. Blood seeped into the water.

San Juan el Bautista stood over him, a gun in his hand, wheezing from his run.

"*¡Maricón!* I've wanted to do that for twenty years."

Leila scrambled to the dry sand. Still on her knees, lacking the strength to stand, she looked back toward Paulo, who tried to lift his torso. The plume of blood from his side expanded and dispersed in the stormy waves. His mouth opened, but he couldn't speak. His expression was shocked, unbelieving, furious. He hovered for a moment, then fell back, and the flame was gone from his eyes.

"You'd better go while you can." San Juan el Bautista's voice sounded distant against the crashing surf.

"What will you do? You'll go back to prison for this."

"Perhaps. Perhaps not. He had many enemies. I won't be the first they'll think of."

He reached down for Paulo's foot and gave it a push. The waves took his body for a moment, but the next one brought it back.

Leila found her feet.

"Thank you."

"I didn't do it for you. I did it for me."

She started back on the beach in the direction she'd come.

"You should know . . ." Juan started to say.

"Yes?"

"Never mind. Get out of here before anyone comes."

She walked away. Her legs felt like jelly, her lungs breathed in knives, and the bruises of Paulo's violence began to smart all over her body. Rain still fell hard, simultaneously chilling her skin and soothing her pain.

Leila stopped one more time after walking about thirty yards. She looked back. San Juan el Bautista talked inaudibly as he shoved again at Paulo's body, which the sea seemed intent to leave on the beach. His gun hung on his hand by the trigger.

She turned and hurried as fast as her battered legs would take her away from the gruesome scene. The man on the transversal bridge was gone when she got there.

45

LEILA AWOKE FROM one of the soundest nights of sleep in her life. The discomfort of a wooden bed didn't bother her. She had slept on worse. She sat up and looked around. This little church comforted her now, just as it had once before. She stretched her legs and arms, waiting for the pains from yesterday's fight to make themselves known in her limbs. It didn't feel as bad as she'd expected.

What a day that was!

Exhausted, soaked, and sore, she had left Isla de Manzanillo in an emotional daze. Not knowing where else to go, she had walked to Alejandra's apartment. Alejandra had been at work, but her grandmother had let her take a shower and had rubbed some aloe vera on her bruises.

Despite Alejandra's grandmother's offer to let her stay the night, Leila had kissed Alejandra's baby daughter and left. Perhaps in the coming days she would get in touch with her friend, but she didn't have the strength to answer any questions now, and Alejandra would be curious. This morning, it was better to wake up alone. So, she had come here to the church that once gave her a little hope after all had seemed lost.

Hope should have been abundant now that fear was gone. Paulo Varga was dead; he would never haunt her again. But the new circumstances of her life still needed some piecing together. After all, she was still here, so far away from her real home. The man she loved was still far away across the sea. Her own daughter—the bones of her bones, the flesh of her flesh—still seemed lost to her forever. The cloud of fear had been lifted, but hope would take more time.

Leila sat up in the pew when she saw the light start to come in. A sharp ache ran up her left leg when she put her feet on the floor.

She waited, listening for the sacristan to come in, just like the last time, and turn on all the fans. She watched for the woman with the lace on her head to enter first and walk to the front. Each entrance happened like clockwork. She liked this church. But she didn't want to stay for Mass this time.

As the church started to fill, she slipped out by the side door. Her bag of things was damp against her shoulder. Later, she would lay out her waterlogged jeans and jacket in the sun to let them dry. She reached into her shorts pocket for her dwindling bills and coins. She could afford a little breakfast. By tonight, if everything went well, she would start earning tips again. She walked up the block toward a café she'd spotted the last time she was here, intent on a cup of coffee and a roll. There was enough time before the end of Mass—and hopefully a call from her family.

The morning was warm and fresh. The air was clean after yesterday's rain, still evaporating from the stones in the early sunshine. The flowers in their pots opened brightly. It would be a hot day with the pleasantness of recent rain and a Caribbean Sea breeze. As a girl, these kinds of mornings used to inspire her to dream about all the possibilities life could hold. It was that way again today. Just like in her childhood, her dreams seemed impossible. If those dreams could come true—and they did—then why couldn't these?

Without fear, she could dream about so many new possibilities. A job could mean more than cash in her pocket. It could really be the start of something. Maybe she could transition from waitressing into real estate here, just like she did before. Once she was established, perhaps she could appeal the revocation of her US visa. She didn't know how that worked, but it was something she could actually think about now.

She didn't have to be so lonely anymore either. She could meet friends without being afraid of them giving up her secrets. She could establish contact with Ashford. If today's call didn't work out—she didn't know if the church could even take a foreign call—then she could email him without feeling afraid. Even in separation, some contact would encourage her in immeasurable ways.

Yes, there *was* a little bit of hope now. Her mind felt clear too as she realized how paranoid she had become. Everything was different compared to yesterday. Even the searing pain all over her body hardly bothered her.

She savored her cup of coffee and her breakfast roll, able to enjoy the simple luxury as more than mere sustenance. She took her time spreading butter on her roll. Delicious. She looked around at the people coming in and out of the café, feeling a desire to know people here and make friends.

The sun was bright against the white outer walls and red trim of the church as Leila returned from the café. There wasn't much movement about with Mass still going on inside. The red-brick square glistened, as did the green leaves of the shrubs in the courtyard, healthy and vibrant after yesterday's rain. She paused at the iron fence at the edge of the churchyard.

Did she see this? Was she hallucinating?

The whole field of her vision glowed, brighter than the sun

would have made it. For a moment, she couldn't move. What her eyes saw, her brain told her she couldn't possibly be seeing. Was it a mirage of the sun? Was she dreaming? She grabbed at the fence to steady her shaking legs.

Her vision returned to normal, and he was still there. It was real. She ran into the churchyard as he leaped up from his bench.

"Ashford! You're really here." She rushed into his arms, still half-unbelieving until she felt him against her, surrounded by his familiar arms and lips, and Cristina—so much bigger now—gathered between them in one embrace. Her tears poured. Her heart thumped wildly.

This man. This child. Where to caress? Where to kiss? She devoured them with her hands, lips, and cheeks. She was blown away by joy. They were both here . . . now. It was so far beyond anything she had dared to dream.

Finally, she pulled her face away from the delight of them, her lost family, and tried to wipe the stream of tears off her cheeks. Leila and Ashford looked at each other for a long moment—smiling, laughing, crying. There was so much to say, but at the same time, nothing that needed saying.

His tears told her how much he had suffered from their separation too. His skin color told her that he had been in Colombia for a while; that meant a great deal. She understood from the way the baby looked at him how deep the bond was between him and their daughter, who had gone through everything with him. Most of all, from all these signs, she understood how deeply Ashford loved her. Many men would tell a girl the lengths they would go to prove their love. Maybe some of them meant it, but few were forced to show it. Ashford had literally crossed the sea for her, giving up everything and putting himself in danger. Everything she went through was worth it to know that. Her heart felt so warm and full.

Ashford loosened the strap that held Cristina to his chest and handed the baby to her. Leila took her daughter into her arms, squeezing her against her chest as she kissed her. The confusion in the baby's eyes had only lasted a moment, and now Leila knew her fear of forgetfulness was unfounded. Cristina knew her mother. Leila's spirit was whole again.

A few minutes later, they were sitting together on the bench. Leila couldn't stop looking into Ashford's eyes.

"Look, you're here! And you brought Cristina too. It's almost too wonderful to believe. But somehow I knew all this time . . . I knew you wouldn't let me go."

"I had to find you." A brief cloud passed over Ashford's expression. He took her hand. "I hate to ask at a moment like this, but are we safe here? I was careful. I don't think I was followed this morning, but . . ."

Leila lifted a finger and placed it on his lips. "There's no more danger. I'll tell you everything later; I don't want to talk about it now. Just know that the danger's gone. There's nothing left that can get in the way of our love. Not Paulo. Not Samantha. Nobody and no thing. We can build our lives together again, starting today."

They hugged tightly. Leila leaned in to smell Ashford's neck—such a delightful remembered scent.

"Do you think I'll make a good *Colombiano*?"

Leila's eyebrows shot up. He had asked the question in Spanish. Pretty good Spanish. She loved it.

"I don't know if they'll let me go back," she said. "You might have to stay. It's amazing to me you'd want to live here."

"Wherever you are is where I want to be. We'll see what can be done. Maybe we'll be able to go back to Arizona in time. If not, I've come to like Cartagena. Would you believe I practically have job offers? I can have a work visa in no time."

"Being a nurse will be tough work here."

"It will be *good* work. That's what I want."

"That's one of the things I love so much about you."

She pressed her face into his neck, closing her eyes.

"What should I call you now?" he asked. "Is it still Leila, or are you Cristina here?"

"Leila, of course. I'll always be your Leila. That's the name you've loved me as, so that's who I am. Besides," she said as she sat upright and looked at the baby in her lap, "the name 'Cristina Cohen' is already taken. And I'll be a Cohen soon, won't I?"

"As soon as possible."

"Let's get married right here at this church . . . this afternoon, if they'll let us."

Ashford took her face in his hands and kissed her.

"*Leila Cohen.* I love the way that sounds. Though nobody here will be able to pronounce it."

They both laughed.

"My bride."

"Darling, I'm going to make you so happy."

Manny had once told her that love was worth anything and everything. It had taken a lot to make her believe him, but now she knew he was right. Love was *always* worth it.

CPSIA information can be obtained
at www.ICGtesting.com
Printed in the USA
LVHW111740280419
615868LV00001B/97/P